BEFORE

WE WERE

BLUE

BEFORE WE WERE BLUE

E.J. SCHWARTZ

flux®

Mendota Heights, Minnesota

First Edition
First Printing, 2021

Book design by Sarah Taplin
Cover design by Sarah Taplin
Cover images by Azyzit/Pixabay, AStoKo/Pixabay

Epigraph on page 7: "Poem Number Two on Bell's Theorem, or The New Physicality of Long Distance Love" by June Jordan, from *We're On: A June Jordan Reader*, edited by Christoph Keller and Jan Heller Levi, Alice James Books 2017 © 2017, 2021 June M. Jordan Literary Estate Trust. Use by permission. www.junejordan.com

Flux, an imprint of North Star Editions, Inc.

Library of Congress Cataloging-in-Publication Data (pending)
978-1-63583-069-9

Flux
North Star Editions, Inc.
2297 Waters Drive
Mendota Heights, MN 55120
www.fluxnow.com

Printed in the United States of America

AUTHOR'S NOTE
WITH CONTENT AND TRIGGER WARNINGS

Books about bodies, how they look, how they feel, how they move, are often unsettling. First, I want to note that there is no universal experience for an eating disorder. This book could never cover the full spectrum of eating disorders, nor will it try to. That said, I do want to prepare my readers. The characters in this novel have thoughts that can be complex, contradictory, and all-consuming. Humor, especially dark humor, is one of the many ways they cope with their suffering. From my experience, dark humor and *writing* dark humor have been some of the best remedies for my own pain. My hope is that some of the catharsis I felt while writing *Before We Were Blue* is accessible to you, its reader.

This book also has mentions of sexual assault and suicide. A book about bodies without mentioning the very real threat that the self and others—family, friends, peers, strangers—can pose to those bodies felt untrue in nature. I tried to tell this story as unafraid as possible and let hurt and healing come through on the page. So, if you make it through this journey with these extraordinary, complicated, vibrant young women, I believe you'll find a world of growth, laughter, light, and love.

Now, without further interruption, this is *Before We Were Blue*.

— E.J. SCHWARTZ

There is no chance that we will fall apart

There is no chance

There are no parts.

—June Jordan

1
Shoshana

Here she is, perched on the ladder of our bunk bed, all botched hair and bitten nails like her body is the one thing she can stand to chew. Rowan's face fits her name. Sharp cheeks, heart-shaped lips, the kind of eyes that feel like a challenge. When I told her that, she said it's because R is a menacing letter and she's the fire-starter type. Today she's trying to expel that fire through one of her favorite games: *What If?*

Last Thursday's was *What if we switched places with the nurses for a day?*

I said we'd quit our jobs immediately, hop on a train, and live the rest of our days as TEFL course leaders abroad. But Rowan said that was too easy. Instead we should separate the nurses, refuse to give them any food, chain them to the ladders of our bunk beds, and laugh devilishly at the sight of their shrinking waists. It'd be the reverse of what they do to us in here: fattening us up for what Rowan deems "slaughter."

"When we get in there, you have to do it quick," Rowan hisses at me now, placing her fingers two inches above her collarbone, on the side of her neck where a baited vein beats blood to her brain, into this idea. *What if you killed me at breakfast this morning?* That's the pretend prompt she's chosen and running with. "And don't hesitate. Stab as hard as you can. Right here."

"Don't you mean slit?" I ask. I've heard of people *slitting* throats before. Sylvia Plath when she was ten. A man in Houston last month to his girlfriend right in the middle of a KFC. Dean during his epic suicide in *A Nightmare on Elm Street*. I've never heard of anyone *stabbing* a throat.

Rowan hits her fist against the ladder's worn wood. "Stab," she corrects. "The knives in there won't be sharp enough for a clean cut and I don't need you sawing off my windpipe. I'm faking suicidal, Shoshana, not sadistic."

Rowan uses the word *faking* a lot. Sometimes I wonder who she was before all this, before becoming a Recovery and Relief patient—everyone here calls it RR—and even before that, when she wasn't sick at all. On her first day at RR, she chopped off her hair, then dyed it eggplant purple with a Kool-Aid packet snuck from the Gray kitchen. The story I heard upon arrival put Britney Spears to shame. In my head, it plays closer to Demi Moore in *G.I. Jane* than Robin Tunney in *Empire Records*. Still, the image of pre-Rowan, Barbie's doppelgänger, never settles. Rowan agrees. She says she came out of the womb early, eager to sin, but never fully met herself until she hacked a pair of scissors two inches above her scalp.

We decide to make Rowan's death swift and painless as we head for the stairs, then are halted by the sight of the other Gray girls. They're huddled by the bottom step, whispering and glancing at the staff room door like nervous schoolchildren.

Our gaze follows theirs. We creep closer, peek at the shut staff room door, and the Gray kitchen past it at the end of the hall.

The Gray kitchen is for Gray girls like us, patients who haven't been cleared to eat by ourselves yet. Rowan and I are late. The rest of the Gray girls should have gone in to eat by now, but they're gathered together, with runny, unblinking eyes.

When we reach the bottom step, Rowan grabs Jazzy's arm, tight and urgent. "What is it? Where are the nurses?"

Jazzy and Donna, the girls who Rowan and I room with, stand in the center of the Gray girls. They're both Asian, with thick black hair and yellow teeth eroded by bulimia. Seeing them side by side, I can't help but think Jazzy, with her full lips and narrow nose and poreless skin, is prettier than Donna. On eyes, it's a tie, both pairs brown and deep set, but Jazzy wins wholeheartedly again on hair, hers longer and glossier with blunt-cut ends.

Glancing away from their bodies, I make a fervent wish I was blind. That we all were. Blind or bodiless. I hate being so judgmental, that my first instinct is to treat Donna as lesser than because of the way she looks. I fight it by turning the observations inward, remembering how before RR, I was prettier. Not pretty. *Never* pretty. Just prettier. Then I stopped eating and clumps of my hair began falling out and now there's a tiny bald spot on the crown of my head just like Dad's. I hide it by clipping the front pieces back. Rowan glimpsed it one time after a shower. Her fingers smoothed down the few strands left, and I thought maybe I would die if it were possible to decompose of shame. But then she went on a tangent about the removable showerheads being one bonus of this place, acting like I was a normal human being.

If I didn't love her before that, I did after.

"You guys remember Alyssa?" Donna asks as she re-adjusts her wide yellow headband. She said she cut off her front bangs in fifth grade and when the hairs grew back, straight up, she started wearing headbands over her ears and around her forehead to hide the sprouts. Then after six months, headbands felt more comfortable that way and she's worn them incorrectly ever since.

I wonder if Donna knows she's the ugly one too, the way I am next to Rowan.

"*Alyssa*," Donna says her name again. "Short. Stumpy. Slurred her *s*'s?"

The Gray girls nod and I do too. Alyssa was a Blue girl a month ago, released back into the wild after we threw her a go-home-and-don't-come-back party, decorated a cake no one wanted to eat.

"Remember how she faked her period so they lowered her goal weight, and she gained the last five pounds by stuffing quarters in her underwear, then got out on early release?"

Rowan nods, but I'm in the dark. Maybe this was during the three weeks Rowan was here before I checked in. She seems so sure of Alyssa's deception, like she played a hand in helping her escape.

"Back up. How do you fake a period?" I ask. Very few things slide past the nurses here. I suspect Nurse Hart would have heard the change clicking between Alyssa's butt cheeks before anything went under the radar at weigh-ins.

"She threw up blood onto a tampon and pretended," says Donna. She talks like a gum-chewer, slow and rhythmic.

"Where'd she get the tampon?" I ask.

Jazzy purses her lips, and her cheekbones round like golf balls. "One of the Blue girls, probably. Bet the nurses just thought one of them lent her a Playtex as a courtesy."

I shake my head a little. "But how would she throw up blood with everything they make us eat?"

Donna and Jazzy exchange a look that makes me want to staple my lips together.

Jazzy rolls her eyes. "You just do it, over and over until it's only blood. Come on, Shoshana, keep up."

"Or you can always pick your nose until it bleeds," Rowan offers, and the rest of the Gray girls nod their assent.

"News is . . . she died yesterday," Jazzy hisses.

Collectively there's an intake of breath. I bite the inside of my cheek, swallow, and it tastes metallic. Teeth grind audibly among the group, anxiety sprouting. But Rowan makes a face that says, *Boo-hoo, you idiots really thought she wouldn't die? Almost a quarter of us do from this, you know . . .*

The fear for Rowan's life, for all of our lives, sits in my body, right below my chin. Rowan shoots me an over-this glare. I feel like I'm caught, something snagged on a sweater. I try to lasso in my emotions so Rowan doesn't see. *Fear?* Her voice echoes in my head, always there, keeping me in line. *We don't know her.*

If this is true, and Alyssa really did die, it's not good news for any of us. The nurses will crack down on regulations, probably be more paranoid than ever, and limit our free time to nothing. They'll be worrywarts and never believe that we're better. We'll never get out of here.

"Supposedly a new girl is coming today, but maybe it's been postponed," says Donna.

Out of the corner of my eye, Rowan deflates like a pinpricked balloon. Her bony shoulders round and her spine curves, the silhouette of a spoon. She's been buzzing with excitement over a new girl joining RR for a good decade; her first victim in weeks.

Behind all of us, the staff door bursts open and the nurses file out, filling the hallway with commotion. Voices rise and fall. Instructions are called. Bic pens click against the nurses' cat-scratched clipboards.

"Sweeps, ladies," Nurse Hart orders, her voice climbing high above the rest. We line up like ducks, prepared to have our hair tied up, our sleeves rolled, and our nails filed so we can't hide anything so much as a crumb under the beds. Once, Donna scraped chocolate under her nails and Kelly, our dietitian, gave her an hour-long lecture about normalizing the stigma of chocolate. Kelly is the only RR staff member we call by first name, probably because she's fun-sized and looks like she could be a patient here herself. Kelly says eating disorders have a sneaky way of holding on to things—even just continuing to fear chocolate after RR could trigger Donna into her eating disorder behaviors again. So Donna had to replace the calories she'd hidden. She didn't choose chocolate; she ate a bowl of ice cream instead. But I swear her eyes were so swollen the next day, it was like she didn't have any.

"Shoshana." Rowan tugs on my already-rolled sleeve.

I follow her puppy eyes and parted lips to see, at the back of the line, a fresh face, her new kill. The new girl is here and she's tiny—like *tiny* tiny. The width of a matchstick. Her face is full of freckles, and her unruly orange, elbow-length hair makes her an Eliza Thornberry lookalike, complete with a mouth full of braces.

Rowan is practically oozing with the promise of a good time. She has a thing about redheads, says they hide secrets in the pigment of their hair. But I think New Girl looks mild. Unextraordinary. The most interesting thing about her is that she's young. Maybe twelve, thirteen at most. The other Gray girls in line chew their cheeks raw with anticipation, waiting to see her break down at her first meal, everyone still buzzed from the gossip of Alyssa's death.

At the kitchen door, Nurse Hart combs my thin dark curls into a high ponytail and I cringe as her fingers, soft and filled with the fluid of age, take my own. She reminds me of my Bubbee. They both have scattered moles on their faces, only Nurse Hart's aren't hairy like Bubbee's, and she has a less raisin-like complexion, darker too. She must be younger, in her forties or fifties. Nurse Hart is bigger though, not just physically big, but aura big. When Nurse Hart is in the room, everyone can feel it. Like a drop in temperature. Like a drizzle.

Rowan and I are given the green light by Nurse Hart, and

Rowan takes my hand, moving us into the kitchen as one. We divide and conquer. She gets utensils. I pick up plates. When we sit, she smirks at me, that magic-craze of renewed spirit in her eyes.

"So, what's your weapon of choice?" Rowan asks, surveying our forks and a spoon from the egg tray.

Can you stab someone with a spoon? I wonder. The mental image makes me queasy.

"Can we hit pause?" I say. I'm not in the mood to play pretend. Not when the scenario is stabbing Rowan in the throat after just finding out about Alyssa. I can practically see Alyssa's dead face blooming behind my eyelids. Her dried-out blue lips. Her marble-gray eyes. Like RR's worst imaginable mascot— the exact blue and gray of our color-coded system.

For the moment I don't want to picture anyone else dead, especially Rowan. Not to mention we're about to eat, as if eating could get any harder.

"Fine." She pinches the fanny pack of fat at my waistline, positioning her fingers in an X, dragging one across the other like the strike of a match. "Tsk-tsk."

I get *tsk-tsk*'d whenever I bow out of one of Rowan's plans. She pinches harder than usual today and I swat her hand with enough power to startle her.

"For Moses's sake, chill out, Shosh," she snaps.

"We don't say Moses like you say Jesus."

"I"—she puts a dramatic hand over her heart—"do not use the word Jesus."

I resist the urge to push back with *You just said it in that sentence right there.* Instead I scoot a few inches down the bench and Rowan puts her arm around me, forcing me back to her, the flesh of our thighs squeezed together. "Oh, come on, Shoshana. You know I'm kidding. Bet you an apple slice the new girl doesn't take three bites before she has a mental breakdown."

I shrug off the attitude and we shake on it, spitting saliva into our palms and sliding our hands up to cup each other's elbows. We grab our plastic drinking cups, the ones we decorated our first week here, and fill them with water. Rowan's is clad with Sharpied smiley faces with *x*'s for eyes, crooked black mouths with dangling tongues. Mine is decorated with half-peeled-off butterfly stickers—all they had left when I arrived.

"Three bites is a cakewalk," I say. "I got to five at my first meal."

Rowan barks out a laugh. "Oh, please. You were a total Boost baby, Shosh."

My middle finger pops up like a Pez dispenser. If you refuse to eat the meals here, they'll give you supplements like Boost or Ensure. She's right that I didn't get to six bites before I settled for sipping on Boost like a baby bottle.

"It took what—three—four nurses to convince you to eat non-liquified foods again?" She covers my profanity with her hand, interlacing our fingers. "Don't get me wrong, your temper impressed me. Look at the weeping willows over there."

She switches her gaze to the end of the table where three girls eagerly place sugar stickers on their tally sheets.

"They're like Reverse Heathers. No power. No self-worth."

I nod. The Reverse Heathers should be in the Blue kitchen,

eating without being stalked by the nurses. I stare at the main Reverse Heather, Hannah P., who's inhaling her orange juice. She was a binge eater before she became bulimic.

I stare at her arms, at the weight she's gained since she got here four weeks ago, then run a hand along my waist where Rowan pinched the fat. *Tsk-tsk.*

"It's pathetic," Rowan spits. "They're the shitshow of the Gray girls. I picked you as my right hand because you're loyal and sane enough to see the lunacy of this Guantánamo Bay replica."

I lick my teeth with laughter because we're in the middle of a town called Friendsville, Maryland, right on the border of West Virginia and Pennsylvania, a place that couldn't sound any less like Guantánamo Bay if it tried. The town next to us is Accident, where the people are called "Accidentals." Rowan said they must've let a five-year-old name the towns in this county. Maryland, according to her eye, is shaped like a gun: her house located in the middle of the trigger, RR at the tip of the barrel, smack on the edge of the muzzle.

Rowan waves an exaggerated hand in the direction of Nurse Hart, whose russet irises narrow at us with suspicion. I pick up my fork and play with my scrambled eggs, telepathically urging Rowan to keep her voice down.

New Girl takes a plate and her cup to decorate. Our gazes follow like a panning camera as she trails along the assortment of food, chin raised like she smells something rotten, like maybe it's us. She picks up a blueberry muffin and clutches it so tight it crumbles in her palm. The berries stain her skin a bruise-like purple.

New Girl looks from Rowan and me to the Reverse Heathers, deciding where to sit. I can feel Rowan's intrigue, an alive vibration swaying between the two of us. It builds when New Girl sneaks to the other end by Hannah P., secretly dissing us.

Rowan rests a hand on my knee, palm upward with the apple slice, hidden. We stare at New Girl, the slo-mo as she lifts a piece of mutilated muffin to her nose, sniffing. The nurses won't let her crumble her muffin tomorrow. Our eating is supposed to be normalized here—no cutting up pizza, no counting grapes, no swishing drinks around in your mouth to buy time. But the nurses first want to evaluate where New Girl is at, what her behaviors are. We all watch as she pops the first piece in her mouth and makes a sour-lemon face, already going for her second bite.

One down, two to go.

I'm buzzing with *I told you so* because New Girl eats the second bite and holds up the third, but then the tears build and I'm so screwed. Nurse Hart whispers to New Girl, "It's okay. Just eat what's on the tally sheet," but Rowan and I can see fire build in the girl's wistful green eyes. Her hands clamp the table. Her taut jaw reveals the extreme hollowness of her cheeks. Nurse Hart repeats herself, voice more commanding, but New Girl grabs the muffin off her plate and slaps it against the wooden table, rolling it like playdough and then hurling it across the room at the cabinets, nearly hitting Kelly in the head. None of us are prepared for when the newbie screams at the pitch of a tea kettle.

What follows: a snot fest. The nurses escort New Girl from the room as she sobs and swears, scrambling for anything to hold on to—the walls, the floor, her life. Her shrieks echo from down the hall, but we ignore them as if they're nothing more than the hum of a heater.

I take the apple slice under the table, a boon for my lack of judgment, and pretend to yawn as I stick the eleven extra calories in my mouth.

Rowan smiles.

I speak with my eyes. *Whatever. I'll win next time.*

She licks her lips. *Not a chance.*

After two pieces of toast, a banana, and the rest of my eggs, I finish my tally sheet. Rowan is the last to complete hers, but she finishes in the mandatory twenty-minute time block. I wait until she's done, and we pass New Girl on the way out, coming back for breakfast number two. This time, if she doesn't comply, she'll be given Boost or Ensure. The flabby texture of Ensure always makes me nauseous, so I'm slightly more sympathetic. We were all new girls once. Even Rowan.

Nurse Hart conducts sweeps of the Gray kitchen carefully, playing detective and fitting the role with her oversized rectangular glasses. She's searching for syrup in our pores, bacon strips under the arches of our feet. It's a mystery how Rowan ever snuck that Kool-Aid packet out of here on day one.

"So, what's the plan?" Rowan asks. "Lock the newbie in the bathroom? Cut her hair off in the middle of the night? I bet we'd make hundreds off those natural red extensions. How long could we get them? Eighteen inches?"

"Twenty if we cut right at her scalp," I say.

Rowan's eyes glimmer at me, the neon blue of food coloring. "That'll be what? Six hundred dollars? Enough for two bus tickets to some small town in Southern California, right where they have ten thousand earthquakes a year. We'll get shitty jobs at Claire's or—what do those Valley girls do—green-smoothie shops? Wait, wait! We can be greeters. You know those girls who stand outside of Hollister in bathing suits and say 'Hey' and 'Sup' all day? It's, like, the easiest job out there. We could totally do that!"

She must know I'm not pretty enough to say "Hey" to strangers and expect a response, let alone have someone pay me to strut my gut around in a bikini.

"I thought you hated demeaning crap like that," I say. She's completely against the male gaze and its tendency toward female objectification.

"I do, but we gotta work the system somehow."

We make our way upstairs to our room with our fingers braided together. The bunk bed Rowan and I split is on the left. Jazzy and Donna's is on the right. Rowan crawls onto my bed, the bottom bunk, and I move over her to squeeze between her and the wall, the two of us staring up at her handwriting—*We're all mad here*, scribbled in Sharpie.

Rowan says forgery is important, a useful skill for teenagers with strict parents. I trace the delicate curve to her *e*'s with my finger, the violent drag of the *w*. The type—a life of its own. I mimic her script on the wood until it's memorized; a quick flick of the wrist and I'm her.

"How come you never told me about Alyssa?" I ask, finger hovering over the *m*.

She lifts up her legs, resting bare feet on the words, toes covering *here.* Now it's just *We're all mad.*

"I didn't tell you because I didn't know about it. Common sense, Shosh. It doesn't matter if you're in the loop or not. You act like you are. Always."

"Oh." I lift my foot and place it next to hers. I'm a size nine and a half. She's a seven. Heel to heel, the tip of her big toe reaches the base of my pinky. She's lucky she's so tiny. So feminine. My growth spurt was painful; it meant I couldn't be a cheerleading flyer anymore, and that derailed my life in so many ways, I can't even count them. The thought of it makes my stomach tighten, breakfast treats pretzeling into one big anxious knot. I usually avoid dwelling on my cheerleading memories around Rowan, never wanting her to see me that messy. If my face slips and shows any sign of discomfort now, she doesn't comment on it.

"What do the rabbis teach you over there in Hebrew school?" She scoffs. "Never lie? Never sin? Never fuck?"

It's not like that, I want to say. *There are no sinners or saints in Judaism. No "Lord I repent my sins" and then they're all forgiven. It's more of a culture.*

Instead I say, "Actually, as a Jewish woman, it's my job to singlehandedly have as much sex as possible. I need to birth enough kids to fill the next synagogue, save the Jewish race."

I make the joke to hear her laugh and it works. Rowan tumbles off the bed, clutching the sides of her ribs, giggling into oblivion. That life I've described: the birthing of babies; the sex chores; the sex, period, doesn't appeal to me at all. For so many reasons, it's hard to figure out where to start. Mostly I think it's something wrong with my body. It droops around me like an unfamiliar, dying plant. I told Rowan once, "It's like someone found a flesh-colored onesie that looks just like me and zipped me inside it while I was sleeping. And I'm aching to unzip it, but I can't." She just shrugged it off, thought it was normal teenage girlness probably.

Rowan's joy wears off surprisingly quick. One moment she's giddy; the next she's lying on the floor, silent. This happens more than I care to admit. Sometimes she's here and sometimes she's only an outline.

"Is that how you ended up here?" she asks me.

"By being Jewish?" I'm the one laughing now. "If every Jewish person had an eating disorder, then—"

"Then what?" she asks, less patient now. "What was it?"

A knock interrupts us: Nurse Robinson, insisting we have mandatory schooling and we're late. Again. Gray girls only have two hours of school a day, and Rowan and I usually sit there with textbooks flipped to random pages in front of us, doodling on fresh sheets of lined paper. Sure, we've written some poor essays, done a few math problems here and there, but mostly we've let the time pass in a blink so we can get on with the day. The minute we leave that wholly converted classroom, we forget it exists.

Every other day after schooling, we have phone calls home. Rowan moves into the staff room to have her call privately, with a nurse supervising, and I always wonder what she's hiding from me, from all of us. She swears it's only so the other Gray girls can't hear her. She doesn't want them knowing about her personal life. We don't talk about her *personal life* much either.

Nurse Hart hands over my white iPhone with the Garwood Elite case on it. It's cracked, the sticker of a cartoon cheerleader sliced by a deep crack from when I threw it against the wall when they first took it away. Nurse Hart watches me dial my home number, mouthing "fifteen minutes" and then stepping away when my parents pick up.

"Shoshi." My father breathes heavily through the line. I can hear his bike shoes scuttle across our kitchen tile. "How goes it?"

I sprawl out on the couch, a fuzzy blanket over my legs that changes color when I stroke it. Upward, the purple becomes lighter. Downward, darker. I draw smiley faces as Dad speaks, the circle made by two downward mirrored *c*'s.

"Good, I guess. We're going to the movies on Saturday." There's bigger news, front-page RR headlines, like New Girl and Alyssa, but I couldn't begin to tell Dad about that stuff.

"Ah," he sighs. "You know, chances are you'll be out of there by January. You could come to my IronMan in Mont-Tremblant. It's beautiful there. They've got luging. A whole list of activities you kids can do while I suffer."

"No one's making you do it," I remind him. He did IronMan

Wisconsin last year. Completed the 2.4-mile swim, 112-mile bike ride, and 26.2-mile run in eleven hours and fifty minutes. We were afraid he wouldn't finish his first one in Boulder five years ago, but he ended up above average in his age group.

Back then, he'd promised it would just be one and done. The registration costs, shipping his bike, putting our family up in hotel rooms for a week . . . He's paying thousands of dollars to "suffer." But less than a week after finishing Boulder, he signed up for his next one in Whistler. That's when we started watching Kona documentaries at the dinner table, inspiring stories of addicts or blind people crawling their way across the finish line. Somehow, it makes Dad feel better, watching a father drag his autistic son all the way through the swim, peddling the kid in a car seat on the back of a bike, pushing him in a stroller for the marathon. It makes me feel sad, like Dad secretly wishes my brother K.J. or I were on the spectrum, so he could be one of those heroes.

"Adam, is that her?" my mother asks. "Adam. Look at this floor. It's a mess. How many times do I have to ask you to leave your bike shoes outside?"

"Shoshi, I'm going to give you over to your mother before she guts me," teases Dad. He's called me *Sushi-Shoshi* since I was eight, when I discovered sushi at Benihana and ate so much I spent the rest of the weekend with my head in the toilet bowl.

"Daughter of mine? Is that you?"

"Hey."

"Oh, honey, we miss you. How's recovery?"

I start drawing frowny faces on the blanket. "Same as two

days ago." She gets a weekly phone call from the nurses and probably knows better than I do how close I am to their definition of recovered.

"The cousins will all be missing you at Thanksgiving this year. Hopefully you'll come home before Hanukkah so we can drive down to Aunt Jill's. Keep the tradition going."

First of all, I doubt the cousins will miss me. The triplets—James, Jordan, and Jackie—only hang out with my brother K.J. The boys will play games like *Kill the Carrier* and use the ping-pong table to play *Slap Pong*. Sometimes, when we were little, Jackie and I would play Polly Pockets together. But ever since James came out as gay, he and Jackie have gotten super close. The last few years she's spent the holiday in the basement with the boys, her and James flirting with K.J. even though we're all first cousins.

Second of all, if I'm still in here for Hanukkah, I might be stabbing my own throat.

"So." Mom draws out a breath. I can practically feel my hair blow back from her exhale, all the way from Westfield, New Jersey. Sometimes I don't feel like I'm that far from home, and other times I can't even remember what my room looks like. I ball up the blanket against my stomach like it's armor.

"I got an email from your coaches at GE," she says. "They want to know if you'll be back in time to compete at Worlds. There's no pressure. They already filled your slot. But the girl isn't you. Their words, not mine. Besides, there's still five months before then and I read somewhere that it's good to set goals, so maybe—"

"Mom." My tone stops her immediately. She waits for me to finish, but I don't have anything to say. If it was just cheer she was talking about, I'd say yes. But there's a lot more to our team, sixth in the world and wildly successful, and she knows it.

Rowan doesn't have a clue about my hardcore cheerleading life. Mainly, she assumes, based on the few comments I've made, which never elicit further questioning since I make sure they aren't wild enough to spark any interest, that I do the *rah-rah pom-pom* cheerleading, the sucky kind my high school team does where the team can't hold fulls without dropping their flyers. If she came to one of my competitions, watched me sign the bottoms of pristine white sneakers, initial bows for good luck, she might understand. The only reason she hasn't found out is because we don't have any technology in here. Otherwise, she would've seen my account, the seventy thousand followers, and seen that I've never been *rah-rah*. I've always been something else.

The nurses must think whatever made us sick is out there, in the mainstream, in our phones, in the parents who only get us for a spare fifteen minutes every other day. I agree with Rowan. They're idiots for not expecting people to return as soon as they chuck us out of the nest, for people like Alyssa to die. If it is out there, shielding us won't help. Then again, I don't know what will.

"I miss you," I say. I peek over at Jazzy across the room, afraid she's heard my admission and will tell Rowan I'm homesick. But she's speaking fast in a foreign language, totally oblivious. I'm jealous the nurses can't understand what she's saying, and I make a mental note to invent a new language with Rowan later, something complex with common phrases she'll love, like *Down with the patriarchy*.

The receiver gives a weighty sigh. "I miss you so much, sweetheart. Get better, okay? I want you home and healthy soon."

"Okay," I say and hand the phone back to Nurse Hart.

I search for Rowan. She's already done and waiting for me with a huge grin on her face. She shakes her head—*no, not yet*—and drags me up the stairs. In our room Donna is performing an Alyssa-inspired ghost story for the other Gray girls. Rowan shoos them out like flies.

She clasps her hands together, beaming at Donna and me. "I just had the most brilliant revelation!"

We blink at her.

This is why I love Rowan. She's darker than me and yeah, that darkness can be intriguing, but it's more than that. Each day with her is different: new excitements, new games, always something that creates enough distraction to make me forget how I really got here.

"Two weeks from today is Thanksgiving!"

Donna and I both wait. That's the brilliant revelation? I hold my tongue, sure Rowan has come up with something more.

"What's your point?" Donna chides, not so trusting. "That we'll be stuck here, eating more food than usual?"

Rowan shakes her pixie cut. "Remember a couple weeks ago when I planned on busting us out of this place? Well, on

Thanksgiving, there will be fewer nurses on staff and I've formed a foolproof plan. So, in or out? Shosh, you're in, obviously. But what about you?" she asks Donna.

I'm in, obviously, according to Rowan, anyway. In the past, her escape plans have fizzled out. I wouldn't take this seriously except she's never used the word *foolproof* before, never looked so eager. I turn to Donna. Maybe she'll say no.

But Donna depends on Jazzy, so we wait for Jazzy to get done with her phone call. When she flies through the door minutes later, wearing an ear-to-ear grin, she sings, "Guess who's getting out of here, bitches?" and thumbs herself. Her pretty brown irises disappear with her smile and I wait for a nurse to come in, to reprimand her for dancing when she's a Gray girl and Gray girls can't move like that. We aren't allowed to burn so many calories.

"They made you a Blue Girl?" Donna asks. Her tongue is bitten between her teeth like she's refraining from sticking it out and telling Jazzy *Nice try, I don't buy it.* I don't either, for the record. After all, it's a Thursday and all Gray-to-Blue decisions are made on Fridays. It doesn't make sense.

"Nope." Jazzy smacks her lips together on the word. "They're sending me home, as in *home* home. Apparently Alyssa is really dead and it scared my parents shit-straight. They're convinced this whole program is crap and that the nurses can't handle us. I'm packing my stuff tonight and I'll be, *poof*"—she shimmies her shoulders—"gone by morning."

So that's how it goes: New Girl shipping in. Jazzy shipping out.

Underneath Donna's disbelief there's palpable sadness, a grief of losing her own version of Rowan. Her eyes take on a plastic-wrap sheen. *Poor Donna*, I think, and swell with relief when Nurse Robinson finds us and tells us to go get showered, dressed, that there is to be no further discussion of Jazzy's release. Showering gives us something to do other than sit around and let the envy build up.

We shuffle in our flip-flops down the hall, passing New Girl sitting half-naked in a solo room with a nurse-in-training, her eyes rubbed raw. Her red hair is soaked wet from a shower, her baptism into RR.

In the stall next to mine, Rowan performs her rendition of Panic! At the Disco's "Hallelujah," a wavy blue curtain between us. Her water shuts off before I'm even done shampooing, and I'm jealous that having no hair cuts her wash time short. I don't have the face or the head shape for a buzz cut. But if I did, I would chop my hair off in a heartbeat.

After Rowan is gone and the stall's quiet, my mind wanders. There's a lot to process with Jazzy leaving and New Girl coming in and Alyssa dying. The only thing I remember about Alyssa is that she was always chewing gum, sneaking it around the center and keeping it at the back of her throat when the nurses suspected and made her open wide. Using it like a workout for her tongue, burning way more calories than the stick itself had. Her autopsy probably showed a whole wad of Bazooka stuck to the lining of her stomach.

Jazzy—healthy or otherwise—is getting released because of gum girl.

I wipe down the closest acrylic mirror. A blurry reflection shows me straight eyebrows and a kangaroo-pouch belly. I glance away. *Since when do I have breasts?*

Tomorrow is Friday, when the nurses will decide who becomes Blue. I find Rowan toweling herself off in our bedroom, thighs sickly small. All nakedness tends to leave me nauseated, but Rowan's body leaves me afraid too. She's breakable. Casper pale. Surely, she won't be moving rooms this week.

Somewhere on the inside of my stomach sits the apple slice, eleven calories Rowan dodged and I downed. Those calories will turn into fat in another three to six hours. I slide my hand over the *tsk-tsk,* the smiley face above the waistband of my shorts, a pot belly grown like the Secret Garden. Suddenly, I feel a burning at my core, a warning that tomorrow I'll be gone too.

Suddenly, I feel Blue.

2
Rowan

We can't all be Jews. We can't all be by-products of rich, every-house-looks-the-same suburbia. We don't all have daddies who pay for their daughters to flounce around in cheerleading skirts all day like innocent angels.

If you're wondering what my point is, Shoshana, it's that we can't all be you.

I've tried to change you. But you know that, don't you? What other reason would I have for telling you statistics on serial killers slaughtering teenage girls or world wars that began from religious conflicts? I've been trying to lure you out of Plato's cave, yet you still wear that hamsa around your neck like the dutiful Jewish daughter you are. You continue to have faith in things. I don't understand it. Sometimes, most of the time, I want to rob you of that.

"Banging your head against a wall burns 150 calories an hour."

I tell you this now because usually you'll respond best to food facts, a reminder of the weight you're gaining and hate to gain but not enough to stop. You barely acknowledge I've spoken, too busy slipping on pajamas, stepping your feet through the foot holes and sucking in the roll of fat bunching above the waistband. Too healthy to care.

"That's what? Two or three calories a minute?" you say, resting your temple against our bunk bed's ladder. "Wouldn't be worth the headache."

Lately I look at you and see an Avatar. Blue as day. The things you say sound Blue too. The nurses hear it. Jazzy and Donna hear it. I need ear plugs because it's deafening to me, like dynamite—a million fucking bricks shooting off at once. I'm not mad, because you clearly don't want to leave me. You're just not smart enough or *dark* enough to find a way out of this. That's my job.

The door shuts and the lights flick off and the four of us marinate in blackness, listening to the sound of Satan's footsteps fading. It's sweet that you call her Nurse Hart. Satan is way more fitting. To be safe, we wait for her checks to end, ten minutes of nothing before we begin our game.

You weren't around when the App game was created, Shoshana, so you don't know it was actually an accident. Jazzy said she missed Twitter, Instagram, Tinder, all the things they keep from us in here. She longed for the instant gratification of likes, knowing what was going on every instant of the day. So, we started piecing it together on our own, deciding what hashtags were trending, which celebrities were hooking up, who of Jazzy's friends had gotten knocked up, and whose boyfriend had cheated on who with Donna's best friend Bitchy Isa.

You mostly lay quiet during the App game and I wonder how you feel about it. How you feel about the things I say or what you think when I disappear inside my head.

Jazzy kicks off her going-away game by opening up the

pretend Perez Hilton app. She whispers in her "E! News" voice, "Liam Hemsworth and Miley Cyrus, back together again on a beach in Fuji. The two lovebirds were spotted getting hot and heavy during a sandy make out session, but pregnancy rumors led Hemsworth fans to believe he's simply putting on a show for good publicity."

"Pregnancy rumors are true," I confirm. "They're naming the baby Orange, which raises another scandal after Gwyneth Paltrow sues for her daughter's copyright."

"Who's Paltrow's daughter again?" Donna asks.

"Apple," I say with a sneer. What a horror to be named after any food.

"I bet she'll get a mega-deal doing ads for Old Orchard's." Jazzy mimics a pathetic seven-year-old girl's voice. "*Hi. My name is Apple and this is my faaaaaavorite apple juice. All natural, just like me.*"

Your Blue belly gives a rumbling laugh from beneath my bed.

"Only by now she's probably had eight plastic surgeries, so that's kind of false advertising," I say.

"Screw you," Jazzy spits, because we all know she had a nose job and a chin implant last summer to balance out her undercut face. Her parents signed the surgery consent form the moment she turned sixteen. At least, Donna and I know that . . . Are you clueless as usual, Shosh? Have you caught up yet?

Our voices trigger footsteps, so even though we've just begun, we go quiet for the night. I listen to your shallow breathing below my top bunk, waiting for it to dip lower and lower until I know you've withered into sleep.

I've always loved girls, especially girls like you, Shosh, late bloomers to seeing the ugliness of the world. But no matter how much Elle Fanning or Zendaya or Ruby Rose get my blood going, my belly warm, it's never been in the *I want your body* sense. Not until you. I was like sky, open and empty, and you swept in like ocean, something I wanted to touch, meet, kiss. You've reflected myself back to me, gifted me with new questions to figure out who the fuck I really am. I'm not in a rush to decide or put a label on it. Lord knows in here, we've got all the time in the world and it's just tick-ticking away. So my thoughts about you lately are just that: thoughts. Although I do wonder how you'd react if I gave you that *What If* in a game. *What if* I kissed you? *What if* you liked it?

You would freak out. I know, I know. It's just your timid nature, Shosh. Afraid of your own Blue shadow. But I warned you when we first met: I ruin things. I told you and instead of running, you latched on like a suckling newborn.

When things inevitably blow up, as they always do around me, I hope you'll remember that: You chose this. You chose me. You chose *us*.

So, back to girls. Girls like you, girls not like you. Girls, the lot of them, like flowers. Art in living form. Until they're plucked. Stomped on. Always saying they're sorry for shitty things they did or, mostly, what they didn't do. Girls like Jazzy and Donna and me. Not you; not yet. Girls like the rest of us, though. Girls ruined simply for being girls.

Boys are like bees. Clever, huh? Sucking the life from the flower's core, making it sacrifice itself, pussy pollen spread around the hive. The bees will buzz over which flowers are loose and which flowers are easy, which flowers have thorns, which flowers are prudes, and which flowers are too ugly to ever stoop that low. But there is no "too low" for bees who hunt honey, boys just looking for a moist hole.

I haven't told you about Jeremy Baxter or the Red Roof Inn. Why not? Because if I did, you'd look at me like you looked at Donna today when Jazzy said she was leaving. With pity. You don't know what that feels like, Shoshana, but I've memorized that look and I'm sick of it.

Sue me for keeping an itty-bitty part of my story to myself.

Jeremy Baxter was a lanky know-it-all, the kind of boy who brags about his one chest hair and a C+ on the Spanish midterm, keen on everyone's approval except his own mother's. He told my seventh-grade class I was a shrub, a prickly legged twelve-year-old who was easy, hot for it, extra juicy for him, and the entire basketball team made a video chanting a nursery rhyme about me.

Row, Row, blows your chode until she makes you scream. Merrily, merrily, chokes voluntarily, a walking STD.

Then they forwarded it on to the whole school.

My guess is that you would have responded like my parents. That is to say, with outrage. They went straight to the male principal's office and my mother said the boys should be suspended, that cutting off their balls was the punishment that really fit the crime. My father stayed silent and moved his hand guiltily over his crotch, as if we'd been pointing the gun at him.

At some point the principal said, "It takes two sides to form a miscommunication," and because we'd been reading *The Diary of Anne Frank* that week, I said, "So the six million Jews murdered in the Holocaust was all just a big *miscommunication* with Hitler?"

You would've gotten a kick out of that, huh, Shosh? Well worth the three weeks of detention and numerous lectures about my unladylike, smart-aleck, in-need-of-much-soap-rinsing mouth.

Spoiler alert: the basketball boys, bees, whatever the fuck, ended up just dandy. The only thing they got was an ironic warning about how their actions had consequences. Karma didn't help a sister out, so I had to make the boys pay myself. Took a little trip to the basketball locker room and soiled their uniforms with jars of pickle juice and mayonnaise and sticky maple syrup. Sounds petty to you, I'm sure, but name one twelve-year-old who isn't petty. Besides, you would've been my accomplice, right? Outraged on my behalf, knife-ready?

The event had the whiff of victory, especially with the mayonnaise, but it wasn't enough. It would never, *will* never, be enough. Those pricks laughed it off, handed soggy uniforms over to mommy dearest for dry cleaning, and moved on. They didn't have to deal with the branding of it in the hallways at school, in the teacher's lounge, outside on the street. The words: *Slut. Snitch. Cock-sucker.*

Maybe it's my fault. Maybe you think I'm dramatic,

Shoshana. That I get off playing God, exacting revenge. And you'd be right. Partially. But you know what? Sometimes we have to be God. Sometimes we know what people deserve and it's okay to give it to them. That's what I abide by anyway.

On our ride home from our meeting with the principal, my mother said I should have remembered that actions lead to consequences for girls, that flowers are meant to sit still and look pretty and say sorry. My father said he'd tried to warn me from diapers: bees will be bees.

Other things you don't know? It was a Sunday, my dark day, when we met. For many, that day is the day of rest, of laundry, meal prep, coffee with chirping birds, bleh. But for me, Sunday is why I am what I am. I think deep down you know something messed me up, an incident like *Row, Row*, but bigger. And that, Shoshana, is the Red Roof Inn. Events like that one cause transformation. A new person instantly. Pink skin ripped from pink skin. Maybe it was fate for us to meet on my worst day of the week, the day that reminds me of why I *can* never and *will* never be like you.

I should have met you at breakfast that morning, church time, just like we met New Girl bright and early. But by the time I got waved in, you'd already been dragged out.

So we met in art class instead, where you looked like a vision meant to be painted. You don't think you're beautiful, and if we're using the conventional standards the beauty industry goes by, you're not. But you're interesting to look at, like spotting an unfamiliar species. To me, that's ten times better than cookie-cutter.

That day, your hair was in a bun and the shower had left your cheeks all rosy. It reminded me of my middle school days, how I used to pinch my cheeks for what was called "a natural glow" and I occasionally pinched too hard and left bruises. You reminded me of me, yet we were nothing alike.

Jazzy had painted a shaded orange sunset on her canvas to resemble a failed Afremov, all choppy colors and mislayered shapes, and I was doing a minimalist interpretation of Frida Kahlo's *The Broken Column*—minimalist because I can't paint that well, *The Broken Column* because I liked seeing the nurses' eyes avoid the breasts.

You—you were slumped on your stool, staring at your blank canvas, looking lost as ever, when I told you, "If you don't paint something, they'll call you a perfectionist, a 'multidimensional characteristic' or whatever in therapy. Even when you're not stressed, you're still stressed, right?"

You said, "Anxiety," familiar with the term. "Maybe it's more beautiful before we touch it, though."

I bent close enough to smell the chemicals on your smock, see the white linen thread on your canvas's base.

"Sure," I agreed. "But unless you want to spend hours explaining that to the peanut gallery over here, I suggest you put something on it. Even if it's just a Malevich dot."

You hesitated. I assumed you didn't know who Kazimir Malevich was. Now I know better. Because at the end of the hour, you had painted a third grader's rendition of Diego

Rivera's *Nude with Calla Lilies*. It was bad, horrible really, if you want to know the truth of it. I mean, Christ, the painting made me look like a Michelangelo prodigy. But you had done it decent enough to recognize and it wasn't prudish. You didn't censor the ass or whitewash it. That meant you understood what I'd been painting, who Frida was and who Diego was, how they were tethered together in a way we were ever after.

Later that night, Jazzy and I planned a mission to get access to your file. There's no lock on the therapy office, so when Jazzy threw a fit that brought the two overnight nurses running, I slipped out, into the office, and beat the lock on the file drawer with a glass dove paperweight. The sound called the nurses down, but it was too late. I read fast and got what I needed, what I'd known the second you said "anxiety," which is as loose a term as any.

No one knows what's wrong with you, Shoshana.

No recorded sexual assaults or rapes, no known physical abuse, no PTSD, no close experiences with death. Your file made mine look like an assault on trees. To this day, I can't understand why you're sick. I guess that was the start of all this: my curiosity.

Shoshana Winnick—my very own Enigma machine.

When the nurses found me, I claimed to have read my own file, so I was only punished for damaging company property and not kicked out for legality issues. My sentence was a call home, a serious talk with my mother, and a loss of all privileges gained in the previous weeks. A do-over button. Push back to start. No going to the bathroom alone. No trips to the movies. No off-grounds activities except for emergencies. But that was what I wanted. Because while we can't all be like you, Shoshana, I'm still hungry for your goodness. That Mary Jane life you lead. Grabbing for it like a life preserver. You, my dear, are my ticket to forgetting the Red Roof Inn and the things that come clawing for me in the dark. That's why I did it. Put the wheel in motion, the both of us in sync. So you and I would be squeaky clean, baptized into RR, and rebirthed as one.

3
Shoshana

The Blue girls have dance class Friday mornings, a show Rowan drags me to before the nurses wake the other Gray girls and "all hell breaks loose," as Rowan kindly puts it. The only problem is that Rowan's a morning person. A six-year-old whose automatic clock rings at five, who jumps on you and says, "I want to play!" whereas I could sleep till noon.

"Up, pup," she demands, licking my cheek.

I shake my head against the pillow, pushing her and her curled tongue away.

"'There will be sleeping enough in the grave.' Do you know who said that? Benjamin Franklin. You know what else he said? 'Shoshana needs to get her cute butt out of bed before Rowan forcibly removes her.'"

She jolts my arm. I let her try a few more methods, including impersonating a scam telemarketer. "*Shoshana Winnick, come on down, you've won a grand prize to be claimed downstairs in the studio!*"

We descend to the dance room with tiptoeing feet, false grace, our pirouettes birthing vertigo stars in front of our eyes. Rowan gives a downright dramatic performance across the waxed wood floor, total *Black Swan*. I can't tell if she's replicating it or parodying it. My money's on the latter.

When we pop a squat with our backs to our reflections, I ask, "So, what's this prize I've won?"

She hands over a note impeccably folded in quarters. "Here."

My eyebrows rise. I thought the prize would be purely fictional. That, or the pleasure of her company. "One secret," I read aloud. "Does this mean I can cash it in?"

"Yes, but obviously the secret is at my discretion and if I'm in a mood, I'll revoke it."

"So I'll never *really* get a secret," I tease. She crosses her arms and I carefully pocket the note, squeezing her elbow to tell her thanks.

The Blue girls warm up, pointing and flexing their feet. One girl, chubby with cellulite on the backs of her pasty thighs, ignores instructions and stands flat-footed, picking lint from her belly button. As Gray girls, we're lowest on the totem pole, too underweight to participate. *Rowan is a Gray girl, though, and Rowan could never be low,* I remind myself. Then repeat it over and over like a mantra. *Rowan is a Gray Girl. Rowan could never be low.*

Lately I've been thinking about Blue and Gray as light and dark, good and evil, and it's not supposed to be that way. Rowan wouldn't dream of it. If anything, to her it's the other way around.

As the music vibrates from the speakers, a slow salsa to start, Rowan snorts evilly, pointing out the pigeon-toed girls who are always a step behind. Maybe I should tell her that she doesn't need to point them out to me. I can catch the girls' mistakes even before she can. It's an eye thing. A cheerleading thing. A Shoshana thing, mostly. But I keep my mouth shut.

My mom says everyone is born to do something and I was born to cheerlead. More specifically, to tumble, because at age six I broke the record for the most back handsprings in a row at our gym—twenty-seven—and my coach, Jim Surgio of Surgio's Gymnastics, put a video up on YouTube that had gyms across the country trying to recruit me for junior Olympic training. That was back when I was still a gymnast, doing Yurchenkos on vault, press handstands on beam, the skin of my hands always cracked and raw and bleeding from bars.

I didn't want to be an Olympian. Actually, that's a lie. I *couldn't* be an Olympian because of the way my mind works. Elite-level girls spend their days in technique training, sitting in splits, holding hollow body rocks until their abs resemble the indents of ice cubes, and I never cared about technique. Back then, I cared about having fun. Goofing off in the pit. Minigiants on strap bar. Trampoline, where if I jumped high enough, I could see over the white wooden divide to where the older girls practiced and try to copy their skills.

At school, with the last name Winnick, I always sat in the back of the classroom. I was quiet, never noticed as anything other than average—a chance for kids to compare themselves against me, the mean. But in the gym, my tricks made me loud. I was the powerhouse of peewees, the only ten-year-old in the state who could land a triple in competition. Parents who came to pick up their kids from practice would watch me instead.

There's power in natural ability, and tumbling is the only thing I've ever been certain I've had it for.

Surprisingly, it took Mom a while to come around to the idea of cheerleading. She was set on my Olympic path to glory, which was never going to happen. She thought cheerleading was a less respectable form of gymnastics. But I liked how none of the cheerleaders had to worry about getting rips on bars or falling off the beam or hitting their back against the vault if they didn't take their hands off the board fast enough.

Cheerleading has a different scale for skills. I went from being a good gymnast to what *Cheer American* magazine called "one of the most talented cheerleaders the sport has ever seen," and I cared more about being a champion than what sport I was championing. I'm built that way. If I were a better gymnast, I would have stayed at Surgio's. It's easier to compete as an individual rather than have a team rely on you. But I'm a better cheerleader, and that made the decision for me.

"So, this was your thing?" Rowan asks, circling a hand to indicate the dancers.

If I had my phone, I could pull up that YouTube video of me at six years old, or show her my team's performance at the World Championships last spring where we came in sixth, or maybe just stand up and do a backflip right here, right now, and that would be enough. But I stay seated, knowing her version of me is whatever she needs it to be, and it's not smart to disrupt that.

"No," I say, because I still can't let her think I'm on the same level as these girls. "Not like this."

Watching the Blue girls' instructor, Ms. Matusick, makes me long for real-world people. She gives the Blue girls corrections, repositioning their arms and legs over and over since, apparently, they have no muscle memory from previous weeks, and she keeps smiling and boosting their egos with fake compliments. *So beautiful! Lovely movements, ladies! Just glorious!*

No one in this dance class could be a real dancer. Not one. And my cheerleading coach Mary-Ellen would catch that in a second. She'd tell them too, because in her world, you're either meant to be an athlete or you're not, and the sooner you find out, the better. The difference between me and Mary-Ellen is that she tells people the truth, no matter how harsh. She believes in girls who can take the heat, in girls who push through their pain, in girls who don't cry. Mostly, in girls who are naturals. Like me, or how I used to be before my breakdown.

"Good. I couldn't be friends with someone like *that*," Rowan says, nodding, amused. She makes a face at a dancer, some raven-haired nonprodigy. The Blue girl is great compared to the others in the class, but a train wreck by any real-world standards.

"I couldn't be friends with dancers, period," Rowan revises. "They're like automatons. Ballet, *this*. Tap, *that*. It's like, chill for two seconds."

I roll out my ankles. "I guess. But it's kind of nice, you know, to love something that much."

Rowan frowns at my disagreement.

"I guess I just admire people with that kind of drive."

"So do I." She lets out a breath. "Jeez-louise, Trunchbull. Don't take everything I say so seriously."

I wish I could take it back, grab the words and choke them down. *I talk too much*, I think. *Excessively. And my voice is annoying. Nobody wants to hear it.* My conscience goes off like a bottle rocket—how much better my life will be, it tells me, if only I stop speaking my mind, if only I stop wasting so much time being a couch potato, if only I lose ten pounds. *If only, if only, if only.*

"I didn't mean it," is all I say.

"I know you didn't." Rowan noses my neck. She puts an arm around me and I feel a little warmer, like maybe I'm not a complete mess.

Before we go into the Gray kitchen for breakfast, we have to do weigh-ins. New Girl stands in front of me, traffic-cone hair swaying to her bony hips. I spend the time in line comparing the size of my calves to hers. She's short. Twelve, we've confirmed through the grapevine. I'm seventeen. Tall. Logically, her calves should be smaller than mine. But mine seem massive in comparison. I can't help wondering what I'll look like to the nurses after they see New Girl, a thin layer of cells stretched flat across her skeleton, and then me, practically an ogre.

The weigh-in door swings open after New Girl, whose face is sullen and clenched.

"Your turn. Go get 'em, tiger," Rowan purrs in my ear. Her

calves fall somewhere between mine and New Girl's, closer to the latter.

The door clicks shut as I step into the clinically white and sterile-smelling room. The walls are lined with hospital photography, the always safe dogs-running-across-a-beach photo. My eyes linger on the container of expired lollipops on the counter. The whole room resembles a pediatrician's office, like Dr. Colwell's, who my brother K.J. and I have seen since we were babies. Dr. Colwell saw the petechiae on K.J.'s toddler face, tiny red dots the size of pinpricks, and diagnosed lupus, leukemia, or ITP. Mom tells stories about taking K.J. to get monthly shots of gamma globulin after Dr. Colwell discovered it was ITP, which meant K.J. had too few platelets in his blood. Mom and Dad only took notice after purple bruises began popping up everywhere under his skin.

Dr. Cowell saved K.J.'s life with an early diagnosis, says Mom, who insists we'll be going to Dr. Colwell until we're forty. I guess that explains why she and Dad never ride K.J.'s case about anything. They still feel like he's that little kid getting blood drawn every month, crying at shots. Like a crack in glass, they're waiting for him to spiderweb, to fully shatter.

I peel off my sweater. Then the jeans. Slip my arms into the holes of a napkin-thin blue gown. Stare at, by Rowan's estimation, fake nursing certificates on the walls.

Nurse Hart doesn't look up from her clipboard, still marking notes about New Girl. "Shoshana, how are you?"

"Fine," I say. Weigh-ins only take about ten seconds, but it feels longer. Your heartbeat gets all fast and suddenly you can hear your own breath, feel the muscles of your thighs dragging you toward the floor, and you're pretty sure the whole world might implode if that number gets any higher or even if it stays the same, because either way it means you're not improving.

Rowan said at the last place she went to, some cheap, indie treatment center in Virginia, they weighed the patients backward on a beam scale so patients didn't see the numbers. Blind weights. At RR, Gray girls start off that way, but quickly we're put on a case-by-case basis that results in most of us knowing what we weigh. RR's philosophy is that weight is just digits, nothing to fear. As much as it unsettles me, seeing the numbers, I think they're right. It's worse to be left wondering.

I step on the scale and Hart moves the bottom weight way to the right. New Girl must be a drop in the bucket.

She announces, "Three gained," and Kelly jots it down with a smile. I note that I only needed two pounds for this week's goal and now I'm up three. I hike up my jeans, sense the extra pressure when they button, and feel less and less sure of myself with each passing minute.

Kelly stands in the corner, petite and pretty, and as far as I know, she doesn't have an eating disorder. It's unfair, really. She's the one planning out all our meals and snacks—three meals and three snacks per day, three different options for each meal—and food has never become an issue for her. Rowan has conspiracies about the number three around here, none of which I buy. Frankly, I'm fond of Kelly, even jealous of her. If I had her body, I wouldn't hate myself.

"You can put your clothes back on," Nurse Hart instructs. They check my vitals, then tell me to send in the next one.

Rowan claps for me, sarcastic as always. "To hell and back again. Mazel tov."

"Rowan," Nurse Hart calls impatiently.

"In the flesh," Rowan announces.

The door shuts behind her. Through it, I hear the nurses laughing. *At* Rowan or *with* Rowan, I'm not sure.

"How'd it go?" Donna asks, eyes narrowed. She's standing with her back against the beige bedrock, a red cloth headband over the tops of her ears.

"Not too bad." I feign superiority like Rowan taught me. "You?"

She purses her lips. "It couldn't be good, right?"

"I guess not. Sucks that Jazzy's gone."

Donna pushes a portion of black hair over her shoulder. "Even if she wanted to call me, she can't. I'll be rotting to death in the Gray kitchen."

"They'll send you home soon. Just do what the nurses say and I'm sure they'll move you to Blue."

"And get out fat?" Her voice is steely. "Yeah, 'cause Jazzy would really want to be friends with me then."

I tap my fingers against my lower lip, stunned. For me it's not about being skinny. Not really. It's about being in shape, controlling what I put in my body. Donna makes it sound like the goal is to be as thin as possible. At least in the beginning, all I wanted was to add more height to my tricks.

The weigh-in room door flings open. Rowan rushes out,

eyes red, nose running. She shoulders past the waiting Gray girls. Sectioned-bangs-and-pierced-nose Bethany snorts, and I wonder what the punishment is for punching a patient.

There's nowhere to run or hide in RR. I find Rowan in thirty seconds flat, in the TV room, where the remotes are locked up by the nurses. She's staring out the window, less existential, more to keep her face hidden until she can pull herself together, which on the few occasions she's broken down like this, she always does swiftly. I slip my arms around her waist, feel the tension in her shoulders lessen, the shake of her weakened muscles quiet. It's the only thing I can do for her. Hugs.

"Everything okay?"

"Like in life?" she spits.

I start to pull away. First the disagreement in dance, now this. I'm two for two today. "Dumb question," I admit.

She laces our fingers together and squeezes, her eyes pinched shut. For a moment, neither of us says a word, but I know weigh-ins will be ending soon. We'll have to go in and eat.

Rowan lifts a hand to her hair, fingering the Kool-Aid strands. Her eyes open to the red rubber track that wraps around the outside of our building, the one the Blue girls walk on if the weather is nice.

"Was it really a Kool-Aid packet?" I ask, wanting to take her mind off whatever's keeping her away.

"Black cherry," she whispers.

"I would've let you dye mine. I mean, the color wouldn't

have shown up since my hair is dark, but I would have let you," I say. *I'll always let you.*

"I hate getting fat," she says, letting it out. The ache in her voice is palpable. "I feel like I'm failing, Shosh. I feel so . . . weak."

I swallow. She always knows what to say to me when I'm upset, but the extent of my intuition stops at hugging her. What now? I could tell her the truth, that *not* eating is what's making her weak, but if I voiced that thought, she'd probably think I was pulling reverse psychology on her, trying to make her gain weight.

"Everyone hates getting fat," I rasp. I start throwing out facts like Rowan does with me sometimes, her recent ones like: *Did you know the sun's going to burn out in four billion years, but before it does, it's going to swell and heat the Earth and burn us all alive?*

I say, "Did you know zero-fat products are actually worse for you because companies just pump insulin into them and then your sugar intake goes through the roof?"

She says nothing.

"But you're not fat, Rowan," I add, hoping I sound reassuring. "Not even close."

"I was maintaining for so long and now I'm gaining. *Gaining*, Shosh. A whole fucking pound."

One pound? The stinging between my eyebrows grows. I know I'm taller by a good half-foot, but is it right that I'm gaining, at least this week, three times as fast as she is?

"You can discuss that in therapy today, Miss Parish," Nurse

Robinson interrupts. She's directly behind us in the hallway. "Until then, I suggest you both get to breakfast."

We move before Nurse Hart appears to back Nurse Robinson up. New Girl stands ahead of us for sweeps and I rub Rowan's back until she shoulders me off. Her fighter-girl energy is building back up and she's glaring at New Girl, who nervously braids her orange strands. There's no way that hairdo is passing inspection. There's a lot you can hide in braids.

Rowan clears her throat until New Girl turns around.

"Got a name?" Rowan pounces.

New Girl hesitates. Her eyes are so swollen from crying that her eyelids droop over her lashes. "Um, Sophie."

"Do you have a nickname 'Um, Sophie' or are we just supposed to call you 'Um, Sophie' for all of eternity?"

She gives Rowan a small head shake, mouth jutting from her braces. "Sophie is a nickname. For Sophia."

"Wow. What a drastic change," Rowan scoffs. "No one ever calls you Soph, or Fee, or S. Murphy, or Smurf as an insult?"

"No." She sounds almost regretful.

"What a shame. Isn't that a shame, Shoshana?"

"Almost as tragic as that reboot of *Scream* last year," I add.

"Long gone are the days of real MTV," she agrees.

New Girl looks at us like she has no idea what we're talking about.

"Have you ever seen *Scream*?" Rowan asks.

New Girl bats her eyes, tearing up.

Rowan stands on tiptoe, leaning over to brush her lips

against my ear. "Remind me. Why are we trying to recruit new friends?"

"This was your idea," I point out.

She crosses her eyes and faces New Girl. "That's one strike, Smurf. You know how this works, right? Three strikes, bye-bye."

New Girl pinches her left leg, a trick I'm familiar with from cheer. Physical pain can block out the emotional. Seeing it, I remember how young this girl is and my first instinct is to step in front of her, sure we've gone too far. But Rowan is grinning. She's on edge. She needs this. This is her world, and I need to reassure her of that.

"Can you tell me what the word abrasive means?" Rowan asks. Two fingers remain raised, an ironic peace sign.

New Girl's eyes get glassier and I wait for her to give in, for the tears to spill over. I can almost hear Rowan's thoughts between my ears. *Break. Come on, Smurf. You know you want to.*

"That's two." Rowan bares her teeth and sucks in, making a *hurting you hurts me, so don't fuck this up* face. "Last try, Smurf. Tell me, faced with the decision to brandish a baseball bat at your worst enemy—"

"—or give a thousand dollars to your best friend—" I jump in, knowing this part.

"—which would you choose?" Rowan finishes.

Smurf chews on her lower lip, giving me and Rowan a glimpse at the overbite she's rocking, orthodontic elastics stained orange from last night's pizza.

"What does brandish mean?" Smurf asks.

"You want a definition?" Rowan baits. The girl nods and Rowan's cheeks push to a hellish grin. "Of or relating to brandishing."

"That's not a helpful definition," I defend. Rowan throws me a *WTF* glance.

"It means waving or hailing," shorts Rowan, and Smurf takes time to mull this over.

"I guess I'd give the money to a friend, because I don't have any real enemies," Smurf answers.

With that, Rowan tunes her out. *Bye-bye, Smurf. Three strikes, she's out.* We stand in line and Rowan makes a point of looking around, avoiding Smurf like she's invisible. Smurf, who I do look at, looks like she wants to be.

Sometimes I think Rowan delights in collecting other people's bruises. Smurf, a snowflake for Rowan to stick out her tongue and eat, gone. When we're let into the kitchen, Rowan snaps her fingers, playing the role of upset and disappointed, even though I see the glint of high bliss in her eyes.

"And I was so sure about her." She feigns frustration. "Redheads. They fool me every damn time."

4
Rowan

The games we play in RR, they aren't all mine. The App game is, but mostly they come from my mother. Picture a woman nearing forty, showing too much skin, wearing thick gold hoops and too-dark lip liner. Put it this way: if she were here, she'd be captain of the RR ship by now, and that includes the nurses. She's a master con woman, elite at making dull situations more interesting, even if it's for the worse.

Chew and Spit is one of my mother's most notable games, the one we started playing together when I was ten. We'd buy all the best snacks we could pile in a basket for twenty bucks at the 7-Eleven and go on midnight drives through town. Bowie looked different in the glow of the yellow telephone poles, with my mother blasting "She'll Drive the Big Car" and "Try Some, Buy Some." I swear she settled us in Bowie, Maryland, just for David Bowie himself.

"Chew what you want and then spit it in the trash." She demonstrated the task with a Milky Way, a string of brown goo swaying between her lips and the bottom of the 7-Eleven plastic bag.

"Just make sure you don't swallow any or it'll go right to the thighs."

I peered down at my still-growing ten-year-old legs, the

knobby knees, the peach fuzz on my calves, the noticeable fleshy insides building up. It didn't occur to me then, or for many years after that, that my mother was anorexic.

Just like I've always believed girls are flowers and boys are bees, I've always believed there are multiple people living inside us. Versions of who we used to be building to the people we are now: Rowan the toddler. Rowan the child. Rowan the preteen. RR Rowan. That last layer is me in the present day, just a version between this and what comes next, a snake skin waiting to be shed.

If the versions of me bear any consistency, it's my disordered eating and it's largely thanks to my mother. She started my "spit, don't swallow" phase and I haven't broken free of it since. In a way, I still feel like I'm ten. Waiting for my mother to point out my problem areas and insist that, though I have real beauty, it can be enhanced with a few fewer calories.

I believed every word that came from her spitting mouth.

You and I sit at the lunch table now, the minutes growing fatter between us. We swallow everything we're asked to. The veins in your arms are like teal-blue zigzags, the color forewarning where you'll be soon: *Blue Blue Blue*. I can hear my own dull-gray pulse ticking like a grandfather clock, slow and agonizing, counting the seconds we have left together, Gray.

"Look," you say, pointing over the Gray kitchen sink, through the window. "A deer."

A lone doe stands past the marked-off RR track, near the edge of the woods a couple hundred yards away.

"Suddenly wildlife amazes you? We really have been in here too long."

"No," you say. "It's a sign."

"A sign?" I spit. "Of what?"

"I don't know. Something good on its way."

I pick up my fork. "Look, it's a sign!" I pick up my spoon. "Look, it's another sign!" I shake my head, catching my warped reflection in the dip of the metal.

You glance at my fork and spoon and look ashamed, and I tighten my fists around the utensils until I can almost hear them. *Don't you dare use us. Don't you dare do anything so vulgar as eat, Rowan.*

You must see my demeanor change because you tease, "Rowan Parish: such a drama queen."

"Shoshana Winnick wouldn't know her personality from a hole in the ground," I parrot.

Too far. I feel the line I've crossed like an electric fence— only you're the one who gets shocked. You physically wince and I quickly hold out my fork and spoon to you.

"Signs. For you, my dear." I hope I sound as sweet as syrup. From the corner of my eye I see Kelly watching us, our exchange, our eating. I'll never forget her supermarket lesson where she made us all pick out paper images of our grocery order and fake scan them for each other. I doubt there's ever been another human on the planet as chipper to talk about our feelings on hunger and fullness than kill-'em-with-kindness Kelly.

Slowly you take the utensils, an acceptance of my apology.

But during our two hours of schooling, you don't look at me, a key sign you need to cool off.

I play M.A.S.H. on a hidden sheet of paper beneath my chemistry textbook, not for me but for you. Forgetting everything I've learned about you, I make up a whole new history. You've never come across as a Jersey girl anyway, Shoshana. New Jersey? The muck, the filth? No way. The way you drop your *r*'s, end your sentences with upward inflection, I would've said Boston.

I add places to M.A.S.H. just to make it more interesting. A *mansion* in Atlanta. An *apartment* in Boston. A *shack* in Friendsville. A *house* in Bowie, right beside mine. For partners I want to give you the options of *me, me, me,* but I decide to play fair and only put myself once, along with Tom Holland and Marie Ulven, aka *girl in red*. You probably love Tom, and don't know Marie, but this is my game for you and if it can't be me, I'm rooting for her.

For kids, I put zero, three, and seventeen.

For cars: horse, hot pink Tesla, and white minivan with suicide doors.

I draw the spiral and you end up with the house in Bowie next to mine, married to Tom Holland, with seventeen kids and the white minivan with suicide doors.

It's pretty much my nightmare—you married to a man and mothering a clan of brats right next door, there for me to watch and witness and groan about but ultimately suffer through. I'd rather you'd gotten the mansion in Atlanta with

Holland, so I could come visit and overstay my welcome, but not be stuck watching the romance permanently.

Donna grunts at her desk beside mine, resting her cheek against her French textbook and trying to read the print from the side. She's muttering about tenses, repeating "*Je ne parle pas français, je ne parle pas français*," fingers drumming against her flash cards. I whisper back, "*Ça dure combien de temps?*" Donna lifts her head, blinking awake, and flips through her textbook, trying to decipher my question. I don't remember much from my French class in middle school, but I always remember *How much time is left?*

Fifteen minutes later, Donna says, "*Trente cinq.*" Thirty-five minutes.

Once we're out, I catch your arm, slip my fingers through yours like they could lock there and force us to be conjoined. Two hours should be enough time for you to forget my words. You keep my hand but don't squeeze back. The urge to *tsk-tsk* you swells because normally we check in on each other, pass glances, pass notes. You didn't look at me once. A new thing I've learned about you: you're capable of holding a grudge.

This time I don't *tsk-tsk* you because it's not your fault. On the outside we wouldn't be like this, Shosh. The bickering, it wouldn't happen. RR just causes all kinds of rifts. Example A is Jazzy and Donna. You and I are stronger, better than them, but even we're susceptible to the pressures in here. It's not each other we get angry with; it's the circumstances. And sure, I get mad at you for simply being you, for winning the life lottery. Two parents who are still together—ones who let you spend all your time on a sport you can't make a living out of. You're here on a fluke, I admit, but it's oh-so-easy to loathe you for that.

My shit is deeper than yours. It's permanent like blood on a white carpet. The first time I was hospitalized, I was Smurf's age. The doctors told me all the same schtick: I would die if I didn't start eating. I didn't care. Eating, to me, was as useless as the rest of it. Brushing teeth. Showering. Combing hair. What was the point of eating one day when I was only going to have to eat the next? The thought of how much I would eat per week, per month, per year, in my lifetime—it made me sick. I told the doctor that very thought and they sent me to River Grove, my first treatment center. I lived there for eight weeks. Those girls had real horror stories. Times in the hospital or other centers when their roommates had hanged themselves, or they found them just lying there like science-room skeletons, cold. River Grove also coincided with my parents' divorce. So, even in this skimming version, it wasn't pretty. I left that place—and many places since—with a golden certificate of recovery. The first time around, my parents believed it. They came to River Grove's ridiculous graduation ceremony and let me tell you, that was a true miracle, since they had to exist in the same room together for over an hour. When I looked out into the group of overzealous parents, I saw them, Shosh. Like, really saw them. My father with his hands halfway down his pockets, saggy eyes pulling to the middle of his face. My mother with her thong peeking out from the sides of her low-rise jeans, all the other fathers clocking her with their eyes.

My parents weren't my parents. They were just people. And messed up ones at that.

Who, I wondered, looking at my father's beer gut and receding hairline, had ever thought *Let me get me some of that*? To this day, I can't believe he's the one who cheated.

Here's what I learned then, Shoshana: Age has no correlation to the shittiness of a person. Kids are not always dumber than their parents. Elders aren't always to be respected. The laws of the universe are bendy. All of us, parts gray and parts blue.

Why didn't I blink an eye at Alyssa's death? Because I heard those River Grove stories and I knew Alyssa had parents like mine. And even if she didn't, you've heard the statistics. Anorexia, the deadliest psychiatric disorder. Eventually, Shoshana, you'll come to expect these things. Signs, even love—they won't save us.

Sometimes I think that's the only way for me to go. At my own hands.

5
Shoshana

When I first arrived at RR and Rowan asked me the question—if I would brandish a baseball bat at my worst enemy or give a thousand dollars to my best friend—I didn't even hesitate. "Bat," I said and pictured my coach Mary-Ellen's face, me swinging like a madman.

That's when Rowan said, "I was right. We are meant to be."

I first found Mary-Ellen in my living room on the TV, when I was plopped down on the couch with a peanut butter and fluff sandwich, hair covered in mayonnaise to get rid of the lice that had made the rounds through our eighth-grade class. I was scrolling through the channels when, by luck or karma, the word *Cheer* popped up on the guide. Aired on X-treme Sports Atlantic (XSA).

Cheer Champions. That's what the reality show is called. Featuring an all-girl, level-five cheerleading team: Garwood Elite, also known as GE. After I watched that episode, I started over from the pilot and binged the rest of the first season and what was released of the second. The show would be on at dinner and I would force Mom to look up from the stove to see one of the flyers land a foot on the main base's face. The base had a split lip and bloody braces and all Mary-Ellen would say was, "No blood on the mat."

Mary-Ellen: a name fit for a woman who smells like children's anxiety.

I watched her scream at the team, kick a girl off for getting fat. "Falling out of shape" was how they referred to it in interviews. Mary-Ellen made her cheerleaders do suicides until they puked their lives away, yet all I could think was, *I want to be one of those girls. Even the one with stitches and a new permanent scar.*

After begging and pleading with my parents to let me switch gyms, drive the extra forty miles to practice six days a week, fly around the country on weekends, pay for hotel rooms and airfare and uniforms and practice gear and the actual practices of course, they agreed. I knew then that they loved me, because if Dad had wanted to do an IronMan every weekend instead of once a year, I would have murdered him.

Everyone tells you *be careful what you wish for*, but no one is. There, in a Garwood Elite sports bra and spandex, running laps, preparing my hardest skills for competition, I knew I wasn't. I would wait around after practice to get interviewed about how I felt—physically, emotionally—and I would lie. When Lorri, the producer, asked me what I wanted, I said what Mary-Ellen wanted me to say: to win.

"When do you think it stopped being fun?" Mrs. Walsh, our RR therapy specialist, asks. She's been sitting silently, listening intently for these last ten minutes. She comes in every Friday, completing half her patient's sessions before the nurses announce decisions on who changes color, half after.

Mrs. Walsh leans back in her suede queen's chair, folding her steady fingers over her knee, waiting.

"I don't know. Probably right before my breakdown," I admit. "I still don't know what they aired. The cameras were there, but . . ." I trail off, picking at a loose hangnail on my thumb. I don't voice it, but I'm thinking, *The not knowing, it kills me. And the only person who takes it off my mind is Rowan.*

Mrs. Walsh rests her pen on her yellow legal pad. "That must have been hard. Having something you love so much become a source of real stress. Can you talk more about what feelings come up with that for you? What it felt like being taped?"

Taped, like *The Real Housewives* or *Jersey Shore.* She must think I'm some sort of Snooki. I wonder if she's seen *Cheer Champions*, researched it for the sake of these sessions. No one in RR has, which surprised me at first, but none of them are cheerleaders and it's not like we're the biggest program on the network. We have a niche following, a small but crazy-consistent fan base.

"The whole team is a part of the show," I say. It's easier to talk to her than it is to the nurses, and I'm not sure why. "But only certain girls are part of the cast—the stars. You follow them for their stories. I didn't have a difficult childhood or a unique ethnicity or a disability like Brittany's, so I wasn't supposed to be one of them. They picked me because I was relatable to viewers. Because, just like them, I watched the show religiously before I was on it. That's how they sold me. *Average teen, now a cheer champion. And you could be too.*"

I mimic the slogan they had me say and feel relieved when Walsh doesn't look at me like I have three heads. *Look at me*, I think. *I'm not stunning enough to be a must-have cast member. I'm not the captain or a vivacious personality. I was picked to play a role because I was new to the team and after two seasons of watching the same girls, the audience wanted fresh meat.*

"So I guess I felt out of place," I continue. "Like I was going to get cut. The on-camera girls aren't invincible. Like Brittany—she was on season two—and she was on camera all the time because of her auditory dyslexia. It affected her timing for eight counts and they did a whole profile on her life outside the gym," I tell Walsh, remembering watching from my couch as Brittany gave viewers a tour of her bedroom, the white walls decked out in multicolored cheer bows. "But after her stunt fell at Worlds, the coaches dropped her like a hot rock. It sparked an online controversy about the show's incorrect representation of her diagnosis, but eventually the whole thing went away. Everything goes away when Mary-Ellen's involved and ratings are high."

Walsh nods, sympathetic.

It's Walsh's eyes, I think. *They're what make me talk so candidly.* Her squinty, soulful gaze reminds me of my dad's, and the thought of him makes my muscles ache with homesickness.

"It sounds like you've been worried about keeping your spot on the team and with the cast," she says. "And that Mary-Ellen and the girls are part of creating that environment."

The sound of Mary-Ellen's name in Walsh's mouth summons her like *Bloody Mary, Bloody Mary, Bloody Mary.* Skinny legs under black yoga pants. Liposuctioned stomach. Cunning fox eyes. The snap of her fake fingernails, filed into tiger-like neon claws. Her curled biceps always crossed over her chest, highlighting her silicone breasts.

Keep 'em up while you can, girls, she'd say and yank up the straps of twelve-year-old Ginger's training bra. One time, she told me to stop sitting cross-legged because "that shit'll give you cellulite." In her words, I was "in danger on that front already."

I hear her more common phrases too. *Get your shit together, kid. I can take you off this team like* that. *Got it? You had a double coming in here. Now you've got a one and a half. Don't get lazy on me. That shit ain't gonna fly around here. Everyone's replaceable. We clear?*

I rip the hangnail off. It stings, and I lean into the pain to keep my emotions level. "People assume it's an act. Scripted and stuff. But that's what Mary-Ellen is like in real life all the time." I sit back on the orange-cushioned loveseat, which is big enough to lie down in if I wanted.

"When you feel like you're going to get cut, when you feel anxious, is there someone on the team you talk to? Someone you confide in?" As she speaks, Walsh taps each finger of her left hand against her knee, playing an imaginary piano. In her right hand, the pen is poised.

I rub my calves out the same way I would before a competition. "Not really. Saying bad things about your own team is sort of anti-cheer. Besides, it's not Mary-Ellen's fault if she puts pressure on me and I turn out not to be a diamond. The other girls are handling that pressure. They're fine."

My voice gives way to heat, frustration. These sessions are supposed to be helping me get better, not worse, and Walsh is clearly not here to help me beat this. Isn't the goal to get rid of my insecurities? Why does it feel like now there are more of them?

"She's my coach," I insist. "She's tough, sometimes really tough, but her teams win because of it."

"Do you mind if I pull out my phone for a second? I'd like to read you the definition of *tough*."

I lift a shoulder. *Fine by me.*

"I'm just going to read whatever Google brings up."

She must think my generation trusts Google like God. I pull a loose string on my sweater, make it long and thin, twirl it around my thumb, right over the fresh wound from my hangnail.

"Tough: *strong enough to withstand adverse conditions or rough or careless handling*." She gives a second's pause. "Does Mary-Ellen *withstand adverse conditions* or *careless handling*?"

I check out my calves again, how meaty they are.

She lowers her gaze to meet mine. "Do you?"

I think about Circle of Death, the game our team plays after practice before anyone can leave. One cheerleader swings her arms back, lifts her fists, feet, wraps her knees, completes her backflip, and before she lands, the cheerleader to her left swings her arms back for a flip. It's a ripple of backflips that moves around the team like an ever-ticking clock. By fifty circles, everyone is hyperventilating; by mid-seventies, half the team are puking their lives away and the other half are looking at the garbage cans enviously, considering doing it just for the minute of rest they'd get afterward. Usually I just keep going and going until by the nineties, I'm landing on my knees.

Here at RR . . . it's the first time since GE that I've seen my knees their normal color. No bruises.

"I get your point," I say. "I'm the tough one. I'm the protagonist. She's Cruella de Vil because she hurts my feelings. You'd probably suggest never cheering for her again. But she wants me to be the best. Whether it's for me or for her, I don't think that matters. She wants me to be a star and if I can't handle the pressure or the way she runs her gym, that's on me. Other girls on the team are fine. They're at home right now, getting ready to compete at the World Championships. So how come I'm not?"

Mrs. Walsh enunciates her speech, so I can tell she's selecting her words one at a time. "You seem to think being used to love and support is a bad thing, Shoshana, and I assure you, it isn't. Can we at least agree that Mary-Ellen is not perfect?"

It's strange, but something in Walsh's voice makes me feel like the cameras are here, like she's Lorri, interviewing me from just behind the lens. Lorri has a notepad just like Walsh's too, her own set of scribbles, most of which are juicy, drama-inducing questions. The whole thing makes me wary, as if my answer might be broadcast to the entire world.

"Sure," I say, "Mary-Ellen isn't perfect." And because I know it's close to the end of the hour and I know exactly what she wants to hear, like what Mary-Ellen wants is a win, I give her the admission. "Nobody is. That's why I'm here. Isn't it?"

We wait all afternoon to get to the one-on-ones, the time where we find out who's going to change color over the weekend and start Monday Blue. Rowan and I sprawl out on the couch, legs tangled, our heads fuzzy from therapy. She's whispering—to herself more than to me—about Thanksgiving and her miracle plan to bust us out of this place. I haven't thought about it in a minute, but by her jittery, animated thrum, it's been one of the only things she can think about.

"And Thanksgiving shouldn't even be a holiday, it should be a time of mourning for indigenous people who were raped and murdered by Puritans. But hey, if the nurses want to leave this place vulnerable, so be it," she mutters right before she gets called.

The fact that Rowan is first up is a sure sign she's staying Gray. The nurses tend to get the easiest conversations out of the way early. It's not an exact science or anything. Like, New Girl goes second when hypothetically she should be first, but it's my best estimation based on past weeks. I'm called ninth, after Donna, who is also still Gray.

"Shoshana," Nurse Hart calls and, although there's no leader, no head of the household, my eyes meet hers and I know she's the one pulling the strings.

"We've taken a long look at your records and your progress over the last few weeks and we're ready to give you more responsibility in your recovery," she says. Her russet eyes are impossibly more red than brown, near paranormal. "We can only do so much. Now, you have to want this for yourself."

"Lead a horse to water," I say. "Preach. Choir. I get it." I play Rowan as best I can. It's easy because I know who she is. Sometimes I hear the things I say and I have no idea who's talking, no clue how to play myself. *Shoshana Winnick, wouldn't know her personality from a hole in the ground.* Rowan, as always, can see right through me.

"How do you feel about that?" Nurse Robinson asks, perched on the stool beside Hart. Because of Robinson's heart-shaped, moleless face, she comes off as more friendly than her coworker. But still not as friendly as Kelly, who beams with her wide cheeks so bright I can feel the sun being tugged closer to Earth.

"Are you sure?" I ask all of them. I don't know how to get out of this one or if I should want to. Putting on weight is one thing, but there has to be more to it than that.

"We know that your friendship with Rowan means a lot to you," Nurse Hart starts, her tone harsher now. She must want me to hear her, *really* hear her. *There's listening and then there's digesting,* she always says. I try to digest. "Life is long, Shoshana. Your health is what's most important here."

"Okay," I say, but I feel my heels dig in. I don't want this. Not if it means leaving Rowan. I don't want to be in RR without her. She's my safety blanket, keeping me warm, keeping me sane. How often will we get to see each other now? How long will I last without her by my side?

"Good. Starting Monday, you'll be on the Blue schedule. Now, go get showered. We'll prep you tomorrow."

Prep me? Like I'm headed for death row? One last meal in the Gray kitchen for dinner and then *bam*, I'm gone?

I stand up, oddly aware of my feet and the space between my steps. I count fifteen before I get to Rowan. The second she sees me, I know she knows. Her eyes go all big and she gives a breathy sigh, like *here we go,* but then the corner of her mouth tips up, mischievous, and I think she's actually happy for me.

"Headed for the dark side, huh?" she teases.

I want to beg her forgiveness.

Donna squeezes my bicep until my circulation cuts off. "You're getting out? Do you realize what this means? You could be home in a month! A *fucking* month, Shoshana."

"It should be you," I tell Donna. Even if she doesn't want to get fat, neither do I. What makes me any different than them?

"Oh, please. Any of us would kill to be in your shoes," Donna argues, smoothing down her purple headband.

"Kill, but not eat." I lean back against the wall, waiting for Rowan's next move. She's too quiet. "Why are you smiling like that?"

Rowan brushes a piece of hair behind my ear idly, like it's her own. "Remember in *Twin Peaks*, when Agent Dale Cooper has those bizarro dreams where he wakes up with a brand-new idea that's so brilliant it changes everything about the investigation?"

Donna positions herself away from us, stepping closer to the other Gray girls because she knows Rowan isn't addressing her and she isn't meant to hear this. I consider for a second if maybe Donna feels terribly left out by us. It can't be easy with Jazzy gone. But Rowan is so tuned into me, I let Donna fade away and grant all my attention to her Kool-Aid hair and Vaselined lips.

"Sure," I say, although I have no idea what *Twin Peaks* is or who Agent Dale Cooper is. But there's enough for me to grasp the concept. *Act like you understand. Always.* I digested that.

"Well, I had a Dale Cooper dream." She yanks me up to our room and mystically pulls out our duffel bags. Half of our clothes are already folded neatly inside. She holds her arms out in a gesture of *ta-da!,* the way a hunter shows off something he's shot. This is her prize, her gift, her talents being put into action.

"Ready to be rescued, Rapunzel?" She grins, taking my new Blue hand in her Gray one. "Because we're not waiting for Thanksgiving. We're leaving tonight."

6
Rowan

If you think this is my first time running away, you haven't been paying attention. No. My first time running away was from mother's womb, a place I knew wasn't safe for a fucking simple clump of cells. It's not my second or third time either. Running away is a family specialty, a recipe passed down through a lineage of women to my mother, who looked at me, a screaming five-year-old dragging her My Little Pony suitcase out the front door, and said if I didn't come back *this instant* there would be hell to pay—as if she hadn't gone on her own Barbie backpack adventures years earlier and been told the very same thing.

At fourteen, I made it halfway to Florida with my then boyfriend, Cheaney—four years older, negative-six-years wiser—before he bailed and I realized what they never tell you in all those glorious let's-ride-across-the-country-and-get-stoned-and-learn-about-life movies: hitchhiking is sketchy as hell.

Running away with you will be different, though. For one, you're resourceful, Shoshana. You'll find a way for us to make money, live off the land, get into good trouble and stay out of bad trouble, and be smart enough to tell the difference when you feel the churn in your gut. You'll make sure we tag along with only semipervs, not the F'd-in-the-head Ted Bundys who cause irreversible damage, the kind that lingers no matter how many showers you take.

For two, you won't bail.

But none of that explains why your skin is a shade of green when I tell you we're leaving. Your eyes dart from me to the duffel bags, then back to me again. Why so serious? Do I have to put on a Joker grin and pry the desperation for escape out of you?

You rake a finger over your hair and say, "We won't make it down the stairs, let alone through the front door."

So, you're worried about getting caught. *How cute.*

"We're not going out the front door," I say. "We're going out the bathroom window. The one above the radiator."

"That's fifteen feet above the ground."

"Twelve, and only seven if we hang by our hands. What? You've never fallen out of a tree before? Seven feet won't break us, Shosh."

You stand with unfocused eyes and audible breath—one of those Pageant of the Masters live-art replicas, frozen in time, the *Mona Lisa* with no half-smile. Then your forehead crinkles. You never cry, but your face builds to something resembling fear or hurt, and call it a soft spot, call it a brain aneurysm, call it an alien host invading my body, but I decide we can't do it. We can't go. Not until you're positive you want to and won't flake. So I do you the favor and decide to play it off, to say, *Ha! You actually thought I would let us go on a suicide mission! Hell, if I really could open that window, wouldn't I be halfway to La La Land by now?*

But before I let you off the hook, you clamp on. "Okay," you say. Your pupils dilate, visibly coming to terms with the plan. I know I should tell you it's okay, that we don't have to go, that I'll stay, for you. But I want this so badly. I want to run and I want you to come with me and screw it if that makes me selfish. In my B.S.E.—Before Shoshana Era—I was rocky. You are the thing keeping me steady now. I need this; I need you.

"So, tonight?" I manage to grant you one more chance to say no. I leave enough pause for the question to sink in.

"Tonight," you answer, more confident this time.

There you are. My brown-eyed girl. You and me against the world.

"Good," I say, pleased, proud. "The signal flies in the sky at midnight."

@

Before our escape, the only activity I have is therapy with Walsh, one hour from five to six. She spends the time making me reflect on my fourth-grade astronomy lesson, the photo we were shown taken by the Voyager 1 space probe in the 90s: Earth from six billion kilometers away. Our teacher, Mr. Scott, had to point out Earth to us five times before we could see it. He circled the whitish-blue speck and said, "Right here. That's Earth."

Would you believe that crap, Shoshana? Everything you've

ever seen, anyone you've ever met, and it can all be covered up by the tip of a fucking thumb.

The rest of my class got over the photo by lunch, but to this day, I haven't. I try explaining that to Walsh, how lonely it all feels, how useless we all are. But she brings out Raggedy Ann dolls and asks me to reframe my emptiness as a different entity, an external factor I can keep out, which means she obviously doesn't get it. You can't keep out what's already inside you.

I bet, if you were in Walsh's shoes, your question would be: *If nothing matters, doesn't everything?* And I get that. You and Walsh both want to understand what my criteria is for things that matter and things that don't. I have trouble with the line myself sometimes, but not all things are made equal. Like, if the president gets shot, it matters more than some Best Buy employee of the month taking the bullet. If a white teenage girl gets kidnapped, people cry for justice, but if a Black teenage girl gets kidnapped, it's lost in a few threads on Twitter. It's not fair, but it's the truth. And you know it. Some things matter to the collective consciousness more than others, but all things have an expiration date in the public eye, even murdered white girls, even presidents, and to me, that makes them all pointless.

"Does Walsh pull that shit on you?" I ask you at dinner. Snap a finger in front of your face because you're zoned out. Thinking about what? Tonight? The great escape? "Walsh," I repeat. "Does she bring out dolls for you to play with?"

Most of what Walsh has me do is channel my child-self to get at my *true* identity. I'm told to visualize little Rowan at age four, eight, or twelve, or imagine her in five years—I suck at all of it. The dolls come later. I'm even worse at taking them seriously.

"Dolls?"

"Yes. *Dolls*. Personifying the problem. I sat there for an hour today talking to *Fearful Farrah* and *Worry Wendy*. It was un-fucking-believable."

You choke on your macaroni.

"I'm being serious. What do you guys do for the hour?"

You shrug. My imagination runs wild to fill in the blank. You and Walsh probably spend the time in silence, nothing to talk about since you are *obviously* perfect and your life is a goddamn dream. I mean, don't get me wrong. Everyone hurts. But your hurt is like a paper cut, and the rest of us are over here with five-inch-long lacerations.

A part of me thinks if you hang around me long enough, Shosh, you'll get it. You'll tell the world to go away and decide the two of us are the only thing that matters. I want that. Dark Shoshana. The version of you who understands happiness doesn't equal fulfillment and that fulfillment is impossible. Another part of me thinks if you get it, if you truly understand bottomlessness the way I do, you won't be the Shoshana I love anymore.

You finish packing in spurts, leaving your bag under the bed, resting the closet doors open a crack so the nurses won't suspect. After dark, I find Smurf, explain the plan, and rough her up a little to make sure she won't sell her soul to Satan and give us up. Not until we're gone, anyway. All she has to do is cry, get both overnight nurses into her room, and keep their attention long enough for you and I to sneak into the bathroom. I can take it from there.

I watch as, sweetly, you try to layer your jeans under polka dot pajamas. I say, "too risky," so you take the jeans off and stuff them in the top of your duffel bag. What we really have to worry about are the sneakers. I order: socks on, shoelaces untied, shoes right under the ladder, ready to go.

Ten minutes to lights out, you start fidgeting. "I'm going to brush my teeth one more time," you say, parting your wet, curly hair.

"You brushed twice already."

"What if we don't have any water out there?" you say, unsure, shy.

"We're going into town, Shoshana, not the desert."

"We're going into town without any money."

"We're seventeen-year-old girls. We don't need money."

You go to the door and walk out, toothbrush in hand, and Donna must be catching on, because she sends me a sketchy look and her eyebrows shoot up like alert caterpillars. She may not have heard my revised getaway plan, but this conversation was enough for her to put two and two together about us leaving. And here she is, desperate for friends, at her wit's end for a way out. Here I am, capable of giving her both.

"No. No way," I say.

She works her pouty lip. "Come on. You and Shoshana can go . . . wherever it is you're going and I'll catch a bus to Jazzy's. I just need help getting out. You were going to let me come before."

"I was going to let you come when it was you and Jazzy. You by yourself is a different story. And FYI, Jazzy doesn't swing that way."

She frowns in that ridiculous, *why, Rowan, I simply have no idea what you're talking about* way, but she's not fooling anyone. Not me, at least. Maybe I know this because I'm batting for her team too, the partly gay team. I'm debating between the B and the Q of LGBTQA+. Not in a rush to settle on which letter yet.

"I'm not into her like that," Donna bluffs. Her red lips pull back to reveal lying, brittle teeth. I used to cut my apples into teeny tiny slices to give the appearance I was eating more— something Donna has never had to do. She's used to swallowing and regurgitating. I'm used to spitting.

"Whatever you say." I wave her off as she moves to the door, arms crossed over her chest like a body guard.

"I'll tell the nurses," she says. Donna, the little fucking tattletale.

"Fine," I snap. "Come along. But as soon as we're outside, you're on your own, and I swear on my grandmother's grave— no, I swear on Shoshana's future grave—if you mess this up—"

"I won't."

She must be serious if she's willing to bet on you, Shosh.

Nurse Hart strides in one minute later and asks what movie we want to see tomorrow. She's taking a tally. You sneak in behind her, teeth pearly white. *We're not seeing anything tomorrow,* I think, basking in the rush of *I know something you don't know.* We list off run-of-the-mill films. We tuck ourselves in.

An hour passes before we hear Smurf's role kick into action. Sharp, high-pitched bird squeaks that sound real—credit where credit's due—ring from across the hall. Sophie's room is diagonal to ours, a few feet before the bathroom, and I can see she's forgotten to shut her bedroom door. All three of us stand ready, our shoes laced tight. But we're compromised unless Sophie closes her door with the nurses inside or lures them downstairs.

"Wait for my cue," I whisper, but Smurf's door stays open as the cries and screams continue. *Shut it,* I think. *Lock it. Buy us time.*

Smurf's hysterics rise in volume and—is it my horror-movie mind or do they sound *too* real? The shrieks swell, loud enough to carry down the hallway and wake the rest of the Gray girls, maybe even the Blue girls on the first floor. A foot kicks Smurf's door closed, hard, but it's not Smurf. Her heel wouldn't pack that kind of power. It must be one of the nurses, trying to shield our eyes from whatever's going on.

This leaves me with two options: run for the hills or, because it's possible others have woken from the noise and could stop us, delay our exit by a day or two. There's no time to deliberate. My impulsive side makes the call.

"Now!" I hiss. We carry our bags to the bathroom, no sign of alerting the masses. Donna closes the bathroom door behind us and in under a minute, I'm at the window above the radiator.

"How are you going to open it?" Donna asks.

I put a finger over my lips to shush her. If I work fast, I can get it open in about fifteen seconds the way my ex-boyfriend Cheaney taught me.

My first day here, I saw this window with its two adjoined panels, the kind where one pane can slide behind the other, and I was sure I could open it. Cheaney and I used to break into places all the time, not out of them, but what's the difference? I would have broken out of here eventually, but I wanted you to come with me and I wanted you to be sure. Running away together now—it will be so worth the wait.

I jimmy the pane up and down. The lock moves jaggedly, but it lifts.

"It's that easy?" Donna shakes her head in shock.

The lock lifts to the top and I slide the left window behind the right, push out the screen. Apparently you weren't kidding about the fifteen-foot drop. I peek out and the ground is barely visible in the dark.

I turn to guinea pig Donna who won't shut the fuck up. "You first, kid."

"Me?" Her chalky skin pales further. "Why?"

"Because I said so. You wanted this. Now go."

She sticks her head out past mine into the fresh air. "I can't see the ground. How will I know when to brace myself?"

"Just keep your body loose and bend your knees. Try to roll forward afterward. I've seen people do that in the movies."

She shakes her head. "No. I can't."

"Fine. Then you're out." I shove her aside. We don't have time for this. "You jump, I jump, Jack. Who first?"

You glance over your shoulder at the bathroom door. What

are you waiting for? Smurf's screams are fading into distant sobs. You listen, then face the window, eyes reflecting the magic of the night.

"I'll go," you say.

"Good girl." I toss your bag out the window, far enough away from the landing spot, as you creep toward the edge. You lift a leg over, straddling the pane, not making the mistake of looking down like Donna did.

"Grab my wrists," I order.

You hesitate but take one hand, then the other, squeezing so hard I can feel the outlines of my bones.

"Put your other leg out. Then slide down as slowly as you can," I order.

I regrip your sweaty skin as you haul your other leg over the edge, your full body sitting on the frame, facing out, back hunched to fit your lengthy torso in the square between RR and the rest of the world.

Neither of us is prepared for what happens next.

What happens: the bathroom door busts open and you turn to see who's there, body twisting before you full-fledged jump. My fingers hold on to you for a single fleeting moment and then they're empty. Nothing. You jumped to get out just in time. You're gone.

"Holy fuck! Holy fuck! Holy fuck!" Donna yells and the bathroom door swings shut behind Nurse Hart, whose hands are streaked with blood. My brain scrambles to make sense of it, but I'm already on the window ledge myself, praying you've gotten out of the way so I don't crush you to death.

"Rowan!" Hart screams.

I don't hang by my hands. There's no time, no thought. On instinct, I hop out. The weight in my stomach lifts and for a second, I think the ground is even farther down than I thought, too far for us to have jumped. But I slam into the earth and the impact jolts up my spine. My knees meet the dirt, palms ramming into the ground a second later.

Heat pulses at my right wrist, adrenaline masking the pain of something worse than bruised. My ears ring. My vision goes wonky. It's the sensation of a badly pulled muscle times a thousand. Like my wrist is on fire, my body forcing me to see what I've done, what I've caused, how I'm always playing a game that tiptoes into getting hurt. I am my mother's daughter. Dreamy yet destructive.

"Jesus *fucking* Christ," I spit, cradling the furnace that is my probably broken wrist. Everything is spinning too fast to stand.

My eyes take a moment to clear the tears. Then I realize we did it. We actually did it. We're out.

You stand above me, staring at the light in the window above us, the darkness all around. You brush the dirt off your knees, then offer up a hand to help me, hoisting me to my feet with my good arm. Nurse Hart leans her head out of the window, peering down, a bloody hand covering her mouth.

In winter air, moon overhead, you look like a mini-Frida, a goddess I could kiss forever.

"I thought you never say Jesus Christ," you let out in a breath.

Less than a second later, the sirens sound.

7
Shoshana

"What were you thinking? You could have been killed," Mom snaps. I practically see her upper row of teeth clawing at her lower lip, her telltale sign for uncapped, motherly rage. She sounds almost as angry as the time I called her from my Jewish sleepaway camp, forced to tell her about how the counselor had bought our bunk tequila and I caved and tried a sip. Then, my punishment was only a lecture about not following the crowd, about how tequila bottles are filled with worms *so congratulations on drinking worm juice*, and about how to implement the "just say no" plan, which I should have already known.

"If you want to leave that badly, there are plenty of other treatment centers—"

"No," I rush. Not now. Not when I've finally made a real best friend and I'm Blue—or will be if the nurses don't change their minds. To be moved somewhere else . . . that would be a fate worse than RR. "I already told you, I didn't mean to do it. I fell. Why else would I—" I peek around and lower my voice, although I'm rooms away from Rowan. "Why else would I have snitched to the nurses? I was never planning to leave, Mom. Not really."

Last night, I went to the nurses to spill the beans. Told

Rowan I was going to brush my teeth and told the truth instead. It tumbled out in spurts. *Don't tell—Escape plan—Not her fault.*

It's a betrayal, my talking to the nurses, but I didn't do it to rat her out or get into the nurses' good graces. My motivation wasn't selfish. I did this for Rowan. This program is only working for one of us and it's not her. If we broke out of RR now . . . in a month, in six months, in a year, she might be worse. She might end up like Alyssa, dead, cold, forgotten. The world is lit by Rowan's tongue, her face, her fire. Blow the candle of Rowan Parish out and we—I—will literally perish. No pun intended.

I swear I won't let that happen.

The nurses promised they'd take care of it. That they'd "catch" us before we made it to the bathroom door. That they wouldn't breathe a word of my betrayal. But who could've foreseen Sophie's seizure? We didn't. They didn't. It was the reason we got to the bathroom window undisturbed. They had too much on their plate. Some pun intended.

Afterward, I told the nurses: *I didn't mean to jump. I slipped off the window ledge. I won't do it ever again. I promise.*

Afterward, I asked: *Is Sophie okay?*

There were musings of information, wisps of honesty. The ambulance was for two; we knew that. Sophie with her seizure and Rowan with a scaphoid fracture in her right wrist. The paramedics called it lucky, all the *What If*s of worse scenarios. *What if Rowan had fallen on top of Shoshana when she jumped out the window? Think of all the possible concussions or spinal damage or extra broken bones . . .*

The paramedics saw "could've been worse," but the nurses saw "could've been better" and "could've been avoided."

"You did not snitch," my mother scolds. "You told them the truth, which was the right thing to do. There's a difference."

"They're synonymous. And if I did the right thing, why am I being yelled at?"

"Adam, talk some sense into your daughter," Mom says. She must throw him the phone because I hear it hit the floor.

Your daughter, like I'm his now, like I'm only hers when she deems it fit. I lean back in the Tempur-Pedic staff room chair. Nurse Hart readjusts her glasses in the corner of the room, her eyes pinned to my mouth. The clock on the wall reads just past seven in the morning; the only people up this early are the ones involved in last night's *incident.* I'm the first to take the plunge and make the mandatory call home.

"*Shoshi,*" Dad sighs. His voice alone makes me regret everything that's happened. He sounds tired, like he's been up all night, like he's disappointed, or even worse, embarrassed. And not the way Mom gets embarrassed when she tells her JCC friends why I'm in here, why I'm not celebrating Rosh Hashanah with everyone. Once, I made a joke about my starvation helping me fit in at Yom Kippur. She didn't appreciate it.

Dad sounds embarrassed, like I'm not who he thought I was.

"I'm sorry," I say, earnest.

"*Shoshi,*" he says again. I see the ghost of his hand lifting, stretching itself through the phone to stroke my cheek. "I know these past few months have been hard and confusing. But if you're going to be there, you gotta *be there,* kid. Does that make sense? We're not sending you away to have a wild adventure or paying them so you'll come home still hurting."

"I know," I say, but a part of me wonders if he's saying this, truly saying it, or if he's reading from a Post-it note Mom has shoved in his face, the way she does to remind him to drive me to practice or pick up the dry cleaning when he's on a conference call.

"Is she going to be back for Worlds?" Mom whispers to Dad. I hear him shooing her away. I'm not meant to hear this part.

"We'll let you go," he says.

I didn't ask to be let go of, I think.

"No more jumping out of windows, okay?"

"Okay."

The phone cuts dead. I hand my phone back to Nurse Hart, wondering if she'll keep me Gray now. To them, it may seem like I changed my mind. Like I decided to make a break for it, to jump and grab Rowan, to say, "Let's do it." But I didn't mean to fall. I just turned my body to see Nurse Hart and slipped. It was an accident. I felt it in my gut. I'm not meant to leave here yet.

Mom spent all those years reading parenting books: *The Blessing of a Skinned Knee, The Strong-Willed Child* for K.J., *Option B*—probably in case Dad died doing his first IronMan and she would be forced to solo parent—and I guess it paid off, because for all the kids in my class who pulled hair or threw fits or came naturally to gossiping, I got the superpower of *knowing better.* It's a disease for a middle schooler, the age where your social status is ranked by meanness. As a girl who had *knowing better*, I posed no threat. I would not yell. I would not add to the gossip. I would not be cruel. And so, in middle school eyes, I would not be interesting.

"Be the bigger person," Mom always insisted, and I had the instinct of what the bigger person would do. But that doesn't mean it was easy or rewarding or anything they say it will be when you do it. Being the bigger person, knowing better, having that gut feeling—it doesn't make you happy. It makes you frustrated. Because for all of eternity, you have to continue to be the type of human being who lets things roll off your shoulders, ignoring trivial drama until it drives you insane. That's why it's easy to be with Rowan. Around her, I don't have to be Shoshana Winnick, good girl, perfect cheerleader, feeble cliché. I don't have to be the bigger person. I can just be.

"Head back to bed," Nurse Hart says. I'm grateful she's noticed how tired I am. "I'll wake you up at noon to walk you through instructions about the self-serve kitchen. You already have your stuff packed, so we'll be moving you downstairs tonight instead of Monday."

A baseball-sized lump leaps in my chest. "I'm still on the Blue schedule?"

She nods.

Yes. Good, I think. *I'll be here, like Dad was saying. I'll do better.* But then I think of Rowan and look at Nurse Hart and the lump sinks. We both know what this means. Tonight, I won't be sleeping in the bed beneath Rowan's. I'll be on the first floor. Moved in with Blue girls. Eating with them. Dancing with them. With them 24/7. The sooner the better, apparently, because the nurses are trying to banish Rowan and me to separate corners as fast as possible. Not that I can blame them. Even I can see how we enable each other.

"Thank you, Shoshana. For telling us," Nurse Hart adds. "I'm sorry we didn't take care of the issue sooner."

She's thanking me, but it feels like a public shaming. I may have done this for Rowan, but she would see it as a betrayal. I lied. Deliberately. Didn't want her face to end up on a milk carton. Would that even matter to her? I doubt it.

When I return upstairs, Rowan is sitting on my bed with a black cast on her right wrist, a silver Sharpie in her left hand.

"We would have gotten away with it, too, if it weren't for those meddling nurses," she says, but her Scooby-Doo impression lacks luster.

"I'm glad we didn't," I say. "You broke your arm."

"I fractured my wrist and it's a teeny, tiny, baby fracture." She hands me the Sharpie and I write my name on the side, curving the bottom of the S so it underlines the rest of my name. I knock my knuckles against the fiber glass to feel its strength. Rowan looks disapprovingly at my signature.

"That's it? You're not even going to write H.A.G.S. like the rest of the Breakfast Club Gray girls?"

"It's winter," I say, but I add *loves you* beneath my name. "Better?"

"Rowan," Nurse Robinson calls from beyond the door.

"It doesn't matter that it's my right wrist because I'm ambidextrous," Rowan tells me, ignoring the command.

Being ambidextrous technically means you're weak on both sides, but I don't tell her that.

"Rowan," Robinson calls again.

"I'm coming!" she yells back. She'll have to make her own phone call home this morning. I wonder who she's going to talk to. Her mom? Her dad? Both? No matter what, it's guaranteed to be shitty.

"If I don't come back,"—she points at me with her new cast— "avenge my death."

"Will do," I swear, but I'm a little too tired for avenging right now. A night with ambulances can do that to a person.

Donna is the one to raise the dead and wake me at a quarter to noon. When she does, she starts by telling me New Girl, Sophie, is still in the hospital, that she won't be back for a day or two and, when she is, she'll be taking my bed. I ask, "Why won't she be using Jazzy's bed?" but Donna doesn't know. She just says Rowan found out Smurf is taking my place while I was asleep and she's ready to jump out another window. In other news, a handyman came this morning and patched up the window we broke out of. Now there are concrete bars covering the opening. A precaution until they can fix it permanently.

The entirety of last night's events doesn't quite hit me until I go to brush my teeth at noon, unable to scrub the aftertaste of guilt from my gums, and see something I shouldn't—a mistake of wrong place, wrong time—in the bathroom, again, which may as well be haunted at this point.

From the window, through the new, shiny jail bars, I spot Nurse Robinson leaning against her white Honda, palms pressed to the sockets of her eyes. She resembles a newly laid egg, squishy and fragile. Sobs shake her as hard as any new girl I've ever seen, worse than Sophie was after she woke from her seizure last night.

"Maybe it's something else," Donna says over my shoulder, looking out, but we both know we did that. We're the ones causing her pain. My *knowing better* gut tells me so.

Random moments like these make me wonder who the nurses are when they leave, if they have any issues of their own. Rowan says no, *not the way we do.* But sometimes I think she wants to believe that, as if *we do* somehow makes us special. Considering her love for Frida, she probably believes the more pain you're in, the more of an artist you are. I like to think that's true for the sake of all people suffering, but honestly, I still believe happiness is the best we can all hope for.

Nurse Hart's Blue Girl talk happens after my lunch, and it's scarily similar to Big Girl talk for toddlers who need potty training. Featuring my new responsibilities, what they include, what I'll experience—how, she tells me, it's okay to be nervous, to mess up, but I need to try.

She leads me through the Blue girls' corridor, a part of the center I was shown on my introductory tour and haven't seen since. The girls' names are written on whiteboards attached to each door. *If Rowan and I had that,* I think, *we would have vandalized it.* Well, *she* would have. I would have added tiny doodles in the white space and been credited for half.

Nurse Hart stops in front of a whiteboard with the names Crystal and Brandy on it. "This is you." She opens the door. I note Blue girls are allowed to fully close them.

The room is simple, clean, and a triple. Two beds—one on each side—and a third at the back. No bunks. All of them have matching pink-and-orange flower duvets. It's cozy, like the college dorm rooms they show in movies.

I stare straight at the window. *They have natural light*, I think, wondering if every room downstairs does or just this one.

"Here's your bed." Nurse Hart points to the one in the back by the window and I set my stuff down.

In a way, it feels like I'm already out, like this isn't really RR but somewhere else entirely. What I wouldn't give for my phone, to just lie down on the bed and scroll through Instagram and see what other people are doing with their lives. I'm the only one whose life has been on pause here. Well, the only person who will have thousands asking about her disappearance. Unless one of these girls is also a secret well-known figure I'm unaware of.

"You'll eat dinner in the Gray kitchen, but sleep in here, then start the Blue schedule in the morning. There's a copy of the hour-by-hour schedule on the back of the door." Nurse Hart motions to the calendar with the rundown. I walk over and read tomorrow's. Sunday: Sleep in. Breakfast. School. Meditation or Art. Free time. Lunch. Personal Projects. Yoga or Movie. Shower. Dinner. Bed.

I'm surprised they have options for some of the slots. Everything for Gray girls is mandatory, and mostly therapeutic.

The yoga gets me excited. Physical activity. Finally. The weekend session of school does not.

"What's *Personal Projects*?" I put my finger over the three p.m. slot.

"You'll pick a passion project, something you can do research on, and you'll present it to the group before you leave. All will be explained later."

"Research?" Usually research requires use of the internet . . .

"There's a lab behind the art room. It's always locked, and before you get all excited—the computers are monitored. Only certain sites are permitted. No Facebook or Tinder or Tweetering or whatever you girls do nowadays."

"I'll be on a computer tomorrow?" Electricity hums in my chest. We've been living like the Amish for months. Even in school sessions, they just give us textbooks or printouts of whatever we need. Finally. A screen. How did I not hear about this? How did *Rowan* not hear about this?

"There are more rules, but yes. How about I take you to ceramics and introduce you to one of the girls you'll be rooming with? Brandy never misses a class."

We walk to the art room, the same one the Gray girls use, but Gray girls never do ceramics, another privilege. The Blue girls work on the pottery wheels with familiarity, their smocks and fingers smudged and their hair tossed in messy buns or ponytails, flyaways crusted with wisps of clay. I have a hard time connecting them to the girls I saw in the dance room yesterday, the ones I thought were so terrible. Here, together, they're a group of gazelles. Captivating, unblinking, and over-all, intimidating.

"Girls."

The gazelles' heads snap up. Nurse Hart is the cheetah that calls them to attention.

"Thank you." She puts her arm around me like we're buddy-buddy. "This is Shoshana Winnick. She'll be starting on your schedule tomorrow."

"Hi, Shoshana," they say in unison.

"Hi," I reply, shyer than intended. They all go back to work-ing, each intent on their own creation. Most of the girls are crafting bowls or flower pots, but one girl, the chubby belly button–picker from dance class yesterday, is sitting with her clay in a mound, unimpressed.

"Shoshana, this is Brandy," Nurse Hart says. It's hard to imagine Brandy has never skipped this class. Unless she's trying to make her pile of clay into a pile of clay, she sucks. "Brandy, Shoshana is your new roommate."

Brandy's eyes are so deep set, the skin beneath her brows droops down to the lids. Her face is flat and puffy like a pancake.

"Okay," she husks.

"I like your mountain," I say, pointing to the dump and trying for sincerity.

"It's a teapot."

I hold back the laugh Rowan would have let go. *Let me guess: a brass one, so you can shoot yourself in the foot and pay your way out of here?* she'd say, and the two of us would giggle, probably the only ones who even know what *The Brass Teapot* is.

"Come along," Nurse Hart says, and I slip out, dreading going back to my new room. We make our way into the Gray kitchen without her sweeping me, which is strange but refreshing. By the time I sit down with my food, Donna and Rowan are mid-conversation, arguing over *Jersey Shore*'s worst season. Rowan says, all of them. Donna says, the first three were good, four and five were the worst, then six picked back up. I say, I've never seen it. Both their jaws drop. Then I backpedal, say I *have* seen it, just not thoroughly. I wonder what they would think if they knew I was on reality TV.

"Whatever," Rowan says. "Nothing beats *The Bachelor*." She mimics jabbing a finger down her throat. "Total crap. The girls will say, 'He cannot possibly bring Courtney back,' but *of course* he will because he'll be forced to by the network, which needs to keep ratings up. It's the dumbest, most commercialized program ever. And that music! God, it's like someone's going to die if they don't get a rose. Everyone's more interested in that than the real people dying in Aleppo."

Donna runs a hand down her sleek ponytail, Kelly watching to make sure she doesn't smear food in the glossy strands. For my last meal in the Gray kitchen I picked pizza, Rowan picked eggplant parmesan, and Donna picked the tofu dish. I can't remember the last time we all chose different things from the daily rotating options.

Donna chose the safest meal, which she does almost every time we eat. Safe foods are the ones considered healthier by diet culture. Like, an apple would be thought of as safer than a cinnamon bun. Oil, safer than butter. The nurses are trying to drill those ideas out of our heads altogether. No such thing as safe or unsafe. I can see Kelly making notes, catching Donna's patterns and preparing another lecture about how there are no good foods, no bad foods, how all food is important. All food: just food.

If we had a dime for every time Kelly said that, we could buy our way out of RR.

"I kind of like *The Bachelor*," Donna admits. Her reluctance is already a flaw in her opinion. If she's going to challenge Rowan, she should stand straighter, not sound so conflicted.

"Exactly my point. You're brain-dead," Rowan snorts. "If you're buying into any of that consumerist crap, you're nothing but a by-product of society. And what's the point of living life if you're just what everyone expects you to be?"

Donna sneers but can't quite refute it. "Every conversation with you makes my brain hurt," she says instead. I can hear her trying, but her words don't bite that way Rowan's do. Rowan has a natural way, a lawyer's way. She'll take her point to the grave, *Blood in the Water* style, even if she changes her mind halfway through an argument. Mary-Ellen would commend her for it.

"That's because every time you watch one of those garbage shows, your brain shrinks, bit by bit by bit, and by this point, I mean . . . you said so yourself. You can't even hold a basic intellectual conversation with a peer without your hollow head threatening to combust," pronounces Rowan.

"Um, guys," I say, trying to douse the fire.

"See, Shoshana." Rowan's eyes bug out. "This is what

happens when you leave me alone for two seconds in the looney bin! It's like you're my leash or something. Without you, without *it*, I'll be turning this place into *Murder, She Wrote* starring me in T-minus twenty-four hours. So, unless you want to write the anorexic's version of *In Cold Blood*, I suggest you find a way to stay Gray."

"It's not up to me," I say, leaving my side of corn bread on the plate.

"What do you mean? All it takes is one outburst and you're back to being one of us."

"*One of us*? You're grouping yourself together with Donna?" I need a change in subject, a way to make sure she doesn't come up with another plan or a hostage situation that ends up with me being captured in the night. I skip *knowing better* and kick the puppy, the easy target, Donna.

"Desperate times," Rowan teases as Donna scoots away from us. I glance at the Reverse Heathers, where New Girl should be. *Sophie*, I correct. *I know her name. I should use it.*

Robinson is at the back of the kitchen in sunglasses.

"Just promise me one thing," Rowan says, her voice low and serious now.

I stare at her cast. It's now signed by Donna and a few of the other Gray girls, but all of their names are smaller than mine. I'm sure Rowan made that a prerequisite for signing it after me.

"Name it."

Her Bette Davis eyes gleam. "Don't forget. *We* are what matters. All the rest is white noise."

"You and me."

"No." She shakes her head. "Closer than that. *Us.* One thing. One word. One entity. That's it."

I taste it on my tongue. "*Us.*"

"Blue. Gray. I don't give a shit if you're a fucking rainbow or grave black. It's us, through all of this. Yes?"

She validates what I already know. That I can be whoever, whatever, I want around her, and she'll still have my back. A best friend. That's what she is to me, and I to her. It's what I've never had in my seventeen years on this planet. Until now.

She can sense the word before I say it, but we shake on it for kicks.

"Yes."

Rowan

Today, I play the *What If* game by myself.

What if the two of us had made it out without being stopped by the EMTs? Where would we be right now? An amusement park? A beach, where grains of sand exfoliate our heels and our flip-flops thud against uneven boardwalk wood? *What if* we found some nearby park, a gazebo, a pond full of mallards, and we raced to the swings, pumping as high as we could and letting our stomachs lift as we flew? *What if* we snuck into a nearby neighborhood pool and, when we were both good and wet, I pulled you close and you didn't freak out when our lips sealed?

Ever since you jumped out that bathroom window, planning to run away with me, planning to give me all of you, I can't stop thinking about how lucky I got. You can't buy this kind of loyalty. I couldn't produce it with Cheaney on the outside. Couldn't with Donna or Jazzy on the inside. Sometimes, there are just two people, at the same point in time, who give themselves over to the magnetism of their chemistry. How lucky am I to have you? Your wholehearted devotion, Shoshana.

That last *What If* has been in the back of my brain for some time now. The *What If* kiss. But in my head, it goes one of two ways. The first is perfect. You kiss me like your life depends on it, our tongues wrestling like those pond mallards, our hands aching for more. Then the second rolls around and you don't even let me get there before you back away, space out, and we're never the same again.

My need to not lose you in reality is stronger than any fantasy I could dream up right now. So I leave the *What Ifs* as *What Ifs*.

It's only been hours, but Smurf is already attempting to replace you in our group of Gray girls. She's sleeping in your bed, stealing your seat in art. She even made a side comment about how Nurse Robinson's walk is more of a waddle, as if I'd be impressed. I was. A little. I suppose I can't blame her for not living up to her predecessor. *We can't all be you,* remember, Shoshana?

Donna is also attempting to replace you. She tries to play games, stupid ones like *Light as a Feather, Stiff as a Board* and *Fuck Marry Kill.* Too hard, she tries, until she sees I won't budge and starts ranting about all the shows she's missing, the movies, the video games, the magazines, knowing I don't care about any of her issues but needing a soundboard to remain sane, which I allow for brief periods of time because things around here are getting dull-dull-duller by the minute.

The magazines she loves bug me the most. *Seventeen*—how to prep your skin so you won't break out in winter. *Vanity Fair*—the best way to grip an eyeliner pencil so your line goes on sharp. *Cosmo*—how to warrant more male attention, sci-entifically proven. A September selfie challenge in *In Touch.* A weekly workout regimen in *Star*. Monday, *Mountain climbers*, all the way to Sunday, *Six pack abs. See results!*

Bullshit. Bullshit. Bullshit. The more we hate ourselves, the more they profit, and that's the whole business in less than ten words. They make women feel bad so they can get them to buy the most ridiculous items, hoping to be happier and prettier like the advertisements promise with individual glue-on eyebrow hairs and chemical tan in a bottle. On and on, they tell us how to do our makeup and keep a man, like any man can really be kept with those things. Eventually, they start coaching us on what to do in the bedroom, taking control of the most intimate parts of our lives with "The One Trick Sure to Make Him Go Crazy!" *Him. Him. Him.* Forever. Those trashy magazines stick with you when you're in it, too, reminding you to disguise your pain under gimme-more moans, assuring him that he did the world's best job, that he's huge, that he's the greatest lover in the goddamn universe, so long as you don't damage his ego. Never make him as insecure as you are.

In seventh grade Cheaney took me to get my belly button pierced. He said it would be hot for him, *a total turn-on*, and I did it. A man in his forties stuck a needle up my stomach in the back of an RV down the shore for only fifteen bucks. In return, I sat on his lap while I filled out the "paperwork." The number of things I've done for men, the amount of money I've spent for their fleeting attention, is sickening. Now, any time I hear "Boys prefer girls who . . ." I tune it the fuck out.

Truth is, Shosh, I chopped my hair my first day here not because I went psycho, but because I'd been wanting to cut it since I was twelve. The hassle of long hair—braiding, curling, brushing—and for what? It was just another *boys prefer girls who…* If boys preferred girls with bald heads, ninety percent of women would be Q-tips right now. I had sworn that off and I needed to believe a person could really do that, could say, "F the mainstream," and follow through.

So I stole a pair of scissors from one of the art rooms, used a fork to lock the door, and started sawing. It took all of two minutes before I set the scissors down, eight inches of blonde hair clumped on the floor. Then, there it was—my face—stripped away from everything. It was the first time in a long time that I felt good about what I saw in the mirror.

Everyone treats short-haired women differently. Blame me for taking the easy way out, for doing it while I'm in here instead of walking into school one day, spikes galore, and saying an F-U to the kids who really need to hear it. But if I had done that, I would have become the subtweet scapegoat. *When that weird girl cuts her hair off and you're like XD hahahaha.* Or *Help find the missing hair!!! #goodluckgettingapromdate #boyorgirl?*

Cyberspace—where people can destroy you in 280 characters.

When you look at me, Shoshana, I have no clue what you see. Make no mistake, most people see my hair and will misinterpret it as a cry for attention, see me as someone who was irrevocably screwed up, the lot of them thinking, *oh those poor parents.* An ounce of that is true. Most of it is total bullshit.

I bet you see me, Shoshana, and think: *Rowan.* The only version of me you've ever met.

My mother freaked when she heard about my haircut over the phone, but she rationalized by thinking by the time I get out I'll be able to tuck it behind my ears. I think if she saw me, the way I looked that day, she would have taken me home. The sight of her daughter, her only child, with a purple boy-cut. It would've been too much to take. But from across-the-state Bowie, Maryland, the three-hour drive to Friendsville seemed daunting. Our love is only worth seventy miles, give or take.

What if I didn't cut my hair? *What if* the nurses had kicked me out for that stunt with your file? *What if* we never met? I'd probably be like Alyssa. Six feet in the ground. Dust for bones. Or I'd be living in the Red Roof Inn again, a more permanent residency. Not physically, but mentally. I'd be there, in room 309.

Sometimes the RR bedsheet brushes my skin in a way that feels just like *the* sheet. Or the door clicks shut and it's suddenly the hotel room locking, with the AC blasting, with my arms chilled. *No, no, no!* I scream myself out of it. I pinch myself, kick myself, pull my hair out of it.

You just think I disappear, don't you? That I go nowhere. On pause, or in a dull void that's not so bad. But I go somewhere, Shoshana. Somewhere you can't see. Somewhere I'd never want you to follow me into. Whether you know it or not, you've been saving me in here, every day, little by little. Rescuing me from that place. Now you're going to be Blue, leaving me alone to revert, to lay there helpless. I can't have that. I need a new plan. That's what the *What If*s are for. Inspiration. Possibility. Where do we go from here?

9
Shoshana

My brain is buzzing with questions about the computer lab. Do they have Macs or PCs? Mouses or trackpads? Can I get on Instagram or Tumblr or YouTube? That last one is the kicker because if I can get on YouTube, I can see everything. What they used of me on the show, how the season finished, if companies like *Hollywire TV* and *Celeb Secrets TV* covered it. If ratings soared when I had my breakdown, how much footage they actually got, who they interviewed afterward to give thoughts on my episode. Probably Meredith. She's by far the best go-to cast member for ramping up emotions. I'm pretty sure they featured her on the show just because she can cry on command.

I dream about going back and getting the last and hardest tumbling pass, proving people wrong, winning Worlds, redemption. Maybe it wouldn't matter. It won't take away what I've done, my breakdown, forever online. But maybe I can shift my character in the eyes of the viewers from sloppy mess back to go-getter, and right now, that feels like everything.

Rowan told me once that everyone can undo the truth. *Everyone has their own*, she said. *That's why no narrative is ever honest. The word* narrative *itself means it's not. It's a tale. It's perspective.*

She compared stories to weaving. Every time a story gets

retold, a yarn is spun around a spool. Spin enough, and you won't be able to see the center, the way it began, the truth. But if you undo the string, back up, rewind, and see the story for the heart of what it is, the core never lies.

When it happened, my breakdown, I could feel it coming. The way you can smell rain. I knew it. And because I knew it, I made a break for it. Ran past the miniteam comprising five-year-olds and headed toward the cubbies filled with Garwood Elite's embroidered backpacks.

Nicole Kartwright, the center flyer and a Garwood Elite legacy, saw my face and readjusted her gigantic bow behind her blonde poof.

"Don't let Mary-Ellen see," she said, as if I didn't already know that. So, I dove for the first safe room I could find—not the women's, but the men's bathroom, where my teammates wouldn't follow me—and locked myself in.

I was hyperventilating. I specifically remember turning on the sink, hoping nobody would hear me cry, and it makes me laugh somewhat bitterly now, since they knew I was losing it the second I didn't come back to the mat for the run-through.

Heath was the one to find me, our ex-military tumbling coach, all cue-ball head and macho muscles, his skin as dark as the black sleeves of our uniforms. I picked myself off the floor just enough to turn the knob. The cameramen were only a few feet away, but Heath slipped in and shut the door after pulling my microphone off and tossing it at the producers in the hallway.

He said something about not taking me off the team, how

I was his favorite, it would all be okay. He poked me in the ribs the same way he did whenever I landed a new tumbling pass. I nodded and wiped snot on my shirt. *Someone is on my side*, I thought. *That should be enough to get me through the rest of this practice.* But then there was a knock at the door, sharp knuckles on wood, and her voice, "Figure your life out, kid! No whining, sobbing crap in my gym!" and I panicked. I started crying again, right there in front of Heath, and when he saw, he left to argue with her. I couldn't believe he wasn't terrified of her, that he was actually defending me.

"What do you wanna do? Let her sit in there all night and lose a Worlds bid over a goddamn bruised ego?" Mary-Ellen shouted.

He must have led her away because their voices grew distant, and I huddled there, wishing I hadn't made a scene in the first place, because Mary-Ellen was right. What was I supposed to do? Hide in the men's bathroom for the rest of practice? I was letting down the team.

I thought about apologizing, but that would require looking Mary-Ellen in the eye and I didn't have the courage for that. Instead, I ended up sprinting out when the next person knocked and needed to use the restroom. I grabbed my bag from the cubbies and raced to the exit. The cameramen followed but eventually had to stop at the end of the street. I kept walking, zombie-style, until the fear of what I had done matched the fear of what could still happen. The headlights of cars passed me; a truck honked, flashing its headlights against my bare legs. With twenty minutes left of practice, I turned back and hustled to the parking lot. The cameras were gone and Mom was there early to pick me up. Heath had already called her. They both suggested taking a week off.

Mary-Ellen doesn't believe in breaks, but I suppose even she didn't protest. If she had, I would've had to choose: get back on the mat or be off the team. And I'm honestly not sure which would have happened.

That was the night I went from eating a little to not at all, and when I fainted the next week at school, shipped out on a gurney to the local hospital, they saw the signs that I'd been "extreme dieting" for months, all summer really. The next thing I knew, I was here.

Before is like a different dimension, a dream, a past life. Or maybe this is the dream. RR. A nightmare, Rowan would say. But no matter how far away *before* feels, it's all real. And it's out there on the internet to remind me. How many Twitter memes are there of me crying uncontrollably? Will people hate me for bailing on the team during competition season, the way I hate myself? They still have a reasonable shot of placing top three at Worlds, but does that matter? Is it the camaraderie that I broke? By this point, they have likely flown in some other, better cheerleader from across the country to replace me, so maybe nobody cares. Maybe this is all in my head.

Lying down in my new Blue bed, I imagine all the things I might see tomorrow on the computer, all those images of me. Nurse Hart said the social media sites are blocked, but one quick Google search and I'd likely find out what the show chose to air.

"So, what kind of name is Shoshana anyway?" Crystal asks. She's in a slinky black nightgown, spaghetti straps bejeweled with silver rhinestones. Her platinum hair shows two or three inches of dark root, so I estimate she's been here three months.

"A Jewish one," I say.

"Oh, so you're Israeli?"

"Unless you're talking about the 'all the Jewish people come from the promised land' thing . . . no," I say.

"Sh," Brandy hisses, her bulging body turned to the wall. Crystal makes a nasty face behind her back and slides her tanned legs under the covers.

I curl up and face the ceiling, no quote or Rowan above me. No App game here, no whispering of footsteps, no footsteps at all. I guess they trust us enough not to check.

The blinds in the window are drawn and I'm pretty sure Brandy would take one of my eyes out if I moved it, but I'm tempted to because I long to see the moon. My eyes bore into the ceiling instead, the nap I took earlier keeping me up now. I think of Rowan. Is she in bed already? Is she in mine, waiting for the nurses to yell at her? Is she whispering to Donna? Does her fractured wrist hurt? Does she miss me?

What's to miss? my conscience chimes. *You're an embarrassment. Without you, she'll realize she's better off. Give it twenty-four hours and you'll be nothing. Smurf Shoshana.*

I lie on my stomach. *Shut up*, I tell it. Usually headphones help, loud music blocking all thoughts. But the room is silent. No way to make my conscience stop until it grows tired or I fall asleep, and for some reason my Olympic sleeping habits don't kick in until well past midnight.

In the morning I wash my face in the sink between Brandy and Crystal, a strange contrast to Rowan and Donna. I hear a toilet flush one level up in the Gray girls' bathroom.

"Are you excited about the kitchen?" Crystal asks. She stands behind my shoulder, staring at me in the mirror. I'm in a comfy Garwood Elite sweatshirt, the kind we wear over our competition uniforms when we walk around the arena. No one here has ever asked me about it.

"Is it really any different?" I ask, wiping my mouth.

"Not really. It's blue, of course, and there are little tables and chairs instead of the long benches. But breakfast is breakfast, you know?"

Maybe this won't be so bad, I think. Crystal seems okay and Brandy keeps to herself. Neither of them are Rowan, but they're not as terrible as I thought. No harm, no foul, so far.

We walk around the bottom of the stairs and I intuitively get in line for sweeps. Crystal grabs my arm and leads me past the Gray kitchen, down the hallway to the Blue one. She pushes through the swinging door, too familiar with it to stop, to pause, to take it in the way I do.

The Blue kitchen: not completely blue. The walls and cabinets are, but the rest is a variety. Green chairs around tiny white tables. Bizarre yellow napkin holders. An orange paper towel rod. It looks like a Skittles commercial. Brighter than the Gray kitchen by a long shot. The food is laid out in trays across the counter. Piles of bacon, eggs, waffles, pancakes.

Little bowls of butter and syrup. The tiny tables preoccupy me. In the Gray kitchen, there's only one long table with two long benches. One place for the nurses and Kelly to keep their eyes on us. By comparison, the Blue kitchen feels scattered. But I guess there aren't any nurses here who need to watch us fill our plates, to check that we're completing our tally sheets.

Habit or instinct, maybe the fear that they're still watching us from tiny cameras in the walls, makes me push food onto my plate. I stare at the open chair next to Crystal, then at one near Brandy alone at a different table. I wish Rowan was here. With her, I always have a place to sit.

I choose Crystal, who seems smug that I did and instantly makes me regret the decision.

"I tried getting an eating disorder three times before it worked," she tells me, mid-bite of her cream cheese bagel. "It's so fun, right? I mean the online chat rooms. All the girls cheering you on. The texts at lunch to stay strong and wait the extra hour before you eat a couple of Ritz crackers."

"I never did that," I say. "The online stuff."

Those pro-ana websites, the few I've peeked at, advertise how to trick your parents into thinking you're eating. They don't publish anything about the awful side effects of starving yourself, like growing hair everywhere, losing it where you want it, passing out, the constant stomach pain from constipation, glamorous diarrhea round the clock. They only show stick-thin bodies. Maybe that's what girls like Crystal want to use the computers for. To log on to websites and start online chat sessions with their pro-ana friends.

"Really? You're, like, the first person I've met who hasn't. So many of us spent our lives on it. I'd be on Pinterest or Tumblr for seriously all day, looking up bikini models for thinspiration."

"Thinspiration?"

"Yeah, you know. Inspiration to be thin."

I know the word, I've just never heard anyone use it aloud before.

"I had this rubber band that my boyfriend gave me, and anytime I wanted to eat, I would snap myself with it. We learned about classical conditioning in my psych class and I thought it would work to associate food with pain."

"Did it?"

"No, but the guilt did. God, anytime I would eat something, afterward, I would feel so bad about it. Like this bad." She holds up a wrist, bumpy scars halfway up her smooth arm. "I'm better now. You'll see. Group therapy helps a ton. It's like you're psycho when you're sick and the extra ten or twenty pounds means your brain and organs can function properly, which means you can actually be happy. If you think about it, ten or twenty pounds—it's not that much. Worth it in the long run. For your sanity's sake."

Ten or twenty pounds? Not a lot? Ten or twenty pounds would mean I wouldn't be able to tumble the same. Of course, when you're cheerleading in uniforms consisting of tiny skirts and bellies out, and you're on camera for millions to see, there's the pressure of how you look. But for me, I stopped eating because of my growth spurt, three inches in a year. If I'd stayed a gymnast, it would have been a hard adjustment, but bearable. Gymnastics judges see long, lean bodies, and that tends to bring in higher scores. But in cheerleading, the new height meant I couldn't be a flyer anymore: too tall, too heavy to lift. And when they moved me to the position of a back spot, it had me crying myself to sleep for weeks, always checking my tummy and thighs and back in the mirror.

Then the growth spurt started affecting my tumbling, my layouts not twisting as fast, less room to run before the roundoff. That did it. I went from being the best to just one of many. Add ten or twenty pounds to the equation and I wouldn't even be in that top quadrant.

For the rest of breakfast, I nod along to Crystal, listening to her run-on sentences about her folk-punk band-playing boyfriend. "At first I was like, no way, I do not want to date some guy in a band and be a gross groupie, but then Brad said he wouldn't take no for an answer and I could come on tour with them in the summer and what can I say? I caved."

I nod but focus on my waffles and eggs until they're gone.

"So, which one are you gonna do? Meditation or art?" she asks as I dart out of the Blue kitchen, ears bleeding. Both of us ate all our calories, yet she never took a breath.

"Meditation." I pick up the pace to get ahead of her. "Gray girls never do that, so it'll be different."

"Gray girls?"

"Yeah," I say. Is she dumber than I thought? "The Gray girls. The ones who eat in the Gray kitchen?"

"You call them that?" She laughs. "It's just Gray and Blue schedules. There's no actual divide."

Rowan calls them Gray girls, has since day one, I think, trusting her way more than Crystal, whose boyfriend story has at least three inconsistencies, starting with his name that went from Chad to Brad.

"Well, meditation it is." Crystal smiles. She reapplies her melon-scented ChapStick, holds the thing like a crucifix.

We pass the Gray kitchen right as the door swings open and Rowan steps out, Donna a quick step behind. They check out Crystal, my replacement roommate, and Rowan's tongue presses against the inside of her cheek, bulging out like an exorcism. Her pupils pulse at the speed of an overworked heart. I read the expression as distaste. And I can see what she sees. A wannabe Barbie, all blonde and pink and a total by-product.

"I see you've become Cady Heron overnight," Rowan says. I'm sure in her *Mean Girls* scenario I'm Cady, she's Janis, and Crystal is Regina George.

"Yeah, traitor," Donna adds.

I put my arms around Rowan immediately, wanting to hug her and never let go. She eases into a giggle, the two of us bonded kinetically.

"You get a Burn Book over there?" she whispers.

"Sure did." I play the game. "Put a picture of you in it. Next to it, I wrote, 'This girl is such a bitch,' and I quoted Donna."

She squeezes me like a teddy bear and my stomach warms, relieved she hasn't labeled me *Smurf Shoshana* yet.

In no time, we're forced to break apart to make it to our

activities on time. It feels like the first of many goodbyes. My first day Blue and I know we'll only have run-ins like this once or twice a day, passing moments to embrace and split off again.

"Hurry up," Crystal tells me, and I follow her into the dance room, glancing back to Rowan, who folds her arms. The lights are dimmed and yoga mats are set up. We take the two empty ones on the outskirts. Ms. Matusick sits at the front. I guess she does dance *and* meditation. Rowan and I never bothered sneaking in for this part. The idea of us being together and silent for a whole hour—unfathomable. Besides, Rowan says meditation is against her faith. When I asked what her faith was, she said, *Nothing that involves sitting around, waving scented candles, or listening to beach waves crashing, calling it spiritual like that's not what every other hippie chick does.*

"Welcome, girls," Ms. Matusick says, her voice low and cool. She has her legs crossed pretzel-style and I fold mine the same way. At GE, you sit in each split for five minutes at a time, ten if your flexibility sucks. I was usually in the ten-minute group, but in here I'm the human pretzel. Ms. Matusick looks impressed.

"I see some new faces. Very lovely. Today I thought we'd start off with breathing techniques." She turns on a spa meditation playlist from her iPhone and readjusts herself on the square gray pillow. "The first thing I want everyone to do is get comfortable. You can lie down if you like, but feel stable. Go ahead and close your eyes and just start breathing for me. Big breaths. In through the nose, out through the mouth."

I inhale, exhale, peek at the other girls who have their eyes closed, then let Ms. Matusick catch the whites of mine.

"Good. Now, concentrate on your hands. Where are they? Feel the control you have over them, to move them, to use them at your leisure."

I slide my hands down my thighs, over my knees to my calves. I miss the way my legs used to feel solid and strong, so my mind drifts to cheer, to the show, and inevitably to the breakdown. How quickly it all floods back.

This is stupid, I think. Ms. Matusick's eyes are closed now, too, and I'm the only one cheating. *I wouldn't be the only one if Rowan were here.*

"Every annoying, fearful thought . . . let's welcome those thoughts. They can't hurt you. Welcome them and then tell them goodbye. Let them leave on your next exhale."

Her voice makes my eyelids feel heavy and so I finally shut them and lie back the way Crystal is positioned. I wonder if I could sleep in here or if I'd get in trouble. Rowan says I snore and also that sleeping is a waste of time. If she could, she'd go all vampire-esque and stay awake 24/7 because there's too much to learn, too much to do, too much to experience here, and *What's the point of life if you spend it all unconscious? Might as well be dead.* When she said that, my conscience agreed, scolding me for the twelve-hour weekend sleep-ins I used to take at home.

I can't remember when my conscience started hating me or when it got this bad. As a kid, I didn't have it, or don't remember having it. So I'm left wondering where the thing came from, if an event triggered it or if I simply developed the self-loathing because I'm a teenager and what teenager doesn't hate themselves?

What scares me is the idea that the voice will never go away, that I'll spend forever like this, trapped between being myself on the inside and seeing myself as others must on the outside, and hating both. I've tried to change it with the lessons they've given me here. Mrs. Walsh says when the bad thoughts come, I'm supposed to ask myself, "Is this useful? Is it kind?" Since the negativity obviously isn't, I'll regain power over my mind, the power to cast the thoughts away.

But it's easier to give in, to let them sit on the sides of my brain and gunk it up. Easier to hate yourself than to love yourself. Not because hate is actually easier than love, but because we're accustomed to it.

Rowan is the one who makes it disappear. I don't know how or why, especially on the days when she's speaking fast to Donna and a tiny part of me sees Mary-Ellen in her eyes. But I'm not terrified of Rowan. How could I be? We're an *us*. Being afraid of her would be like being afraid of myself.

Ms. Matusick comes around and touches our temples, the bridges of our noses, under our ears where she says our lymph nodes are, where toxins drain and built-up stress can dissipate.

"Wasn't that great?" Crystal says at the end, and I try to gauge if she really liked it that much or if she's just the type of person who sugarcoats everything, who says, "Isn't that just wonderful?" or "Wasn't it the best ever?" even when it wasn't.

Then again, she showed me her scars. She's not blindly faking happy or she would've hidden them.

"Not bad," I say. "Can I ask you a question?"

"Always," she bubbles.

"What's your personal project?"

"Fashion," she says. "Brand names versus local stores. How vintage gets way too much attention. The prices people are willing to pay for dirty old rags is seriously disturbing."

"So, you can do it on anything?"

She wavers a bit, twirling a lock of blonde hair. I see the Regina George that Rowan picked up on in a second. "I'm sure there are some limitations. Like *Brandy*." She whispers the name low and I realize, by picking Crystal, I chose a side in a war. "She's writing a report on market sales, something about *Fifty Shades of Gray* versus Pulitzer Prize winners. Can you believe that? So strange. Most of the girls aren't that weird. They usually just focus on internet stuff. One girl's doing Apple products and how to use them. Another one's doing social media apps and their individual meanings, kind of like how Facebook is for old people now."

I regret picking Crystal. Big time. The report Brandy is doing sounds interesting and I like how she keeps to herself.

"Is anyone doing theirs on eating disorders?" I ask.

"Not a chance. We get enough of that in here, don't you think? But if you wanted to, I bet you could. You can incorporate art, too. Music. Things like that. Alyssa did an interpretive dance and I swear I could actually feel her pain. What a shame about her. She was such an angel."

"You were friends with her?" I ask. At this point I can't picture Alyssa's face or really remember anything about her. Just the gum thing.

She nods. "But Brandy knew her best. They were roommates for a while. I guess Brandy helped her get out, you know, and fake it with the quarters. That's whose bed you've been sleeping in."

"Brandy's?"

"Alyssa's. But don't worry, it's not haunted. She didn't die in here."

I shiver anyway. I slept in Alyssa's bed last night? It's not like I'm fated for death just because I've been sleeping in the same sheets as her, but I'm preoccupied with the notion that my skin has touched hers. That even washed, a pinch of Alyssa's DNA, a particle, has come into contact with mine. A dusting of her hovering over me as I sleep.

I don't believe in fate, but I do believe in God, even if it's in the loosest sense. How can people not believe when there are the stars and the moon and the sun and the ground beneath our feet and the wind at our backs and more ocean than land, so much we'll never get a chance to see it all?

Rowan doesn't believe in anything, not Mother Earth or *some invisible guy in the sky who tells gay people they're wrong and leaves the priests to enforce his laws and molest little children while they do it.* She says most churches disregard half the Bible and what's the point of believing a portion of something that's supposed to be sacred? It's all or nothing. "Nothing," she says, because although there are some good rules like "Don't F your wife's mom," there are too many "Kill anyone with a religion different than yours" to take the Bible seriously.

"And don't get me started on the 'No alcohol in church, *lest ye die*' thing," she told me. "I mean, if there's no alcohol, how the fuck are we supposed to make it through the sermon?"

I admitted then that I'd never had alcohol, not besides a sip of wine at Passover or a taste of Dad's beer during summer barbecues or that one sip of tequila at sleepaway camp where I just barely put my lips on the rim. Rowan nearly fell to the floor. She told me the second we get out of here, she's going to buy me orange juice and peach schnapps, because I seem like the type to want something "sweet and easy like a five-year-old," and we're going to "cheers" by the ocean. "The only thing worth the calories," she said.

Crystal sticks by me the whole day, right up until the anticipated personal projects. Nurse Robinson opens the door to the computer lab and I'm surprised Rowan doesn't know about it or didn't tell me about it. Maybe she kept it from me for my own good.

I tell Nurse Robinson I'm thinking of doing something with photography or sports or high school statistics. Partly true, but also partly false since I haven't got a clue what I'm doing. All I can think about is the World Wide Web.

"You have a half hour, ladies," Robinson says.

I nod and take an open seat next to Brandy, who's already clicking away. I can't believe this is it. There are six computers. Old iMacs with half-working mouses, but who cares. They're functional.

Nurse Robinson turns around and I click on the Safari icon, watching it bounce for what seems like an eternity. It pulls up a window, Google, and I blink at the logo I haven't seen in so long. In the web bar, I type it in, sure there's no way it'll work. My fingers move and push the buttons and hit enter. Brandy's eyes flicker to my screen as the page loads and loads and loads and loads and then there it is.

YouTube.

"Don't," Brandy cuts, reaching over to take my mouse and hit the back button that reloads Google. Her thick fingers peel away from my clicker, one by one, as she watches me. "It's not worth it. Believe me."

I'm going to see it eventually, I think. *Why not now?*

As if Brandy has tracked the thought, she says, "You've been Blue less than twenty-four hours. Practice some willpower. See if you can make it in here before you make it out there."

Willpower. Do I have even an ounce of that? My eyes rest on Google again, fingers reaching for the mouse.

It won't take me long to find out.

10
Rowan

You've been Blue for five days, eight hours, and twenty-five minutes, and blow my brains out right here, right now, because if nothing changes I'm going to have an "accident" soon, one that ends with me at the bottom of the stairs, limbs bent incorrectly. Or maybe that'll be Smurf, my new best-bud Shirley Temple bunkmate. Your replacement, Shoshana—as bad as Venus being sent in for Serena.

One little push. That's all it would take for Smurf to go flying. Easy to claim *mistake* or *didn't mean to* or *I'm sorry, it was totally a "miscommunication."*

"You look insane," Donna says, watching me scratch at the wooden bed board with my bitten nails. I tear at them with my teeth so often the edges zigzag like a saw. They're bleeding by the time I finish carving my initials into the wood. R.I.P. There's no I. My parents never gave me a middle name, but it feels fitting. Irene. Iris. Isabelle. Pick whatever. R.I.P. Rest in Peace. An omen I've welcomed since I was thirteen.

The nurses must see us in shades. Various tones of grays and blues, hues of how deep we're in it. New Girl: dark gray. Like gunmetal. Donna: a lighter gray, like smoke or aluminum, still fidgeting for the extra two or three calories when she thinks no one's looking. You: navy as a blueberry, making your way toward a bright sky blue. And me? Some sort of black ash that, no matter how much blue or yellow or white you throw on top of it, never relents to changing its color.

"Stop talking," I command Donna. At night, I've been itching to turn her headbands into blindfolds, play a game to make her afraid of me again, like she was, like they all were, in the beginning. Now she sees my soft places for you as a weakness, and I don't want her looking at me like that. Like she thinks I'm a freaking Beanie Baby.

"In a week, when I'm Blue like Shoshana, you're going to miss the sound of my voice," she says.

"False." There's no way I'd miss bland Donna. There's only one person I'd miss, the same person I'm missing right now, the same person who's been gone five days, eight hours, and twenty-eight minutes, and that's you. Yesterday, I didn't see you at all, not even in passing, but I heard the Blue girls down the hall laughing and recognized your own. My mouth went all sour grape and my skin went prickly as a pinecone.

So, give it to me, Shoshana. The truth. Are you enjoying yourself over there? Is this what you wanted? I can only imagine that it's the other side of crazy. But maybe Blue suits you? Maybe you're waiting to run away on your own, back to your family and your blasé life. I won't blame you, if that's the case. Or I'll try not to.

Smurf whispers goodnight to me when we're told lights out. I used to stay up late, just to feel you press your feet against my bed board, checking to see if I was up too. Now I lie awake with my itchy arm, wondering what'll happen when I'm alone, like Donna said. Eventually, Gray or Blue, they'll have to let me go. They can't hold me here for years, and even if they could, I'll be eighteen soon. What then? Go back to school? Run away on my own? Find the next best thing to you, Shosh?

Smurf's tears are silent, but I can hear her sniffling most nights, tiny shudders that Donna might miss from across the room, but I certainly don't. I want to make fun of her for it, but lately I feel like crying too. Without you, the darkness is an invitation for all kinds of thoughts, some about you and what I want, others about what led me here. Most are about the Red Roof Inn, why I'll ruin you if I get too close.

On Friday morning, Donna drags me to go see you dance, the both of us ready to have a good laugh because you're not the dancing type, not with those gawky limbs and harmless eyes. I'm sorry—I'm really not trying to be mean, Shosh, but the idea of you being smooth on the dance floor . . . I can't picture it without choking on air.

We arrive at the room early. Donna and I check ourselves out in the paneled mirrors, so many reflections around the room it's impossible to not see ourselves. Donna turns around, checking out her own ass, pinching the inch of thigh fat and smoothing a hand over her waist.

"Standing up burns forty more calories an hour than sitting," I tell her, just like I'd tell you if you were here. She squints like she thinks I'm checking her out and noticing whatever flaws she's noticing. I am. But I'm checking myself out too, the purple hair growing out with blonde roots, the short frame, the round baby face.

My body was my first lover, but now it feels more like an ex I can't get away from.

The door swings open. The Blue girls file in. You're at the back, standing with the blonde bimbo again, the one who looks like she drives a hot-pink bug convertible and lives by lip gloss.

"Look what the cat dragged in," I say, but Bimbo is speaking and you're listening, too distracted to hear. When you look up and spot me, your face screams of guilt.

"You're going to watch?" you ask, cheeks flushed.

"Just because you're Blue, Shoshana, doesn't mean I'm going to stop enjoying the entertainment us Gray girls get." I smirk. "Better give the performance of a lifetime, Pavlova."

"Girls," Ms. Matusick says, pushing through to get to the front. All our eyes go directly to the little nugget following her. "This is my daughter, Elly. She's ten. Her teachers are on strike for higher wages, so I had to bring her with me. She's excited to be here, aren't you, El?"

Elly smiles and gets all squirmy. She has a gap between her two front teeth and wide-set eyes just like her mom's. The way she stands, arms behind her back, hands clasped together, speaks of mischief. Everyone takes her in like an Apple product. She's that playful and distracting for us.

"Aw," coos Donna, weak at the sight of the girl's curly ponytail and velvet scrunchie. The kid's T-shirt says *Happy girls are the prettiest.* Clearly, she doesn't know a thing about the harsh realities of the universe yet.

"I prefer babies," I say. "They may sleep and burp and shit all day, but they're as pure as Poland Spring."

Elly takes in the group, gaze moving swiftly over Donna and me, but slower over the Blue girls, who are stretching. Ms. Matusick kick-starts the music and almost instantly, Elly erupts into a bloodcurdling scream.

"What! What is it?" Ms. Matusick tries to regain control of her Mexican jumping bean daughter while we all wince at the pinching sound.

"It's her! It's her! It's her! It's her!" Elly bounces on the balls of her petite feet, putting her hands on the sides of her head and spinning in a circle. "You," she says, pointing into the sea of Blue dancers. "You're Shoshana Winnick!"

It's like getting my blood pressure taken—I can feel my heartbeat in my arm. My feet go pins and needles, and my lungs wait impatiently for me to take another breath as I look to you for an answer.

You go beet red. Blink twice. Rub your arms like there's a wind chill. Ms. Matusick flushes with embarrassment and attempts, unsuccessfully, to settle her daughter.

"Mom! She's from *Cheer Champions*!" says Elly, vibrating with fangirl energy. Ms. Matusick pulls her daughter close, whispering, with a tight grip on her arm. Elly stops jumping. She doesn't stop staring at you.

I want to cross my arms or scowl or do something to show you I disapprove of this breach of our unspoken agreement. How does she know you? What the fuck is *Cheer Champions*? What on God's earth have you been keeping from me? I can merely glare as you stare back, frozen, lips parted, eyes fluttering from me to the floor. You try to form words, but you swallow the air and nothing springs up.

"Let's begin!" Ms. Matusick claps her hands, raising the volume of the music to cut off any further discussion. She starts without her usual intro and you move to the back of the Blue girls, Bimbo beside you, the two of you watching Ms. Matusick dance, slowly following the steps because what else is there to do but pretend things are normal? Elly is beside her mom, grinning from ear to ear, gawking at you with OMG heart eyes.

And you . . . your brain stops the moment your body starts. The panic drains from your features as you keep on beat, shifting your weight like you can feel the rhythm, where it's going, strike the next position at the precise right time. All those days we sat here watching the Blue girls and I never put two and two together.

You're good. More than that. *You're naturally rhythmic.*

"Did you know she could dance this well?" Donna asks.

I didn't, but I nod. Apparently, there's more to you than meets the eye.

You keep dancing, eyes trained on the mirror, and I decide to do what I do best—make people nervous. In your case, the best way to do that is to get up and storm out. The door slams behind me and even with the music still going, I know you're stinging with the absence of me. You won't follow, won't risk making a scene or getting in trouble or losing Blue. Not goody-goody Shosh. But you'll feel it and maybe, just maybe, falter in your step.

I hear the door open behind me and I expect you to prove me wrong, to be there, to say everything that just happened wasn't real and you're exactly who I think you are. But it's not you. It's depress-me Donna.

"You gonna flip out?" Donna asks, dark eyes buzzed at the new potential of soap opera drama.

"Stop acting like you're my backup," I hiss. "You had your chance and you chickened out." I wave my broken arm as a sign of our attempted escape.

"All right, so I didn't jump out a window. At least I still have two working arms and didn't pretend to be someone I'm not."

"Everyone pretends to be someone they're not," I snap. It's the wrong answer. I should have said *Shoshana isn't pretending*. But I can't lie for you there, not when I feel like you've left out something major. We're all guilty of lying about our reputations. We all undergo mental plastic surgery for every room we walk into. But I thought you were different, Shosh, and you're not. It's a shame, not a sin.

"Is she on *Sesame Street* or something? That girl was, like, five."

"Ten, and she's not on *Sesame Street*."

"How do you know?"

"Rowan? Donna?" Nurse Hart makes a beeline for us. "Either you're watching the girls dance or you're not. You can't stand out here unsupervised."

"Why not?" I demand. "Shoshana gets to do whatever she

wants and she jumped out the window too." I don't say this to throw you under the bus, but to prove the point that I'm already under it, suffocating, and no one cares.

"She did not jump out the window and this isn't up for discussion."

Normally, that comment would make me laugh, prompt a middle finger or an eye roll. Didn't jump out the window? You may not have broken any bones, but you sure as shit went out that window before me. But after what just happened, I betray us again and say, "What did she tell you? That I pushed her?"

"Ms. Parish." Nurse Hart shakes her head. Behind rectangular glasses, her eyes loom with warning. "I'd say we should call your mother again, but I think she's heard plenty from you this week."

"Call her a hundred times, she still won't show up here."

I play the orphan Annie card for all it's worth. The same card I've used since pre-K when I went to school with a locket and did my own version of *Maybe,* told everyone "my story" about the parents who left me as a baby but promised to come back someday. It worked for sympathy points from my teacher until a mother called mine to set up a playdate, so happy to hear her son had a fellow adoptee in the class. It was one of the only times my mother spanked me.

"Your mother is not my concern. You are. Now go get in line for sweeps. The rest of the girls will be down soon." She crooks a finger at a new nurse, some med school trainee they hired for extra help, an unpaid intern idiot.

Her name is Hope, she says, and she smiles too widely at

us. Her lower lip trembles to reveal the tiniest gap between her front teeth, like Elly's. I match her smile, but mine drips with polymer, a falsity that moves through the air and taints whatever *hope* she actually has for us, for me. My ears let out low whistles as I realize who my anger is really directed at.

Have you been playing tricks on me, Shoshana? Deceiving me? Deliberately lying to my face? My feelings need sunscreen right now. It burns, loving you. The more you love someone the more damage they can do, and here you've been, secretly singeing my skin all along like some newly formed star. I wish I could pluck you from your shiny blue sky, roll you in my hands like putty, and shape you into whatever I need you to be. Because I don't know the person who was dancing today. And you've reminded me what a punishment it is to live so alone in our bodies. To live with no promise of the truth, the possibility that everyone around is not who they say they are.

Is that you, Shoshana? And think very hard before you answer. Are you the person I knew from the start or someone I've never known at all?

11
Shoshana

She just left. Walked out of the dance room and then Donna went next, her new second-in-command, and how could I explain it? *You see, I'm actually on one of those TV shows you hate and I've been lying to your face this whole time, but we're still us, right?* She would have laughed in my face, told me to go to hell, or since she doesn't believe in hell, someplace real and horrible, like Afghanistan in the middle of a firefight.

Crystal hasn't stopped pestering me about "life in the spotlight" since dance class. She asked why, after the class ended, Ms. Matusick asked me to sign a napkin for Elly. So I told her about the show, and now she won't shut up.

There are older fans of *Cheer Champions*, loads of teenagers and twenty-somethings, and even mothers who used to whisper to me over their daughters' shoulders at competitions, telling me I was their favorite cast member. But the older fans can mostly contain themselves. There's nothing subtle about a ten-year-old.

Elly—the scream heard around the world of RR.

"Who cares what she's famous for?" Brandy says, shutting down the gossip. "She's a kid."

Calling me a kid to my face feels a bit out of place, given Brandy's only a year or two older than I am, one of the only patients willingly in the adolescent program who is over eighteen. But I appreciate the knockdown from the imaginary pedestal the rest of the Blue girls have me on. I nod a *thanks* to her. She nods a *you're welcome* back.

Ever since Brandy stopped me from peeking at YouTube on Sunday, we've shared small moments like this. She still doesn't like me, but the ice between us seems to be thawing. Crystal has noticed it too, and she's much less eager to talk to me as a result. The prospect of my fame has earned me a few extra bonus points, but not as much as I would've thought from someone like her.

"What's the movie called?" Brandy asks me later, during our downtime. She missed dance this morning in favor of making more clay. She only heard musings of what happened.

"It's not a movie. It's a reality show," I tell her. Her asking seems way more sincere than the other Blue girls', and after this morning, I'm eager to talk to someone about it.

The whole of it hit me when I was dancing, how much I miss the choreography of routines, cheer in general, the baskets, the tumbling, stunts, pyramid—I even miss miserable jumps. And another thing I remembered: I'm still on the team, still on the show even if I haven't been present the last few episodes. In the grand scheme of things, my time at RR isn't going to make or break my reputation. I can fix it. My life is waiting for me back home. It's like Nurse Hart has been saying. *Life is a long time.* There's a lot to look forward to. Like Worlds, if I want it and am willing to chase after it.

"Cool," is Brandy's big reply. She doesn't ask any more

questions after that, and I think she might be the type of girl I'd avoid at school for social damnation by association purposes, but in here, she's a gold mine. Sensible, kind, straightforward. And unlike a lot of the other girls here, including myself, she's not a people pleaser.

"Gonna include me in your project?"

"If you want to be in it, then sure," I say.

My personal project: a photo collage of the girls in here and what they hate about themselves. I came up with the idea by researching self-portraits, recollecting the one Rowan drew of herself weeks ago in art, just the back of her head in the middle of a storm cloud.

"It's not about drawing yourself. It's about creating your-self," she said. "However *you* see *you*."

"So you think you're a bunch of condensed water drop-lets?" I teased. By that point in our friendship, I had picked up on her sarcastic tongue and could continue it like a baton she handed off.

"Can't you see it's me?" She looked at the ominous, if slightly cartoonish, cloud. "I'm the sky. I have the power to bring you rainbows or wreck you like Katrina."

It got me thinking about the way we see ourselves, why all these girls ended up here, and the power of pro-ana websites. I suspect we don't hate our bodies as much as we hate the way other people perceive them. Judgment and ridicule, those are the things we worry most about.

I asked Nurse Robinson for permission to use a camera

and some Blue girls to volunteer small portions of their bodies they distaste the most.

"My ankles."

"That's the part you hate most about yourself?" I ask Brandy in disbelief. I feel shitty the moment the words leave my mouth, my tone an insinuation that there are worse things to her appearance than her ankles. It's the very opposite of what I want my project to do.

"Well, I'd say you could take a picture of my entire body, but contrary to how people think I'm supposed to feel about myself, I don't actually hate every part of me."

"I'm sorry, I didn't mean—"

"Doesn't matter what you meant." She shakes her head. "If someone gets hurt by what you say or what you do, it's your fault."

Her words sound profound, but I think about Mary-Ellen. If Brandy is right, it would mean that it's Mary-Ellen's fault for my breakdown, my feelings. I don't believe that. I don't buy that we're responsible for how other people feel about what we do.

"How'd Hitagi Senjougahara take the news of your show?" Brandy asks.

"Who?"

"Purple-haired girl."

Rowan. My stomach bloats and knots. "Not well, really, since I lied to her about it." *Not well* feels like a gross under-statement. Rowan walked out. The slammed door was a clear indicator that she wants nothing to do with me.

"You told her you weren't famous?"

"No, but I didn't tell her I was."

"And you think she's never done the same to you?"

"Lied about not being famous?"

"Lied, period."

I shrug because I'm not dumb. I know Rowan hides things from me, like her family, like what haunts her from the past, but she hides those things from everyone. It feels different coming from Rowan. Less of a betrayal, more just that it's in her nature to be mysterious. The same way she likes me innocent, I like her unknown. And maybe that's wrong, but it's the way we've been from the beginning. With me playing the role of an open book. I'm not supposed to lie or have secrets of my own. I broke our contract.

"If you're worried she'll hate you, then don't tell her. Call it a fluke. She won't know. At least not until she's out of here. Deal with it then."

Lying won't work. Rowan knows me too well. She'd spot my guilt in a second and flag it red.

But she didn't catch you when you told Nurse Hart about the escape plan, my conscience hisses, playing devil's advocate. *Turning Blue is strike one. This could be two. One more . . .* My conscience feeds the solution. *Lie again. Two wrongs don't make a right, but they will cancel each other out.*

I take the photo of Brandy's ankles during our Personal Projects session. They're thick cankles, and her feet are big too. Size eleven. She wiggles her stumpy toes and I try not to pick her apart.

"These are nice, Shoshana. It's Show-shon-a right?" a

nurse—I think her name is Dream or Hope or some cliché—asks, flipping through the photos and pronouncing my name correctly. I nod, then cringe when she leaves a fingerprint on the photo of Crystal's self-harm scars. I take the photos back from her and she hands over the craft bin. It's filled with rhinestones, stickers, dollar store 3D flowers, heart buttons, anything that sparkles, as requested.

"Thanks," I say, holding the box.

She grins from ear to ear; it's probably the first nice acknowledgment she's received here. I wonder if she's met Rowan yet.

I spend the next hour repositioning the photos on a poster board. With all the Blue girls offering more than one sore spot—more than one thing they hate about themselves because there are too many to pick and they can't narrow it down—the photo collection has grown. Hope—she introduced herself to Brandy—tapes the photos to the places where I set them down, and I can see what the girls see, why they hate their big noses, thin eyebrows, curved bellies, narrow lips, drooping necks, broad shoulders. They don't look like the photos in the magazines: retouched and positioned to highlight the model's attractive parts. They don't look beautiful. They look flawed, like most humans do up close.

K.J. used to like taking pictures of people like this. Portraits and stuff. In Georgetown, the big leagues for little league baseball, he snapped the team picture. There's a photo of Mom, Dad, me, and the whole team on the fridge at home. His event, yet no proof he was there.

A part of me always thought he was pretending not to like being in front of a camera because Mom and Dad had it on me no matter what. Even when he was on the mound, pitching, the perfect opportunity to get a clean shot with no chance for him to put his palm over the lens—they still switched the camera to my backflips on the sidelines.

But K.J. stopped taking photos a year ago, so I feel like I'm channeling the creativity he's dropped. I might feel bad for my brother, firstborn and least loved, but it's hard to feel bad for a zombie who spends all his time in the basement playing video games. *Call of Duty. Fortnite.* Some virtual-reality baseball game, since he won't play real baseball anymore.

Dad says if one of us is going to follow in his IronMan footsteps, it'll be me. I think he's right because K.J. never leaves the couch. But the IronMan is too crazy even for me. My muscles aren't trained for seventeen straight hours of exercise. They're trained for two and a half minutes of agony and to smile through it. It's Dad's dream to do a father-daughter IronMan. He wants to star in an IronMan documentary, more obsessed with the camera than K.J. or I have ever been. His only way to get in front of one now is by standing next to me.

The *Cheer Champions* camera crew came to my house once. Lorri walked my parents through procedure. *Answer questions honestly. Unless it's during an interview, DO NOT LOOK DIRECTLY AT THE CAMERA. No, a house tour and an interview are not the same thing. Relax and be genuine. They'll love you.*

Dad lived for it. He even listened to Mom and whitened his teeth beforehand.

In the middle of the house tour, K.J. came up from the basement to grab snacks, and our next-door neighbor since preschool, Zach Breeden—Breezy to everyone at school—walked in on the action and grinned like he was in a life insurance commercial, like it was his own camera and crew and just another episode of *Life Is Breezy*. He volunteered to pose as my friend or my boyfriend, sliding me the courtesy of "if that's cool." I said no and Lorri agreed. But she wanted the boys anyway. I mean, two fit, attractive teenage boys, one of whom was my blood relative—she'd struck a gold mine. I bet she would've come to my house every week to get updates if K.J. hadn't shaken his head, grabbed Breezy by the skin of his neck, and padded back down to the basement. But not before Breezy skidded in his socks and shouted, "I've been in love with Shoshana Winnick since she threw rocks at me in pre-K!" at the blinking red camera.

That line never aired. The network didn't like the idea of *innocent Shoshi* pelting rocks at boys she liked and it leading to affection. After all, girls like Elly might get the idea to hurl boulders at their crushes. I'm a role model. The *Cheer Champions* producers taught me how an audience can be swayed by words and images. That's what I'm trying to do with my personal project, with the photography here. Change the girls' perceptions and by extension, my own.

After Personal Projects, the sun moves down and the moon lifts up. We settle in for bed, and I'm almost grateful for Crystal's constant stream of irrelevant information. It keeps me from thinking about Rowan, how angry she must be with me.

"Brad is coming to visit next week," Crystal says before she turns the lights out. Neither Brandy nor I care very much about Brad or Chad or his folk-punk band. We've heard enough about this over the last few nights. *Brad took my virginity when we were fifteen. Brad is an insane guitarist. Brad is actually the son of John Mayer's third cousin.*

Brandy and I pass each other a look in the moonlight from the window. How did I not see it before? Crystal is a pathological liar.

"How'd you clear it with the nurses?" I ask.

"I've been good lately. Family can come when you're Blue and they approve it, so he's going to pretend to be my brother."

"What happens when they see you kissing him?"

She scowls but tosses her extra blankets off the bed at my interrogation, like she has nothing to hide. "We'll wait until our goodbye to do that."

"So, we'll meet him, then?" asks Brandy, speaking up. This time Crystal hesitates a moment too long.

"I mean, he's only stopping by for a little. Like ten minutes."

"Plenty of time," I add, fluffing my pillow.

Crystal leers like a cat. "So, Shoshana, do you have a boyfriend? I mean, you must have offers if you're famous."

I'm the one scowling now. I've never had a serious boyfriend and she knows it, the same way Rowan knew it when I told her I was still a virgin and she said, *Thanks, Captain Obvious.* I don't know what it is about myself that reads "inexperienced," but it's a scent everyone can smell. It's also a scent I'm not eager to change. I've never longed for a boyfriend or for some spontaneous sexcapade. That's not who I am, never has been.

"Or is it a girlfriend? I don't want to assume—"

"Neither," I say, not willing to lie the way she does in order to feel good about myself.

"No one?" Crystal frowns. "Jesus, that sucks. Is that how you ended up here? Depressed because no one wants you?"

I think about Breezy, what he said during that home interview, how it struck me so hard because the rock thing was true. He'd made fun of me endlessly when we were kids—pulled my hair on the bus, raced me home and called me a slowpoke when he beat me every time, wrestled me in the mud until someone found us almost killing each other and tore us apart. One day, he made fun of my favorite shirt, a yellow long sleeve with a monkey eating a banana on it, and I picked up a rock and chucked it at his head. I could've done real damage, too, if I hadn't missed by a mile. Breezy proceeded to make fun of my aim and I cried and later threw the shirt in the trash.

Anytime I talk to his friends now, K.J. shoots me a look to kill. I wonder if he's happy I'm gone, if his friends have noticed. I wonder if they ever ask about me, wishing they would and wishing, for K.J.'s sake, they wouldn't. It's not like I even want to be with any of them, but it's nice to be noticed. They're practically the only people at school who truly know me.

Corey Westler, one of K.J.'s best friends, stole my first kiss in a game of hide-and-seek. We were hiding together when, out of nowhere, he kissed me so hard I bumped into our basement boiler. It burned the side of my shoulder and I still have the small textured scar to prove it.

It was an awful kiss. Maybe not *awful*, but definitely boring. In fact, all my kisses—of which there have been three—have been pretty bland. I'm not sure if it's me or them, but I was always just waiting for it to be over, usually making a list of conditioning drills in my head that I should do before the next cheer practice.

"Isn't anyone going to ask me about my boyfriend or girlfriend?" Brandy asks, her voice husky with exhaustion. I can't tell if she's joking or actually wants us to ask.

"No," Crystal says. "Because no one cares what a murderer has to say about her love life."

My eyes flit to Brandy, then to Crystal, my hands growing cold, my mouth instantly rigid to the point where I can feel the grooves of my teeth grind together. *Murderer?* My spine and neck lengthen, as if an invisible string above my head is pulling me upright, red alert, red alert.

"*I'm* the murderer? You're the one who tortured her."

Crystal sucks in a breath and holds it. She lets the air out dramatically before she speaks. "I *never* said a bad word to Alyssa."

So this is where the rift comes from, I think. *Alyssa and the blame for her death, who actually dealt her hand.*

Brandy stares down Crystal. I debate calling out for a nurse, because this feels like *Silence of the Lambs* right before Hannibal jumps from inside his cell, but I bite my tongue and watch instead.

"Yes, you did. We were on the Gray schedule together. I remember all of it. Everything you said. Everything you did. Build up your fake boyfriend and awesome life all you want, but deep down, you're as miserable a bitch as the rest of us, and worse because you take it out on other people."

Crystal and I are stunned into silence. For the five days I've known her, Brandy has never uttered more than a line here or there. Now she's on the verge of a monologue.

Crystal storms out, slamming our door behind her. No doubt, she's going to get one of the overnight nurses. Brandy must not be worried, though, because she curls up against the wall without a word. When Crystal doesn't return, I follow Brandy and hit the hay.

I wake up at four a.m. wet and sticky, the inside of my thighs dripping in warmth.

It's like déjà vu from when I was thirteen. I know what this is. But I'm momentarily confused about etiquette. If I climb out of bed now, the blood will drip onto the floor. I need to remember what this is like, how to plug myself and stop the flow.

Schultz's and Robinson's names are written on the chart outside the overnight nurses' door. Crystal was asleep in her bed when I woke, so the two of them must've talked her down. I knock twice.

"What's wrong, Shoshana?" Schultz asks, glancing at the floral bedsheets wrapped around my waist. I whisper it shamefully, wishing she were my mom. For all her annoying management control over my life, my mom would assure me everything was fine, that it wasn't a big deal. She'd take care of me and wash my soiled clothes and pull me in for a hug. But everyone knows everything in RR. My blood is fire. It's just a waiting game to see who smells the smoke.

I readjust the bedsheets, opening them just enough for Schultz to see a drop of blood spider-web itself down my thigh until I catch it with the cotton at my knee. She grabs a tampon and a pad from a side cabinet and puts an arm around me as we head for the bathroom. "You've been spending too much time near me," she jokes, even though she hasn't been here for almost two weeks—on a vacation in the Caribbean with her college-aged sons. "Our schedules have synced."

I choose the tampon but oddly enough, I can't get it in, so I exchange it for the pad while Nurse Hart is called. She's about as thrilled as I am with this reentry to womanhood until, in the morning, she stands in the stall with me to verify the soiled cotton is of my body's real making. After I wipe leftover blood onto a clean pad and she believes me, she's as happy as a clam. All of the nurses are chirping enthusiastically, practically eager to clean up on aisle Shoshana and wash my crime-scene sheets.

"She really is the ghost of Alyssa's past," Crystal whispers to some of the other Blue girls behind me on our way to breakfast. I keep my head straight, not flinching.

So what if I got my period and am sleeping in Alyssa's bed? That doesn't mean I'm destined to kill myself. She faked her period. I got mine for real. I'm no ghost.

I decide to wait outside the Gray kitchen for Rowan, whom I haven't spoken to in almost twenty-four hours. A new record and not a good one. There's nothing I can say to fix what happened, except lie like Brandy suggested, and I don't plan on doing that. But I'm praying the right words will come when I see her.

Her purple head rounds the corner and, like her self-portrait, I see only the back of her head. The face next to hers is Sophie's, animated and laughing, and my brain blanks.

Why is Rowan with her? I thought we kicked her out? Three strikes—didn't that happen?

Maybe it's my period, but the jealousy rolls in, hot. *This is all your fault,* my conscience snaps, and it's on the mark. This *is* my fault. I should have told her the truth. I should never have tipped off the nurses about our escape plan. I promised to be Thelma to her Louise, swore we'd stick together. I promised her we'd stay one, even if it meant not getting better. And I failed.

When Sophie stops laughing and Rowan turns her head, I rush in.

"Can we talk?" I ask, my insides screaming. Beside her, Donna sneers at me. Surely they've talked about me behind my back by this point, blamed me for switching to the dark side.

"What's there to talk about?" Rowan asks. I can tell she's itching to fire on me or scoot past me out of the kitchen, anything to get the last word. Doesn't she know I'll always let her have it?

"Everything." I resist the urge to hug her to me and force her to forget this whole ridiculous I'm-on-a-TV-show thing. "I didn't tell you because I didn't think it was a big deal."

Donna laughs as if she's a part of the discussion. "It's the biggest deal about you."

"No, it's not." Rowan cuts her a glare.

Even like this, Rowan is defending me.

"I'll explain everything," I plead, and her eyes soften, polluted blue blinking back to clear Atlantic.

"When will you explain? We never see each other."

"I'll talk to the nurses. They'll let us hang out—"

"So they can babysit us? Any way you slice it, this ends with you walking out that door and me still in here."

Rowan's not mad like I thought she'd be. It's worse. I expected her to fight for us, but she's not even trying.

"That's not true," I say.

"They'll be sending you home any minute now, Shosh. Believe me, this is for the best."

"So, that's it?" I hear my voice getting audibly shaky. "No more us because it's *easier.*"

I throw the word *easy* at her, knowing she hates when people take the easy way out. But if this is ending, it can't be my fault. I'm trying to fix this. She only has to let me.

Rowan casts down her eyes, smiling at me like I did a good thing, like I've been a good girl, unexpectedly impressive. But she's also sad. Her shoulders slouch like this very conversation is paining her, each word, a knife to her back.

"Don't . . ." My voice comes out choking. "Don't run away. Please."

"I tried to take you with me." She leans her head against the Gray kitchen's doorframe as Hart examines her nails. "And you fell from that window, didn't you?"

My heart sinks. My stomach heaves. Her tone tells all:

she doubts my commitment to her. A nurse must have tattled or insinuated my betrayal. Rowan was supposed to think I jumped, a sign of my full commitment to her. Falling, slipping, it's just another reminder of my cowardice. Strike two. Or is that three? Am I out already?

"Have fun being Blue," she says and walks into the Gray kitchen that, supervised and censored, feels like the privileged kitchen to be in right now.

12
Rowan

Sometimes, when I picture you out in the real world, in temple, praying, I find peace in your belief, Shoshana. In how you say God is your safety blanket and, although it's hard for most people to believe, for you it's easy. *Better to have faith that someone's always with you than to feel truly alone.*

I don't believe in the whole God schtick. You know that. I don't believe in the whole "the idea of God is what makes people do the right thing" thing either. If you tell a little kid not to touch a hot iron, versus if you tell a little kid that *God* told him not to touch a hot iron, it'll have the same result. And when that kid inevitably touches that hot iron and gets burned and it hurts like a bitch, he'll learn his lesson. Not because of God, but because actions have consequences. And consequences are what *really* keep people moral.

When I ask you why there are kids with cancer, why there are world wars and so much hate if God exists, it's only because I want you to be more like me. I want you to see there's no God, no higher whatever. There is only me and you. But your answer is that you don't know why there's suffering, no more than the next person. You've hypothesized that maybe God wanted it this way: not a utopia, but the craziest jigsaw puzzle imaginable. It's a cute answer. Of course, there's no logic there. You're completely clueless, just as much as I am, possibly more so for believing something without any evidence. But no matter how much I pride myself on atheism, I always end up resenting your faith.

I think about us, the way we were last week and all the weeks before that, the way Elly screamed, the way you danced so beautifully. What jigsaw puzzle is this and how do we put it together? That's the question I've found myself circling these last few nights.

It's close to midnight when Donna teaches Sophie the App game. If the nurses hear, they'll think I started it, but I don't care. *Let them hear*, I think. *They're going to hold me hostage anyway. Might as well have a little fun.* We play the Shoshana special edition to guess who you are on the outside.

"An actress," Sophie says first. "Or a random viral meme."

Donna guesses, "A famous person's girlfriend."

I hate that one the most.

Cheer Champions. That's what Elly called it. I've been guessing what it means all day. A club? A team? A summer camp? Could be anything. But I suspect, given that Elly screamed at the very sight of your face but you'd never seen her in your life—and also given the *Cheer* part—it's some sort of reality program. A cheerleading documentary.

Sophie goes for *16 and Pregnant.* A YouTuber. A model. Despite all her wrong answers and her strikeout when we first met, she's smarter than I've given her credit for. After only minutes of their wrongful assumptions, I spill my personal approximation.

"It's a reality show, like *Dance Moms*."

They both sigh at the same time, like their brains have clicked the way mine did hours ago.

"But cheer teams are bigger than those small group dances," I say. "She's got to be one of the people they focus on. Elly knew her name, first and last."

"So, she's like the Maddie Ziegler of cheerleading?" Sophie asks.

I nod. That would explain your ten-year-old fan base.

We iron out the details. *Why did you hide it from us?*

"Embarrassment," Sophie offers. "Maybe she's not the Maddie. Maybe she's the JoJo."

"JoJo still has her own fan base," Donna says.

"And Shoshana's not annoying like that. She's more like America's sweetheart. Think Selena Gomez. Couldn't hurt a fly," I add.

"If she's here with us and not filming anything, they're probably off-season," Sophie says.

Donna lifts her head off her pillow. "Off-season?"

"TV shows take only a couple months to film. My dad works in entertainment and he does the postproduction stuff. Maybe Shoshana waited for the season to end and then she came here to get better."

Maybe that's why you're here, I think. *Something happened and they sent you away. To us. To me.* I never gave you enough credit, never expected you had been through real shit. I still don't think it's on the same level as the Red Roof Inn—my dark day, Sunday shit—but yours is shit nonetheless. It feels out of place for the demure, spotless Shosh you play so well. But I let it make you more interesting and appealing, because we both know this scale of who's-hurt-worse will never balance between us.

I guess I should've known the only reason your file was empty when Jazzy and I found it is because you didn't come from a previous treatment center. This is your first one. You're brand new and they hadn't taken any notes yet. Now, I bet your file is thick, juicy. If only I could get my hands on it . . . or on Elly. That rug rat has to be your personal encyclopedia.

"If you guys could go anywhere in the world right now, where would it be?" Donna asks, mid-yawn.

"Neverland," Sophie whispers magically. She might be decent at the App game, but she's still twelve. Still loves the whitewashed Disney version of Peter Pan, still believes in a world where the good guys always win and the bad guys get eaten by crocodiles, where children are never left alone like we've been left alone here. *Lost girls*, I bet she thinks. Every one of us waiting for a Pan to come to our rescue.

"The original Peter Pan was a villain, you know," I tell them as I measure my thighs with my fingers, thumb-to-thumb, pinky-to-pinky. "J. M. Barrie wrote it as a satanic story where Peter kidnaps children and preys on innocent girls. Captain Hook wasn't even a part of it until they made the novel into a play. The stage crew just needed to distract the audience while they shifted scenery so they invented Hook."

"Is that true?" Donna asks. Whether it's to me or Sophie, who knows.

"Who cares. I like the Disney version," Sophie decides. "*To die would be an awfully big adventure*," she quotes wistfully.

I make a gagging gesture no one can see in the dark. That quote has been butchered by Tumblr, overused by teens who write it in glitter on their walls or tattoo it on their flesh, not really understanding. The point of that line isn't that Peter wants to die, which is the way emo kids read into it, or that he believes the afterlife is a choose-your-own-adventure, the way gamers read into it. It's that he's aloof. And no one—*no one*—is aloof about death. That's what makes Peter special. It's one of the only lines Disney kept from J.M. Barrie's O.G. Peter.

"Of course you prefer it," I tell Sophie, rolling eyes she can't see. "You're all about raindrops and roses and whiskers on kittens."

I thought you were my version of Disney's Peter, Shoshana. I felt it in my toes, in my bones, that you could save me from this. But now I'm worried I'm *your* Peter, and not the Disney kind.

"What about you, Rowan? Where would you go?" asks Donna.

If I could be anywhere right now, it'd be on top of some breezy warm mountain with you, Shosh. Not Neverland, a place that doesn't exist. A real, sunny mountaintop, where no one could find us. Yellow wheatgrass and a soothing sunset. A book or a movie on an iPad, full service in HD quality. Our own little slice of heaven. You would be there—but not the confusing you who broke our number one unspoken rule, breaching our friendship with your lies—the you from last week. The you I actually knew.

In my dream, I'm driving on I-95, windows down, Brendon Urie up, and my hands slip off the wheel. Less slip, more jerk. Purpose, not accident. The wheels screech and slam me into the guardrail, tear it apart until I'm upside down, my blood and brains dripping down the inside of the windshield. A flash of white and then I'm in the hospital, my parents rushing in, their love for me and each other revitalized. I see myself happy with them. But then I blink and I'm still driving. My hands lie steady on the wheel.

A dream within a dream.

I wake up at two a.m., my lips wet, tasting like salt. My back is soaked and smells like muck. It would be so easy to do that in real life. *Have a science test tomorrow?* Turn the wheel. *Want to skip homecoming and prom and all the stereotypical rom-com rites of passage?* Call it a muscle spasm. *Want everything to stop forever?* Cruise control your way into oblivion.

Millions of people get in their cars every day. The choice is at their fingertips.

Maybe once upon a time, I was a Wendy in Disney's *Peter Pan*. Sweet. Nurturing. But I bolted my windows for fear of all the sketchy Peters who might sneak in while I slept. A large part of me still thinks this is all my fault.

"Are you okay?" Sophie whispers below me, and I wish she were you. Sophie described the Ana voice in her head like

Nurse Hart's pro-ana doppelgänger. Before RR, she even refused to lick envelopes, petrified of the calories on the sticky flap. She's been obedient with the nurses' requests thus far, but she's due for a setback soon. I suppose she's already had one with her newly diagnosed epilepsy: the two white pills she swallows each morning and the two she swallows each night that keep her brain waves inhibited. She told us that she'd felt fuzzy the night of our attempted escape, like the pixels of her body were fading in and out. Afterward, she only remembers the ambulance and the hospital where they put her in a dark, quiet room, with a bunch of wires on her head, and waited for her to fall asleep. An EEG. Diagnosis: epilepsy. Medication: levetiracetam. So I doubt she'll make it out of here before she turns thirteen in June.

"Rowan?" Sophie checks again.

Rowan Parish does not let others see her down, I remind myself, keeping silent. *She does not associate with baby twelve-year-olds who don't have a clue.*

Sophie starts to hum, her voice threading a blanket in the night, wrapping itself around us until the room is less cold and my soul feels less bleak. Maybe one day we'll live in a world where people can choose how they want to feel. Take a dose of happiness or sadness or pride or confidence. Alcohol and drugs can do the trick for oblivion, but having a range of feelings to choose from—that would change everything. I wouldn't be here right now if I could just shoot up with some satisfaction and be done with it.

Sophie falls asleep shortly after that, and without her

voice, there's nothing. It brings on what I've been avoiding, what I overheard and what you don't know yet. What the nurses said—you're going home for Thanksgiving. A trial weekend. Your parents will be here in no time and, from what I inferred, you're gone for good after that.

I was right, Shosh. You're going home and I'm being left behind. The story's already been written and all we're doing is living it out.

Rip the Band-Aid off, I think, because that's what will hurt less. Despite everything I feel for you, the only thing I want now is to stop hurting. So that's what I plan to do. Break all ties. Cut the umbilical cord. No more born as one.

Here we are as two.

13
Shoshana

"They're here," Nurse Robinson tells me. I still don't believe it—being sent home for a trial weekend so soon. Getting my period must've done the trick, because one day I'm Blue, the next I'm Blue with extra privileges.

I can't imagine how Rowan feels right now—betrayed, angry, left behind without a thought. But there is a thought. So, so many thoughts that I just don't know how to translate into spoken words. Rowan's the one who's better at repairing things. I'm the one who's better at messing things up.

With my duffel bag slung over my shoulder, I make a break for the door. My parents are outside, pacing in the parking lot with Hart and Robinson, who appear to be running through a list with them. Mom takes the papers and folds them in her pocket.

Dad's the one I crush first, squeezing him around the middle, hearing his *oomph* followed by a laugh, then a sigh. Mom's the one who crushes me.

"Look at you!" She's already crying. "You got taller!"

Or you got shorter, I think. She's self-conscious about the two inches she's shrunk already. Her face is barely up to my neck.

"We're so glad to be taking you home, kid," Dad breathes. He kisses my hair, then gives me a noogie to ruin it.

My cheeks flood with blood in front of Nurse Hart. She seems eager to say something as she hands me my iPhone from the plastic bag of cells, but nothing makes it to the surface. I spot Donna's rhinestone Blackberry and Rowan's plain Android in the bag. Mom sees the crack in my iPhone and immediately offers to get me a new one for Hanukkah. I wonder if my body selfies are still on my camera roll, the ones I used to take every morning to play spot-the-difference from the day before. If they are, I'll have to find a way to delete them without looking too closely. I don't want to see that body compared to the one I'm in now.

"If everything goes well at home, you'll come back here, do one more week, two max, and then go home for good," Robinson says. She stands next to Nurse Hart with an unwavering stare, clearly trying for the coldness Nurse Hart perfects.

Robinson is in charge of alumni support, a side of her we never see as inpatient residents. I guess "aftercare coordinator" is her official title. Basically, she keeps tabs on the girls who graduate RR and checks that they're continuing to eat okay, that their mental health hasn't gone down the drain. I picture Robinson in her sunglasses after Sophie's seizure and our attempted escape, in tears by her car. She must feel partially responsible for Alyssa's death, thinking maybe she could've reached out more, somehow made a difference. It's easier to tell what Robinson thinks than it is to read Hart's mind.

Going by Robinson's stern expression and Hart's approving one, Hart is trying to beat that softness out of her.

"One more week?" I ask. My throat makes a sound between a cough and a gag.

A week left at RR means only a week left to fix things with Rowan. A week before I possibly never see her again.

Nurse Hart squeezes my shoulder with finality, like she can read my mind. "Have a good Thanksgiving and we'll see you on Sunday," she says. Then she turns on the heels of her white Keds and she and Robinson head back inside.

"I'll take that." Dad grabs my duffel bag as Mom pops the trunk open. I move past them to hop in the back seat. It's surreal. The last two months of my life have been spent here, confined to Gray and Blue. Now here I am, outside in a world of every color.

"Excited to sleep in your own bed again?" Dad asks, backing us out of the RR parking lot.

"Excited to have my own bathroom," I admit. The car smells like coffee and leather, and I forgot how nice it is to just lie across the back of it.

Mom reaches over the console to stroke my cheek. "Tired, honey?"

"Still hibernates in winter. Good to know our Sushi-Shoshi hasn't really changed."

He thinks I haven't changed? If I didn't, what was all of this for? My conscience has been better in the last day or two, sedated from the shock of this long trial weekend, Wednesday through Sunday, tomorrow being Thursday, Thanksgiving. But all the muted bad thoughts have begun to rear their ugly heads. *If you didn't change, what's to stop you from having another breakdown?*

I sit up and rub my eyes, staring out the window, where the world runs into a blur of everything and nothing. Our route home is 326 miles. I start to use my phone, but having not been in a car for so long or gone on my phone for more than five minutes at a time, it makes me too nauseated. The only thing I manage to do is swipe my thumb and delete my old body selfies without peering too close. *See! I am better!* I tell the voice in my head, tell Dad telepathically. *I have changed!*

When we stop for a restroom, I re-download all the apps I deleted on my cleanse quest before Mom and Dad forced my hand and found RR. Instagram. Twitter. Snapchat. Tumblr. Facebook. I had gotten rid of them all. They load with creeping circles on the homepage, spirals that look like tornadoes beginning to bloom.

"How much longer?" I ask, assuming Mom's response will be "Every time the wheels turn we get a little closer." That's what her mom used to tell her as a kid, and she always says it to K.J. and me on road trips.

Instead, she responds with, "Another forty minutes," and switches to be in the back seat with me. I lay my head on her lap.

"Shoshana. Wake up." Dad's voice is gentle. He opens the car door. "I'd try to carry you, kid, but I think you've gotten a little big for that." He smiles for a minute, then spaces. "Not *big* big. Just . . . tall."

The garage. The white exterior. The black shutters. The neatly mowed lawn and blue stone pathway. My house. I've forgotten its familiarity.

We enter through the garage, pass the laundry room, and

head into the kitchen where K.J. is eating Chipotle and watching ESPN. He probably hasn't moved from that seat since I left months ago.

Mom forces him to get up and give me the world's most awkward hug. I'm relieved when he goes back to eating and zombie-ing.

"I told you to wait for us, Kaleb," Mom scolds. "You didn't even offer to get your sister anything."

K.J. pushes his brown paper bag across the island, not looking away from the television. "I thought she didn't eat anymore."

None of us know what to say to that.

"What do you want for your welcome home dinner? Pasta? A protein shake?" Mom asks.

I wonder if she remembers that's my usual post-practice dinner. I nod. "Sure."

"Good. Give me fifteen minutes."

I head upstairs to my room. Dad drops off my bag and leaves me be. My bed has been made neatly with all four corners tucked in, which means our cleaning lady, Lili, came by recently. I sprawl out with the fuzzy purple pillows and curl up in the turquoise comforter. Everything is so clean and so *mine*.

On my desk is my MacBook, covered in various stickers like my iPhone, but not shattered. It's right where I left it and the sight of the thing almost kills me.

I dive over and power it up, not thinking of Brandy's warning to stay off social media, but of all that I've missed these last few weeks. In the search bar, I click on the Instagram icon and it logs me in automatically. There's a video at the top of the feed, *SnapsCheer*, a page for cheer updates on various teams. They posted Lady Claws's i5 team stunting. Difficult, but clean.

And just like that, I'm alive in the world again.

Before I scroll down, I click on my personal page. Over a hundred thousand followers, and an extra ten thousand since I've seen it. My last post was two and a half months ago, in August, a photo of me in my Garwood Elite practice wear, a one-shoulder blinged-out sports bra and barely there spandex. My caption: *You want to be the girl in black and gold. Oh hey, that's me.* It was a line from last year's cheer music, a voiceover right before the dance.

The Instagram photo before the last one is of me, Bri, Meredith, and Angela, a photo Lorri had taken, branding us the "Fantastic Four" of *Cheer Champions.* Another publicity stunt. I didn't think it would stick since we aren't really friends, but turns out, people believe most anything they see. Either they don't know it's manipulated, or they don't care.

I scroll through comments, some as recent as this morning, strangers asking where I am, hoping I'm okay, saying the show isn't the same without me, that I should come back ASAP. It doesn't help that I haven't seen the show. Maybe then I'd understand what some of the comments mean by *Did you see what happened to Angela?* or *The team needs you. Your stunt never stays up anymore.*

One Angela fan account accuses me of bullying the rest of the "Fantastic Four" girls, who are apparently now the "Triple Threats."

After five minutes of reading, I can't stand it anymore. I open YouTube. Search "*Cheer Champions* episode trailers" and filter for the most recent.

Season four, episode twelve promo: "A Bad Break."

I click the title and take it in with my eyes. Red and blue lights. Loud sirens. A 911 dispatcher's voice cutting through the madness. "911, what's your emergency?"

Cut to: Angela's face, an arm covering her sweaty forehead. She's in tears.

Cut to: Mary-Ellen, pushing girls away. Heath ordering them to back up and give Angela space.

Cut to: Meredith in an interview, brushing away a tear. She says, "I don't know what we're going to do without her."

Then it's over. I blink at my reflection in the blank screen. My face is recognizable to most nine-year-old girls, but hardly recognizable to me. This goes miles beyond looks. Since when do I bail on the team and get an eating disorder? Since when do I have to watch Garwood Elite promos for intel? I'm on the show. I'm supposed to be the one who creates the scoop, who's in the loop, not the one who's totally clueless.

"Shoshana! Dinner!" Mom calls. I close my laptop reflexively and head down without being asked twice. Eat all the pasta and down half the shake just to show them I'm okay. Dad flips through a triathlon magazine, shoveling in spinach and washing it down with organic chocolate milk.

My iPhone vibrates. Lorri, who usually does all her business through her assistant, has chosen to text me directly. She writes: *Are you back?*

Someone must have tipped her off, and that someone could only have been my mom. There's no point in lying.

Yes, I type.

Her response is immediate. *Good. Come to the gym Friday. Need to talk.*

"Adam, help me clean up this kitchen. Lili had it spotless this morning and I don't know what K.J. did to wreck it."

Dad helps her on command, the two of them wiping down the counters, piling miscellaneous papers against the tiny kitchen TV. When Mom cleans around me, she lists off all the people coming for Thanksgiving tomorrow. The triplets and their parents, Aunt Jill and Uncle Jerry; our neighbors, the Breedens, and their son, rock-dodging Breezy. Add Bubbee and Zaydee on Mom's side and you get fourteen total.

"Do they know I was at RR?" I ask.

"Oh, no one cares, honey. Everybody loves you, our little family superstar."

I deadpan and she gives in.

"Yes, they know. Although the Breedens don't."

"And Breezy wouldn't give a damn anyway," says K.J., grabbing Chips Ahoy! cookies from the cabinet and leaving an empty chip bag on the counter Mom just cleaned. It's amazing he's not fat. Dad's genes work miracles on him.

"Kaleb, I just cleaned that counter," Mom says.

K.J. rolls his eyes and makes a show of putting his chip bag in the garbage.

"See. Was that so hard?"

"If it's not so hard, why couldn't you just do it?" he grumbles and exits with the cookies.

"That boy is graying my hair, I swear."

"I'm gonna go shower," I chime. Mom doesn't let me leave the room without a hug.

The shower feels amazing. Hot, strong water pressure. I can even lock the door. When I go to get changed, my closet opens right to my Garwood Elite uniform, the new one we ordered in the summer: long sleeved, mesh arms, cropped right at the ribs. A gold metallic skirt with built-in black shorts underneath. It must have arrived around the time I went to RR.

It's more blinged-out than our previous uniforms, probably why it cost almost four hundred dollars. I decide to try it on and see how it feels, being back. But as I slide up the skirt, it squeezes unbearably at the bottoms of my thighs. My arms get stuck in the sleeves, threatening to rip the mesh. All the weight I've gained, it means I can't fit into my uniform. I probably can't fit into half the clothes I own. The dress I imagined wearing for Thanksgiving tomorrow, it'll never work.

Pajamas are the only thing that fit okay. Baggie and soft. I try to forget about the clothes by preoccupying myself with social media, reopening my laptop and going to Twitter. I contemplate tweeting something. Maybe: *I'm back.* Or: *Happy early Thanksgiving.* Or: *If anyone wants a GE uniform, size small, please DM me.* Instead, I do what's best—wait for Lorri and see what she thinks I should post to reenter social media.

Cradle-to-grave producer, part publicist, Lorri doesn't

just run the show; she runs our lives. She'll want to give me advice on my online profile and how to reenter the spotlight.

In the morning, there are two new dresses on the door, each in size four, six, and eight, and I'm ridiculously grateful. They're Free People dresses, pretty, frilly things Rowan would hate. I choose the green flouncy one.

Mom covers her mouth when she sees me in the eight, then circles her finger in a sign that I should twirl.

"One in a million," she breathes.

"One in seven billion, statistically speaking," Dad corrects, looking up from his book, *Life Without Limits* by Nick Vujicic. The guy on the cover has no arms or legs. "But yes, you look lovely."

Being told I look good makes me feel bad. Always. Any comment about my appearance just reminds me that I'm stuck in this body that people can see and formulate judgments on. I remember Rowan talking once about awareness. About how she's fully aware of where her eating disorder started, can break down the capitalistic beauty industry and the media's fat-phobia, but the awareness doesn't absolve her of the problem. Being able to locate an issue doesn't squander it. How unfair, she said, to know these roots that lie so deep within us and not be able to yank them out.

"My string bean all grown up," Mom coos.

Not such a string bean anymore, my conscience sneaks in, like it's saying Rowan is right. It's too late to change my own mind.

The doorbell rings and Mom jumps. "That must be the caterers!"

"Caterers for fourteen people?"

Dad waves me over and I sit down. He massages my shoulder. "I know, but even I have to admit they make a better turkey than your mother."

It's not the caterers. It's Bubbee and Zaydee, here an hour early to help set up. There's no setting up to do, so I sit with Bubbee at the piano and let her teach me "Mary Had a Little Lamb" even though I don't play piano or care to. Zaydee sits with K.J. on the couch, talking sports back and forth until James, Jordan, and Jackie show up and the kids are all sent to the basement, also known as K.J.'s lair. I tell Bubbee I'll learn the rest of the notes later and secretly hope she forgets. I've never been a musical talent like her. My talent is cheerleading and that's all.

There's a game on the basement flat-screen that hypnotizes Jordan and K.J., Jackie and James feigning interest. It's hard to remember a time when James was still in the closet, when Jackie swore he was public enemy number one and we would play dress-up in my room. My fame on the show drove her away, like it did so many girls at school. There is an endless parade of peers who ignore me, as if to say, *We don't care about your following.* It sucks when the audience at home thinks you're popular and, in reality, you have no one to partner up with on science projects.

"WINNICK," a voice calls, heavy feet thudding down the basement steps. Breezy is the only person who calls K.J. "Winnick," so I idly tuck hair behind my ears and wait for him to round the corner.

K.J. waves him over, simultaneously motioning for Jackie

and James to make room. I'm standing by the ping-pong table all by myself. We lost the balls to K.J.'s friends playing beer pong, so I've just been spinning the paddle and trying to guess which side it will land on, red or black. When this one lands on black with a bang, everyone but K.J. looks over.

Breezy's in dark jeans, a gray button-down, and blue Sperrys. His face turns from confusion to recognition to a shit-eating grin. "Holy shit. Wifey's back."

He comes over and bear-hugs me, lifting my feet off the ground. His hug is warmer than K.J.'s last night.

"How've you been?"

"Good." I subtly pull my dress back down. His arms rode it up a little. "You?"

"Yeah, good. But seriously, you go off on me, Sho? Haven't seen you in ages."

Just like he's the only one to call K.J. "Winnick," he's the only one to call me "Sho." He created the nickname after I went to a baseball game of his and K.J.'s and did back handsprings on the sidelines until I was too dizzy to stand. *Sho the show-off*, he said. I loathed it at the time, but in the last few years it's become more of a funny nickname.

"No. I've been around," I say, a half lie.

"Breezy, you gonna watch the game or not?" K.J. asks, obviously wanting me to make myself scarce.

"Nah, man. I'll check it out later." He looks to me, a hint of a dare as he observes the ping-pong table. "Wanna play?"

He passes me and grabs a paddle. When I tell him there

aren't any balls, he bites his tongue and hunts for one in an old bin of LEGOs. Like a miracle, he finds an orange ball.

"Don't worry. I'll go easy on you."

"Is that going to be your excuse when I win?" I challenge.

"Still competitive as shit, I see."

I see it too—how I've held this part of myself down for so long in RR with Rowan. It all floods back now, the way I trained on Dad's treadmill to try and beat Breezy on our races home from the front of our development, how I woke up at five a.m. to do workouts before school to get center spots for cheer. There was the time Mom almost had a heart attack when she found me in the kitchen at midnight, upside-down, doing a handstand against the back doors.

I'm a lunatic when it comes to winning. I've forgotten that.

"Your serve," he says.

I take the ball and serve. Right into the net.

Breezy's dimples deepen into his cheeks. "You always talk a big game, Sho, but you can't back it up."

I make myself look uncertain and then I hustle him. He loses. Badly. Tries to claim a weak wrist, then insists best two out of three, but I beat him a second time and then a third just for kicks. Put an L up on my forehead and he grins like I'm sweet rather than obnoxious. Even with K.J. glancing over at us like he has laser heat vision and is going to slice me in half, I'm having fun.

"You're supposed to let me win once. I'm a guest. It's polite."

"It's pathetic, is what it is," I say as Mom calls us up for food.

Breezy spends the rest of Thanksgiving with me. At the table, he eats beside me and I manage not to think too much about what I'm consuming. He puts his plate in the sink next to mine and, unprompted, follows me up to my room. He lays on my bed like it's his. For five minutes, he pretends to be asleep from a food coma and I reorder my books according to height. Then he opens his eyes, picks up an Expo marker, and begins doodling on my whiteboard wall. The last time I wrote on it was years ago. In the top right corner, half-erased, are old workout routines. The reps and sets are scribbled and half-faded.

"You better make sure no one erases this," he says, capping the black marker. He's drawn a stick figure with oversized muscles and upturned feet. There's an arrow pointing to its head and it says, as if I had written it: *I <3 Zach Breeden.*

"I'm erasing that," I say, because there's an implication there I don't like.

I get up to take the spray bottle and washcloth, but he guards his doodle. I hold the bottle up, threatening to spritz him. I'm not sure if this is flirting or not, but I guess it is because he wraps an arm around my waist and moves me away from the drawing to protect it, putting us on the bed. I'm nervous that I'm heavy. Maybe his wrist was actually weak from lifting me the first time.

I'm even more surprised when he pulls me flat against him and outright, no warning, kisses me on the mouth.

His lips are warm and eager and my body waits for a stirring, a foot pop, a tingle of butterflies in my belly—anything. But there's nothing except a desperation to shove him off, a longing to get his moist lips and curled tongue out and away from my body.

It's my fourth kiss and it's the same as all the rest: unpleasant.

I don't want to cause a scene or upset him, so I let him go on. I open my eyes in the middle of the kiss, honestly bored, and see K.J. in the doorway, pissed. I jump away from Breezy just in time, as two of my brother's other friends come into view. Corey Westler, my first kiss, which K.J. still doesn't know about, pushes into the room.

"Hey douche-face," Corey says, punching Breezy on the arm. I stare at my brother. Breezy didn't see that he caught us, but I know he did. Will K.J. say anything about it? I wait for him to.

"Hey," Breezy says, punching Corey back.

The no-name kid glances around my room, then at me. "Yo, I'm Smith."

Smith. He's new, K.J. had mentioned once. He left out that Smith looks like the kid from *Shameless*, Carl, when he goes through his gangster phase, white with appropriated braids and a chunky cubic-zirconia chain around his neck.

"Hi," I say, aware of how very girly my bedspread is. Rowan would say *puke, puke, puke.*

"What are you doing here?" Breezy asks.

"We're going to Cassidy's in fifteen. You in?"

I stand still, feeling out of place in my own room. "That's what boys can do," Rowan told me. "They take up space and dominate the air with the ownership and entitlement they feel over everything."

Corey and Smith start laughing. I don't know why, until they point at Breezy's drawing on my wall, the black lines still shiny. K.J.'s jaw works and Breezy admits that he drew it, as a joke, *obviously*.

Corey spits as he speaks. "You're starting to look like a real pussy, Breezy."

"Fuck you. Your dick looks like a pussy."

"Your dick looks like a Tic Tac."

"That's why your sister's breath smells so good," Breezy says.

The line doesn't refer to me, but to Corey's older sister, high school dropout Tara, but the word *sister* somehow drags me into the conversation.

Corey tackles Breezy and gets him in a headlock, both of them nearly smacking into my dresser. My mouth opens and I'm about to cry out for them to "quit it or I'll tell Mom" like a five-year-old, but Corey lets go and they both start laughing.

K.J. shakes his head like they're both crazy, the same way I feel. He scoffs "idiots" like a frat boy calling, and the boys follow him out.

Breezy shoots me a quick "See you around" before he goes.

I'm left alone, staring into one of the small flower mirrors on my dresser and parting my mouth with my fingers to peer down the pipe of my throat. I want to see if anything's changed, any physical result of that kiss. The texture of Breezy's tongue just irks me and I dwell on the revulsion, the sense of *thank God* that swells now that he's gone. Why do I always feel this way when I'm kissed? Why does the idea of anything more than that, especially sex, make me practically jump out of my skin?

Since my mouth looks perfectly normal in the mirror, I let it go. Some three hours away in RR, Rowan is still Gray and still mad at me, but I feel like she would have answers. I lie down on my bed and stroke the hem of my green dress, waiting for her to burst in and sweep me away.

In less than twenty-four hours, I'll meet with Lorri at the gym. I'll see what Mary-Ellen and Heath and the team are up to. I'll look different to them, fatter, and Lorri might not want to put me on camera like this. I consider the idea that Mary-Ellen might kick me off the team, just as she did with that other girl who packed on the pounds. I won't be able to take it if she screams at me in front of the entire gym again.

On my laptop, I download all the available episodes of *Cheer Champions*, reading the summaries until I find the one I'm looking for. Season three, episode twenty-two: *As pressure builds leading up to the Garwood Elite showcase, Mary-Ellen worries the girls are unprepared. After a six-hour practice, Shoshana walks off the mat, leaving the team in hot water.*

The episode of my breakdown. This is it. Before I go back into the gym tomorrow, I need to know what everyone saw, how they view me. As the small talk downstairs drones on, I shut the door, crawl into bed, and press play.

14
Rowan

I've had a lot of bad things happen in my life, like the time a bird crapped on my head when I was seven and again when I was nine, the second time right on my forehead so when the shit hit, it dribbled down into my mouth and my tongue tasted like bitter grains for weeks. But watching you jump in your mother's and father's arms, and zoom off without even a quick peek over your shoulder . . . it tastes a lot shittier than that.

It's Thanksgiving, the fake B.S. holiday where I'm supposed to be thankful for something—anything—whether it be the RR roof over our heads or the nurses for their hard work. I don't know. When it's my turn at the dinner table, I say, "Virginia Woolf's *A Room of One's Own.*" The other girls give me confused *I'm not well-read* looks, and we move on.

We do all the generic crap: turkey and gravy and an extra phone call to our families.

"I'm thankful for being here," says Sophie, and you should see how sincere she is. It's nuts.

"So, what else does your family do?" Donna asks her after we've gone full circle, the three of us picking at our turkey. Ever since she found out Sophie's family is crazy superstitious, Donna can't stop asking questions. *Do you ever walk under a ladder to piss off your parents? What about the whole "black cats" thing? Salt over the shoulder?*

"Do you hold your breath when you pass graveyards?" she asks, taking a slice of cherry pie.

"No, but if we see three red cars in a parking lot, we sign the cross." She does it on herself. Forehead, chest, shoulder, shoulder.

I ignore both of them, staring at the slice of pie I can't *Chew and Spit.*

Fuck this, I think. *Fuck this whole fucking program.* I wish I had a lighter. Then I could burn the whole place to the ground. Tear it down like they're doing with me.

Donna and Sophie get dismissed after their plates are cleared and they don't wait for me like you would. My plate is still filled with turkey and pie I refuse to eat. Robinson waits. They've left me with zero control, but this, at least, I can choose.

"Why don't you just force-feed me?" I ask Robinson. We're the only two left in the kitchen now and I can't help my attitude. This place sucks in general, but it's pointless without you, Shosh.

Robinson eyes the slice, thinking of cramming it down my throat and suffocating me, I'm sure. If Kelly were here, she'd give me extra time. She'd offer a substitute food. Robinson is a Hart wannabe.

"Haven't you heard of people who just don't like to eat?"

Robinson frowns. She's skinny-ish—to the point I bet she doesn't eat much either.

"You know," she says, "with decisions being made

tomorrow and Shoshana coming back in a couple of days, I thought you'd be more motivated this week."

I bore my eyes into hers because she's being smart for once. Using you to get to me. Is she saying what I think she's saying? They've been talking about me shedding my Gray skin and turning into a bluebird? Is there a chance to be bunked with you again and repair the damage? I pick up the fork, slowly, and let her watch me stick each bite into my mouth. Chew, swallow, chew, swallow, again, again. The turkey and pie slowly disappear.

Robinson doesn't need to give me permission to leave because when I exit the kitchen, my plate is licked clean.

The three of us—Donna, Sophie, and I—head to watch *A Charlie Brown Thanksgiving* with all of the RR girls, Gray and Blue alike. If you were here, we'd be sitting together, already having patched the gaping wound between us. You're not here, though. I don't know where you are. Your house? A family member's? A friend's? What's your National Day of Mourning like?

I try not to tumble down the route of *What If*s.

Everyone enjoys Charlie Brown. The Blue girls are laughing; even some of the Gray girls find Peppermint Patty hilarious. They don't see the show the way I do. Charlie tells Lucy he's afraid: afraid of his friends, including her, tricking him into getting hurt. Lucy assures him she won't, not again, only to laugh when she tricks Charlie and he falls on his back. He doesn't die because he's a cartoon and that doesn't happen in PG programs, but reality is, it's a F'd friendship any way you slice it.

I told one person about the Red Roof Inn after it happened: my one, albeit not super-close, friend Carly S. Lipton. Carly was a weirdo and the whole town knew it. Long, greasy black hair that covered her dark eyes, jeans always an inch too short. She was a target on sight and had gotten a shitty reputation for supposedly stealing frog hearts from the dissection lab. People spread rumors that she would chew the hearts like gum around school, that she was on crack. But Carly's knowledge of drugs stopped at Elmer's glue and Sharpie markers. She took the frog hearts to give them proper burials outdoors by the baseball field. Nobody really knew her except me, and that's what I initially liked about her. We bonded over our hatred of our algebra teacher, Mr. Salter.

One day after school when I was still an open wreck, I told her about the Red Roof Inn. Just slipped it into conversation, almost made a joke of it. Carly didn't laugh, but she also didn't look up from her rock drawing. Human affairs were beneath her interest. She cared for animals and animals alone.

"Why don't you tell Cheaney?" she asked.

I pictured Cheaney playing my hero, a role he was dying for even as my ex. Another toxic person, always one excuse away from ripping someone's eyelids off.

"If it was really the way you said it, why didn't you report it?"

How many times had I wanted to tell someone—anyone? And that was what she said.

So on instinct, I hit the reverse button on our conversation, teasing, "It wasn't really that way. I was kidding, Car, God." And Car said, "That's fucked, Ro." And I said, "Whoop-de-doo, Ms. Sensitive."

To forget about the Red Roof Inn, and the me that told the truth and then took it back, I tell myself that that version of me, high school messed-up Rowan, is a layer buried so deep I'll never be able to find her. That's the thing about morphing into a new person, Shosh . . . you can convince yourself your sins are no longer your own. You make yourself believe that the new you wouldn't make the same mistake twice, even though you very well might.

Wah wah wah, goes the grandmother on screen, same as all the parents and teachers and principals and anyone other than the Peanuts kids. I bet Walsh would say Charlie Brown has *anxiety*. I also bet none of the girls have noticed Woodstock is a cannibal.

"That's what the nurses sound like," I whisper to Donna. Two Blue girls in front of us turn around, shaming me with their eyes. I recognize Bimbo, blonde-haired and white as Wonder Bread, lip gloss applied directly after her shower. She looks like who I wanted to be when I was six and who I'd never want to be now.

I want to claw her eyes out just for talking to you, taking up your valuable time and space. But I can't say or do anything bad if they're going to make me Blue like Robinson said. One day. Less than that. Just tonight. *Be good and be Blue tomorrow,*

I convince myself. *Be good and be with you again.* It should be that easy.

You told me once that you hate the idea of people relying on you, of being walked over, used like you know you are by people who see your kindness as weakness. I told you: get used to it. People will use you your whole life. Hell, I use you, just as you use me. Scratch my back, I'll scratch yours. That's the way friendship works. I made us comrades, Shoshana. I made us what we are. Friends, with some dependency issues, I'll admit. You're my heroin(e), with and without the *e*, and without you here I'm having all the symptoms of a real detox. Shaky, nauseated, desperate to get you back.

The only time you don't use someone is when you love them unconditionally. When you love someone that way, it doesn't matter how much they take from you or how badly they F you over, you can't stop giving yourself away to them. I wonder where our limits are. How far you'll go for me, how far I'll go for you.

15
Shoshana

"Do you want me to go in with you?" Mom asks. We've been sitting in the Garwood Elite parking lot for almost ten minutes, watching the six-year-olds make their way inside, enormous cheer bows hovering high over their dainty heads.

"No," I say. "I'm going."

I open the car door and slide out in my workout gear. Mom suggested that, if I came back to the gym, I should go in wearing clothes fit for tumbling. She figures I'll be tempted by the mats and trampoline, and she's probably right.

Last night I stayed up watching *Cheer Champions*. They didn't catch as much of my breakdown as I'd thought, or had chosen not to air it. The cameras only glimpsed my ducking out of my double, the way I almost cracked my skull open on the mat, my legs folding into my chest like someone had shoved me into a suitcase. It was my fault—a mental block I'd been having on and off for weeks. But the camera crew recorded Mary-Ellen's blowup: "*Do everyone a favor and quit! You're a shell of the talent you used to be! Snot-nosed kid like you ain't gonna win me shit!*"

Then they aired Heath coming into the bathroom, throwing my mic out the door. They didn't air more than that. In fact, the whole thing sort of made me look like the victim, although that could just be me feeling sorry for myself. Everything Mary-Ellen said was the truth, but on camera it came off as her being stressed, taking it out on me because I was there, not because I deserved it. It was as if she were the one having the breakdown, not me.

In the next episode, they used footage of me from last year, when Mom and Dad took K.J. and me on vacation to the Bahamas, me saying, "So I won't be here for a little while. It'll be nice to take a break and clear my head and come back ready to work harder."

I'd said "clear my head" because we had just lost NCA before vacation, a huge competition that meant we weren't ready for Worlds. But it fit perfectly with the episode. They made it look like I was choosing to take a leave of absence, not being taken out for health reasons. I sent Lorri a thank-you text.

"I'm going on a Starbucks run, but I'll be back here in twenty minutes. Take as much time as you need." Mom blows me a kiss.

Garwood Elite's front door has a sticker of the initials GE outlined in gold. When I push it open, our secretary, Chloe Crist—the cheer girls all call her CC—is at the front desk, on the phone, trading off between reciting a rundown of expenses and sneaking peeks at her speculative fiction book. She does a double take. She must have been told to expect me because she waves me forward, thumbing Mary-Ellen's office. "In there," she mouths.

A thick black curtain covers the window between the front

waiting room and the practice space. Parents aren't allowed to view our practices. No one is allowed in but us. What happens in the gym stays in the gym. I walk past the front desk and the curtains, where Mary-Ellen's office is. Her door is wide open, and Lorri's voice is flooding through it.

"No. That's not what I'm saying. I'm saying we need her to do this, otherwise our ratings are questionable at best and with the network up our asses, we need a fast turnaround. Believe me, talk to them all you want, but if the numbers don't hit, they're gonna pull the plug. Viewers love a protagonist. She'll fix this. She'll testify to your character. That alone will do more than the entire rest of the team could—"

I knock on the open door lightly, but Lorri's neck whips to the side like I've rammed my fist against it.

She stops speaking and gets up from the bare wooden chair to give me a hug. She's tiny, but warm. "Hey, superstar!"

Mom calls me *superstar* like I'm Aly Raisman, a real cereal box girl. Lorri calls me *superstar* like she just thinks I'm a good kid.

"Hi," I say, too afraid to look at Mary-Ellen. She likes eye contact though, so when I pull away from Lorri, I face her and take her in. Her hair poof is smaller than usual, but her breasts are bigger than I remember and her black pupils multiply like cancer cells. She takes me in, not happy about my reappearance.

"Welcome back," she cuts.

I didn't know this was a *welcome back* meeting. I thought it would be a "you're a fool to darken this door again" meeting. I've been preparing myself so I don't cry.

"FYI, kid, you're only here for the show. If it was my call, you'd stay wherever the hell it was you just came from."

I swallow, my right eye twitching. My shoes are glued to the carpet. They're letting me back on the team because they need me for the show, not because I'm good enough as a cheerleader.

Mary-Ellen sits back in her chair, turning away. Lorri gently guides me outside to the cheerleading mat. She keeps her voice low and neutral as she says, "She doesn't mean that. She just wants you to work hard and prove to her that you belong here."

My head is swimming and my knees feel wobbly, weak.

"Is that Bagels and Lox?"

Heath stands on the edge of the mat, hands on his waist. He calls me Bagels and Lox because I'm the only Jewish girl on the team, the one who doesn't pray "in Jesus's name" during the occasional team kickoff prayer. It always makes me antsy, the nickname, uncomfortable to the point of potential rashes. It makes me think of the Jewish slurs K.J. and I learned in Hebrew school. How we're supposed to stand up for ourselves, but I don't or can't. I just grin and shrug it off, the same way I ignore that kickoff prayer, which the cameras caught one time—me standing awkwardly to the side as the team clasped hands, their backs to me—and when it aired, people called it exclusionary, praying at practice. In my head, I call it antisemitic.

You wouldn't pray at school, would you? parents wrote online.

Mary-Ellen wanted to pray, though, and that was that.

Not participating set me on her bad side from the start. She likes to be right, with no opposition. She believes in Jesus and my refusal makes me Judas. Although I have no proof of it, I suspect this is one of the main reasons why Mary-Ellen doesn't like me. The gold cross that hangs around her nipped-and-tucked neck and sits between her lifted breasts taunts me like it's true: her antisemitism, the root of her hatred.

You're only here for the show.

"You want to try tumbling? Warm up?" Heath asks. Typical. The first thing he wants to do is get me back in shape. Admittedly, I do need to start soon. My muscles have shriveled and I can only imagine the pain it'll take to repair them.

"Here." He waves me over to the floor, points at where to stand, and tells me, "Throw me a back tuck."

Gym lights glinting off his black bald head, he still sounds like a sergeant, even fifteen years post-deployment.

I move to the spot and Heath positions his arms like he's going to spot me. I swing my fists back, set and wrap my knees as fast as I can in the backflip. I land without his help, but it's low, like *end of a practice, last round of Circle of Death* low. Nothing like *Shoshana Winnick at the start of practice, fully fueled.*

"Again," he says, and I robotically throw another one. He spots me this time, giving me the air I need so I land with my chest up. "Good. We'll start fulls next week. Come in tomorrow and we'll put you back in the routine. We're redoing the running tumbling section, adding difficulty. I want you doing the Arabian pass at Worlds."

I nod, astonished at their accommodations, acting as if no

time has passed. RR is basically nonexistent. Rowan Parish is a girl I've never heard of.

I watch a cheeky cheerleader in the level-one Minis do a back walkover. She's cute, with promising form and familiar eyes. I love cheerleaders like that, committed, determined, in it for the joy, not the tiny uniforms or the prospect of fame. It's the one nice thing about *Cheer Champions*. It's not just a reality show you can make with random people you pluck off the street. You need level-five cheerleaders, which means Lorri can't just hire people to replace us. Mary-Ellen can, though. She has girls lining up around the block, amazing cheerleaders begging to be on her top GE team.

Before Heath can ask, I do a third back tuck on my own, giving it all the energy I have left. I land solidly on the blue mat, my white shoes vibrating from the springs.

Heath pats me on the shoulder. "Good to have you back."

"Excuse me," a tiny voice speaks behind us. The cheeky back walkover girl. The Minis are on a water break and she holds out a Sharpie and her practice bow. "Can you sign my bow?"

"Sure," I say. "What's your name?"

"Daphne."

"Daphne." I sign my name against the gold part of the bow. "Your back walkovers are pretty clean."

She beams, never expecting I'd notice.

"Keep your elbows by your ears and you'll go faster, maybe into a back handspring and that'll put you at level two."

She nods and runs off, immediately practicing in the corner with her arms locked. She takes well to the correction, even setting up like she's ready to connect the handspring. I give her a thumbs-up and she keeps going. Over and over and over. Energy I don't have anymore.

"You always were the best with the toddlers," Heath says, crossing his gigantic muscles over his chest.

"Not all of them," I say, remembering the ones at Reach the Sky who took selfies with me in the background, assuming I wouldn't notice. I was just trying to eat dinner with Mom and Dad at a local restaurant after the competition. I was paranoid they'd get an awful one of me with sauce on my face. I kept shooting them looks to kill.

"You should go practice with them," says Heath.

"With who?"

"The Minis."

I shake my head, sure I've missed part of the conversation. "Those girls are level one."

"Some technique training would do you good. Can you even do a back walkover anymore?"

No, I can't. Back walkovers require back flexibility, and once I learned back handsprings and stopped flying, I didn't stretch for bridges.

"The Lox I know would do this, without question. Tumbling with toddlers, anything. Whatever it takes to be the best. And that's always been my plan for you. Number one."

I believe him, but as pathetic as it sounds, those three backflips wiped me out. My heart is still pounding and I didn't even stretch.

"I need to borrow her," interrupts Lorri. She wraps an

arm around me, moving us off the mat, away from Heath and toward the tumble track. Heath doesn't like Lorri or the show. He wants us strictly focused on the routine. *Cheer first, fame later.* That's his motto.

Lorri and I sit on the tumble track, our weight dipping the woven black material.

"First things first: how are you feeling?" she asks.

I stretch out my legs. At Thanksgiving, Bubbee and Zaydee didn't mention my eating disorder. The last person to ask me how I was feeling about things was Mrs. Walsh in therapy.

"Better," I say.

"Good. Because if you're going to come back, we want it to be for the long haul. There have been some issues with XSA renewing us after this season and I believe you can sway the network."

She looks at Mary-Ellen's office, the door suddenly closed. "You're the kind of girl our audience lives for. A nice, wholesome kid, in this sport for the right reasons. These last few episodes have been the most difficult for our editing team to polish. They're less . . . redemptive in nature."

She waits, but I haven't a clue what I'm supposed to say. "What do you want me to do?" I finally ask.

"Well, we're hoping to get you on camera as soon as possible. And then, have you tell the audience you're ready to be back and work hard for Mary-Ellen."

Work hard for Mary-Ellen. That's their spin.

Cheering is like chess. Right now, I'm a pawn. I don't have a lot of skills compared to the best girls on GE and that makes me more disposable. Mary-Ellen is our king, to be protected at all costs. Kings in chess aren't so powerful though, and it helps me breathe easier in the gym when I imagine Mary-Ellen, protected by the lot of us, nearly powerless herself.

"I need to go back to the treatment center for at least a week," I say. "I won't be back at practices until then."

Lorri smiles. "Not an issue. We can film your interview tomorrow, if you're free. That way, we can cut it early. We can shoot you with the girls whenever. Oh, and we'll have to re-create you coming in, as if we'd taped you walking into the gym this morning, seeing Mary-Ellen and Heath and the girls, but easy enough. I already have the angles worked out for them to run and hug you."

Running to hug me? It's laughable. She knows as well as I do that I'm not close with any of the girls on the team. They don't talk to me unless it's to pass along instructions. I still live by the "don't speak unless spoken to" rule here.

"If you haven't heard, GE isn't doing so well in competition this season. People like to watch winners, or at least graceful losers. Mary-Ellen is not graceful," Lorri says.

One thing we can agree on.

"I have to talk to my mom," I say, using the line to buy me time. Lorri knows my mom, who says yes to anything the crew asks for. "But I can probably do the interview tomorrow. Heath wants me to block the new part of the routine anyway."

"Two birds, one stone. I'll let the camera crew know," says Lorri, already on her cell. Heath nods at me from afar, now helping the Minis. I head for the exit and see Mary-Ellen's door is still closed, like she's the one hiding from me.

I eat a peanut butter sandwich for dinner. All of it, because Dad is watching, but I wish I didn't have to. A PB sandwich is over 400 calories. That's supposed to be a fourth of my day and I've already had a 600-calorie breakfast, 500-calorie lunch, and two snacks of 180 calories each. I'm almost at 2,000.

As a Gray Girl, I ate roughly 3,000 calories a day, which sucked but didn't feel as shitty as this, even when I'm eating less. Maybe it's the setting or wanting to get back in shape, but each bite pricks my brain with a *Stop* from my conscience. *Stop. Stop. Stop.* I don't. Then finally: *Fine, but you can't complain when you're not the best because you're the one doing it to yourself. Stop. Shoshana. Stop.*

We go to temple for Friday night services as a family. Well, without K.J. He's hanging out with his friends, so I go with Mom and Dad and sit with my siddur, the three of us listening to our rabbi read from the Torah on the bema.

The Hebrew is all gibberish to me, even after years of Hebrew school and a bat mitzvah. I can say the prayers on Shabbat, memorized, but little else. Still, the rabbi speaks in English about mitzvot, good deeds we can do for other people, and I like listening to him. Rowan hates religion, but I think she would like temple if she tried it. We're not Mormons or super orthodox, being told what's right and wrong like it's clear-cut. We're just listening to stories about how people help each other.

"Do you remember that time you almost dropped the Torah?" Mom whispers, getting tired after forty-five minutes. She always finds that story funny, but for me, a thirteen-year-old who could barely lift the Torah, it was terrifying. If it falls, the person who drops it has to fast for forty days. Thirteen-year-old me couldn't imagine not having ice cream sundae Pop-Tarts for a minute, let alone five weeks.

"The important thing is that I didn't drop it."

"And you and K.J. on the high holidays . . . I had to bring you both books to hide behind your siddurs to get you to sit still. Do you remember?"

"Yes." I read Junie B. Jones for hours.

Dad shushes us. He's more serious about Judaism than we are, which I always find interesting, considering he converted for Mom when Bubbee and Zaydee wouldn't give him their blessing otherwise.

After the hour service, Rabbi Saltzman comes up and shakes my hand. Rowan would die if she saw this freeze-frame, but I smile and say, "Shabbat Shalom," and he does the same. If we were orthodox, we'd walk home and spend the next day without light or power. No iPhones or computers—like at RR. Instead, Dad runs the heater in the car and we drive the two miles home with the radio playing cool jazz.

K.J. and the boys are in the kitchen when we get there. He always brings them home like stray dogs, feeding them pizza and garlic knots, their own sacred service.

"Go say hi," Mom orders.

Walking into the kitchen with my sweaty hair and no makeup makes me insecure. Rowan would knock sense into me if she were here.

Does it matter what they think? No.

Does it matter what boys think, period? No.

They're all numbskulls, Shoshana. Forget 'em.

I miss her, like an aching bruise that flares up whenever someone touches it. I wish I told her more things about myself, like how much I enjoy wearing heels, even if I do hate how they make me feel gigantic at well over six feet. I wish I told her that I love competition makeup, that applying it feels like painting, therapeutic. I wish I told her that I don't see the harm in things the way she does and that's okay. We don't have to agree on everything.

But she'd say: *Every tube of mascara you buy—remember—that money goes right to the white man's pocket. The same man who fuels all those advertisements that make you feel like shit for not having it in the first place. Cycle of corruption.*

I can hear her voice. I long for it so much I search for her on social media. On Facebook, I friend her, but I can't track down her Tumblr or Twitter. On Instagram, she has seventy followers. I go down her list, more guys than girls. You can see her slimming down as the photos become more recent. She's always thin, but in the last ones, she looks like a skeleton, hand on her hip, taken in the mirror, posted with the caption *Just a girl with an existential crisis. HMU.* Taken almost two years ago.

It catches me off guard because selfies don't strike me as

the type of thing she would post. But maybe I'm wrong. *Gotta work the system somehow.* That's what she said. Maybe selfies are working the system. Then again, maybe selfies *are* the system.

Still searching for Rowan's Twitter account, I decide to make my official debut. I forgot to talk to Lorri about it today, but surely she won't mind. She's happy I'm back on the team, and it's only normal I'd announce it. I press the blue button and the little blue check mark pops up next to my name.

Hello, world. I'm here. What'd I miss? I tweet.

Less than a minute is all it takes. Replies. Dozens of them. Happy I'm alive, back, so relieved I'm not lying in a ditch somewhere. Am I coming back to the show? Am I going to open up about what happened? Am I going to stick around this time, or is this one last-hurrah tweet before I go full dark and delete my account?

I don't have answers for them about the show, but I tweet out *Tomorrow* with a winky face.

That'll keep them on their toes until I find out more, I think. For now I surround myself in the warmth of strangers' concerns and praise, hoping it will be enough to get me through GE's practice tomorrow, and back in shape in time for Worlds.

16
Rowan

Today is Sophie's first one-on-one. Her step-right-up-and-get-a-chance-to-look-at-the-psychic's-crystal-ball to see her future for free. A real photo-worthy moment, too, because a girl only hears she's staying Gray for the first time once. I mean, technically she's already heard it, but no one goes Blue in the first two weeks. This time, she gets to wonder, to hope, and then be let down. It's as they say: nothing's like the first time and it always fucking hurts.

Sophie's name is called. Quick, like a bee sting. Boo-boo all better. Donna and I cheer as she rejoins us, playing the roles of proud parents. Our beautiful Gray girl, the shade of tin and the moon, and us, oh-so-proud.

Sophie asks me, "Will you be Gray again too?"

"Not t-t-today, junior."

She's too young to get the *Billy Madison* reference, but she understands enough.

Today, I'm going to be Blue. Robinson practically said so: *With decisions being made tomorrow and Shoshana coming back in a couple of days, I thought you'd be more motivated this week.* Insinuation, as powerful a tool as any. So I've stayed motivated, I've followed their rules for the last forty-eight hours so we'd be together, Shosh. Once we're Blue, we'll be whole again. Maybe we'll even get to be roomies; all will be right with the world.

Sophie sighs with relief when Donna comes out shaking her head. It means I'm definitely switching colors. Otherwise, it would have been Donna this week.

"Rowan," they call, and *first time for everything* because when I walk in, it's without complaint.

"So," Nurse Hart sighs, my thick folder sitting hefty between us. She doesn't bother building the suspense. She spits it out, my arms already prickled with goose bumps. Maybe now I'll actually try. You and I can go clean, the nurses' way, and get out of here together. No more window stunts necessary.

Then the words hit me. "We have decided to keep you on the Gray schedule."

It's not the first time I've heard that. It's the eleventh time, actually. Eleven weeks in a row and this is the first time it really stings. I can't tell when I'll ever not be Gray. Because to them, I'll always be the girl who chopped off her hair and ruined her pretty face, corrupted you until you turned away from them. It's their narrative. I'm just living in it.

In my eyes, you, Shoshana, are a part of me. You swore it, remember? *Us.* And as that part, this whole mess belongs to the both of us to clean up. They can't just send you home and leave me here. They can't love you and hate me. It can't work like that.

I would just walk out, but today I can't. Today cannot be another day of the same thing. I'm supposed to be Blue. If they think I'm going to keep listening to them say the same things for another week or month or year, they've got another thing coming. That thing: tidal-wave Rowan.

"You can't just keep me locked up in here. My family pays for this. We're already broke. I was supposed to be Blue weeks ago. So either do your job and make me Blue or send me on my merry way," I spit.

"Every patient's recovery time is different," Robinson starts. "You jumped out of a window last week, Rowan. We can't just—"

"So did Shoshana!" I slam my palms down on the table and the nurses share looks of disappointment and exhaustion, strategizing how to deescalate. They must think this is example A of why I can't be Blue—that I'm out of control, throwing hissy fits when I don't get my way. They don't see that they are the ones driving me up this wall. With zero control over my life, I'm going certifiably insane. And I see through their tiny ways of trying to make me feel better, pretending I have control by letting me sit where I want to at the breakfast table, like that's putting me back in the driver's seat of my life.

I slam the door in their faces on my way out and the effect startles the outside Gray girls. Sophie and Donna watch me dart up the stairs, where I shut our door and sit against it because there's no lock.

Once, after a fight with my mother, I put cheese sticks in a bag of ice and took it to my bedroom, pushed the dresser against the door to keep her out, and convinced myself I could survive on Polly-O for the rest of my days. It took only an hour before she came upstairs and made me open the door, half my lifetime supply already diminished.

I plan to last longer this time. At least a couple of days now that I can restrict myself food-wise.

It takes all my strength to move my bunk bed against the doorframe, the legs leaving skid marks across the floor. Unfortunately, the sound is so loud that by the time I almost get there, the nurses are pushing back with everything they've got.

Everything they've got: a whole lot more than me. They move the bunk bed back into place and Hart tells me I won't be spending the day on the Gray *or* Blue schedule. I'll be spending it with them.

I think, just maybe, I've finally struck gold. That this has been the final straw and they'll give up and send me home, tell my mother I'm broken, and I'll go back to the way things were. Not that things were good before; they weren't. But they also weren't this. Even those dumb indie centers, Sunrise Peaks and Life's Carousel, weren't so strict.

A mandate for being with the nurses is that I eat in the staff room. They don't talk to me. No one does, including Sophie and Donna who, for the few moments I see them, look the other way. The instruction is clear and centerwide—keep your distance from the deranged, possibly rabid Rowan.

Silent treatment. The nurses know how to use it, just like we do. By the end of lunch, I feel less important than I did yesterday, and the urge to talk to myself aloud grows stronger by the minute. I resist. If I give in, it's all downhill from there.

Slipping. Now, I understand the word. Not jumping

purposefully. Not sliding, which has the connotation of playground fun. *Slipping.* Not from a window but from within. Day after day, slipping away. RR wants me to have a clean slate—a do-over. I'm big enough to admit that it's maybe what I need, but that doesn't mean their Kool-Aid tastes any better going down.

I play mind games to get myself through the day. Not tic-tac-toe or twenty questions. Things you need two people for. More like people watching, imagining how a person will react to something and then seeing how close my approximation is. I imagine pinching Nurse Hart on the arm. Her reaction would be a quick shake, a "do it one more time and see what happens."

"What do you think you're doing?" she asks, my arm outstretched, fingers poised to pinch.

I put my hand down.

"What is it going to take for you to take this program seriously?" Hart asks. The tip of her nose is red, her glasses rubbed too tight. "Because if you're not going to follow it, we're going to have no choice but to send you home."

She says that like it's a threat.

"Except you can't. My mother won't let you until you send me back as someone who's not her spitting image," I say. "And Robinson is right. I jumped out a window and broke my arm last week. If my mother was any sane parent, she would have pulled me from this institution already, or come to see me at least."

"Shoshana's parents didn't pull her out," Hope says, hidden behind Hart.

"Yes," I say. "And we all know the Winnicks got that Thanksgiving 'trial weekend' because of it."

The nurses quiet and I assume it's because I've hit the nail on the lying, scheming head. You see, Shoshana, your parents worked out a deal with the nurses. They were dying without you. It wasn't your period that got you out, which I've heard about so many times you'd think you parted the very first Red Sea. No, it was the fact that your parents could've sued the shit out of RR and they didn't. What other explanation is there? I mean, no one goes home that soon. I know people are typically Gray for longer than they are Blue, but percentage-wise, you've been Blue for, like, a sliver in time.

I'll tell you—what I wouldn't give to have a parent who loved me enough to commit blackmail. Your mother is a shark, Shosh.

"Being here might not be what's best for your care, Rowan," Nurse Hart says, "and if we make that decision, we'll refer you to other services."

What she's saying is that sooner or later, they're going to give up on me. I'll have to go home or be sent someplace new. They have the option to put me out with the trash, whereas my mother doesn't.

There are times—very rare times, I should add—that I feel bad for my mother, the end product of seven siblings, a woman who wanted to be an attorney but got pregnant her freshman year of college after a one-night stand with my Phi

Kaps president father, forced to keep me by her church-loving father. The tale of how I came to be. I could play *What If?* with my mother's life forever.

Starting with: *What if* she had just gone the coat hanger route?

"Is this the part where you tell me if I pull a stunt like that again, I'll be out on my ass faster than you can say 'thank-God-that's-over'?" I ask.

"This is the part where I tell you we love you," Nurse Hart says and plops her stiff hand on my purple head. She strokes my hair and smiles, almost as if she likes the color and isn't repulsed by the shade like most older people. "We want to help you, Rowan, in whatever way you'll let us. But we can't do anything without you."

I should shove her off, say I don't need hers or anyone else's help. But I'm tired and no one has spoken to me in what feels like years. Her skin is soft. I close my eyes, refusing to let tears burn their way to my eyelids as they always do when I finally find comfort.

"Let's get some fresh air," Hart says. Without pause, she gets up to walk out the door. I follow, the two of us bathed in the licking winter chill in no time. She reaches into the waistband of her scrubs and pulls out a lighter and a pack of Marlboros.

"Not for you," she says.

I watch, stunned as she lights up and blows out gray puffs between her nostrils. She doesn't even look like Satan or Hart or anyone I've ever met. She looks like a lady who gardens and sits on her paint-chipped porch eating black licorice.

"Smoking kills you," I say.

"So does starving yourself." She sits on the curb. "Now, give it a go."

"Give what a go?" I look at the open parking lot, the long road in the distance where the driveway pulls off. We're literally in the middle of fucking nowhere.

"Whatever you want." She takes another drag and even though she's just lit up, she puts her cigarette on the ground and rolls it under her Ked. "Scream. Cry. Cuss. Whatever will make you feel less shitty."

Her voice is uncanny. Usually she'd say, "Do what will make you feel better" in her calm, reasonable nurse's voice. Here, she has the hint of a Georgia accent.

I think of which to choose. Screaming, crying, or cursing. None of them will change a damn thing, but the frustration of trying to choose brings hot tears to my eyes and they don't need my permission to fall against my cheeks.

Hell knows how you never do this, Shosh. You never cry. Either you're a robot or you have the best poker face in existence, because silly me used to think you were an open book— good girl by day and good girl by night. Now, I know better.

"Keep going," Nurse Hart encourages, and the pain rolls in hot. I keep going, part command, part out of control. It shakes me, and I can't think of what's making me sad besides everything. Everything, all the time. I put my face into the crook of my elbow, snot dripping down my forearm. My mouth makes a sound like a dying animal until Nurse Hart wraps her arm around me from the side and my sobs rack both of us.

"Forget about all the Rowans inside you," she says. "Forget being multiple things at once. You're one human being. Inhale as one human. Exhale as one human. Screw the rest."

There, for just a moment, Nurse Hart becomes something that resembles a friend. She's not you. Far from it, Shosh, but she knows me well enough to do the job.

She breaks my armor.

17
Shoshana

"Let's start with your absence," Lorri says, standing directly behind the camera. She's checking to make sure not a hair's out of place in the shot, instructing Mark and Lee on what she wants it to look like. It being me.

The crew move around me, checking audio and lighting my face for the most flattering view on the monitor. It's been months since I've taped anything, so rather than scroll on my phone until the last minute, I pay attention to the green screen and my image.

"You don't have to lie. Just be vague," Lorri advises, finally satisfied with the picture.

I go to itch my nose but stop, not wanting to screw up the face Alisha, the makeup artist, put on me. No one asks if I'm nervous, but it's obvious Lorri is. She needs this to work to keep her job and so do the rest of the crew. *Cheer Champions* was Lorri's first big win, and almost four seasons later, it's dwindling.

"Remember, don't slouch. Use present tense. Work the eyes," Lorri directs.

I nod, then with the red light blinking, start spilling.

"Most of you probably noticed I haven't been in the gym for a while now. It's been . . . a necessary change, just something I

BEFORE WE WERE BLUE

needed to do. But I'm back! I'm ready to train for Worlds and be better than before."

Lorri digs her finger into her cheek. *I'm not selling it enough. I need to smile wider.* All the blush and concealer in the world can't keep me from looking out of sorts right now.

"Today I'm getting worked back into the routine," I say, smiling so wide my cheeks hurt. "Hopefully it won't take me too long to get back in the swing of things. We'll be nearing Worlds soon."

Lorri gives a thumbs-up. *Yes. Focus on the future.*

"I remember watching the girls on this show compete at Worlds before I was on the team, and now I'm prepared to give it everything I've got. This team wants to win and Mary-Ellen and Heath can get us there. This year, we're gunning for the rings."

I hold up my hand and wiggle ring-less fingers. Every cheerleader wants a Worlds' ring. Only the number one team in each division get them.

"Okay, good," Lorri says. "We'll have some of the other girls make statements on your behalf. For the sake of limited time, let's film some of your reactions to today's practice and we can choose which one depending on how it goes. After that, we'll call it a day."

Getting the interview done early makes sense for everyone. This way, I won't have to wait after practice for them to set the equipment back up. Alisha won't have to redo my makeup on a sweaty, cherry-red face.

I react four different ways. Tell the camera:

1) Practice is going great. It feels like I never left. All I can think about is getting out on the competition floor with my sisters and getting a Worlds' bid.

2) Coming back is harder than I thought. This practice was a struggle, but that's to be expected. I'll keep working hard.

3) I'm out of shape, clearly *laugh* but I'll get back into tip-top shape in the next few weeks. Really, I need to focus on the mental part of cheer. It's all in my head.

4) I don't know if I can do this. I'm not sure I'm good enough anymore.

Lorri claps at the first and nods reluctantly at the last.

The statement they'll use for the episode depends on how today's practice actually goes. I've already re-created my entrance, Alisha doing my makeup before I phonily went back outside and reopened the door and the girls came running up to hug me. I don't remember the show feeling this organized or strategically produced.

"Anything else you want to say before we wrap up?" Lorri asks. I'm not like Meredith. I won't cry for them or get any more dramatic than option four. So I say, "No," and Jay moves the boom mic away from me, cutting the audio. Alisha hands me a makeup wipe.

Practice moves as quickly as it did before RR. In front of me on the floor, Angela throws a full, the same thing as a double but with one twist instead of two. The ambulance episode must have been a ploy or filmed a while ago because she's here, training and flipping, in great shape. Likely, she got roughed up a little bit and the crew called 911 to boost ratings. Also, they probably got Angela's mother going crazy on camera. The audience is in a love-hate relationship with Angela's mom and her heated meltdowns.

Gretta, whom everyone calls Ginger for her flaming red hair and zany spirit, stands in the opposite corner and goes next, power-hurdling into a roundoff whip double she makes look effortless. She's a rubber band when she tumbles, just a flash of her strawberry hair and white shoes as they punch the mat, flipping for days. She's far better than everyone else on the team and she's only twelve. The red hair reminds me of Sophie, only Sophie's like a newborn kitten and Ginger's like a gnawing tiger.

I sit beside Heath, stretching, watching how everyone's improved while I've fallen behind.

"Switch to plank," Heath orders. I hold it as the girls warm up. After only thirty seconds, my arms shake and my abs burn. "Good. Now get up and join the rest of the lot. Roundoff handspring rebounds only."

I get up and move to the end of the line, Ginger in front of me. She's the youngest on our team, having just aged into the level-five division. Before RR, I was her back spot. A fairly easy task because she's so small and I'm tall enough to hold the back of her knee when I'm on tiptoe. But Bri has taken my place in Ginger's stunt group. A new girl named Frankie has filled Bri's spot with Angela.

Ginger tumbles again, landing her full and punching right into a front tuck step out, tumbling back toward me until she's gone all the way up and down the mat. She's incredible, finishing the pass with a neat twisting double.

Time's up for me. I start to gain power as I run and hurl myself into the roundoff back handspring rebound. My body is used to going for the tuck, the full, the double, but I just rebound and stretch my arms up, so when I add on, my muscle memory will push for the extra height.

Mary-Ellen gives me a nod of approval as I walk to the back of the line. Her nod takes credit for my work, for all of our work. It's as if she's the one doing Ginger's flawless doubles. Our wins are her wins first. The name, Garwood Elite, is more powerful than any individual who belongs to this gym. As long as I have the letters GE on my chest, everything I do belongs to her.

A few more rounds of tumbling later, Heath lets me throw tucks and even a full. Coming back is easier than I'd anticipated. I'm winded, exhausted—slightly dying, actually—but the skills are still there.

"We're going to try something new," Heath says after everyone's blood is pumping. He places his hands on my shoulders and shakes them in front of the rest of the girls, loosening the muscles for whatever strain he's about to cause.

"Here's what's going to happen. Everyone needs to be listening to my voice right now, otherwise someone is going to get seriously hurt." Heath crosses to Ginger. He motions for her to stand up and walks her over to her running tumbling spot. He tugs playfully on her ponytail, grinning.

"Oh no," Meredith breathes to Angela behind me.

I swallow down the bile rising in my throat. *Oh no* is right. Heath only grins like that when he has an insane idea, one that could end in paralysis.

Mary-Ellen takes a seat on the stacked mats beside the floor. She crosses her legs, posture overexaggerated with her shoulders back, boobs out. Her job is to watch and criticize. Our job: to be flawless.

"Ginger, you're going to start in this corner. Shoshana will be in *this* corner." He walks me over to the opposite side. "Your passes are going to be synched. Ginger, you are going to go on the number five. Throw me a front tuck step out through to a double. Got that? On five." He holds up his hand to Ginger. "Take three steps before the front tuck so you flip in the center of the mat. What number do you leave on?"

"Five."

"And how many steps do you take?"

"Three."

He smirks and faces me.

"Bagels and Lox, you're going on three. Two steps before the power hurdle. I want you to do an Arabian, roundoff through to a full, for now. We'll work on the double later."

An Arabian is a jump half-turn into a front flip. Before I land, I'll have to split my feet midair and connect the roundoff. Arabians can throw off the rest of the tumbling pass, but if done with the right form, they're jaw-dropping.

With the counts Heath's given, I work out that Ginger and I will be in the same place at the same time, the center of the mat. Without there being a collision, one of us must go over the other. Common sense says that, since I've got a foot on the redheaded dynamo, I'll be higher in the air. Over the bridge, not under the tunnel.

It's exactly the kind of badass stunt I would have loved to watch on *Cheer Champions*. I would have been sitting on the edge of the couch, mouth sticky with fluff, waiting to see the paramedics arrive.

"Everyone else, throw your synchro passes on the following one. You should be starting your steps exactly when the two of them are in the air, somewhere around one," Heath announces. He works his way back to me and clamps a hand on the back of my neck. "Relax. We're going to mark it first. You don't have to do the Arabian today."

I pause to survey the cameras just off the mat. If I don't do the Arabian, they'll be using reaction number four. Mary-Ellen trails a pointed fingernail down the line of her jaw, then taps her chin in anticipation.

"I'll do it," I say.

Heath pokes my side. "Atta girl. Everyone mark it!"

We dart in the direction of our tumbling passes when he counts, but no one flips yet. Ginger and I run toward each other, meet in the middle, and pass one another. Ginger widens her eyes.

She says, "Better make your Arabian high."

I say, "Better make your front tuck low."

The closer we are to hitting, the more hype this section of the routine will have. Audiences want to see wild things in all-star cheer. GE will stand out in competition with a stunt like this.

"Ready to go full-out?" Heath asks. Everyone says yes except Ginger and I. We are the "awe" factor of this section. If either of us is off by a second, we're dead. She'll be crushed by me or I'll be taken out midair, dropped five feet to the ground in any number of positions.

Heath begins counting. There's no backing out now.

Red hair fills my peripheral vision as I sprint and punch the mat. It should be enough height not to kill her. We flip and it's over in a flash, something whipping against my leg. I connect the roundoff, but don't finish the rest of the pass—eerily similar to the way the breakdown went. Pausing. Hesitation. This time, I'm not midair, though.

Mary-Ellen claps her hands from atop the mats, her throne. Heath rubs his chin. I look at my teammates, their mouths hanging open like fish looking for food.

Ginger hasn't completed her pass either. Her left hand is over her heart, covering the Garwood Elite logo on her sports bra. Her right hand holds her ponytail like it's a safety rope. I scratch my leg where her hair whipped my shin. One-inch difference and I would have punted her head off like a football.

"I'll keep playing around with the counts so you'll have more distance from each other," Heath promises.

For once, I think even he is afraid.

After suicides, sprints, handstand walking, and ankle weighted jumps, the team starts Circle of Death. I'm already having trouble breathing, my muscles screaming, but I push myself to participate.

Angela stops to find the garbage bins after two circles, which is the groundhog sign for *it's going to be a long night*. I hear the sound of her coughing and throw another back tuck. By thirty, everyone, even Ginger, is half knocked out. Mary-Ellen yells at us to pick up the pace but I literately can't do another backflip if my life depends on it. I watch the square outlines of Ginger's abs form and disappear as she breathes in and out, going for another one. She's a robot, I swear.

"You," Heath says, grabbing my arm, "you're done for tonight. Go home."

I silently thank him for saving me from having to tell Mary-Ellen I'm too weak. At least this way it looks like he stopped me and I'm not the only one gassing out.

I toss my gym bag in the back of the car and settle into the passenger's seat. Sweat sticks my legs to the leather and I readjust, watching the younger girls pile into their carpools. My sports bra could literally be wrung out.

"How was it?" Mom asks, pausing her audiobook. She looks at me with concern, hands at ten and two on the wheel. "You're as red as a tomato."

"They kicked my butt," I say, leaving out the parts about Ginger and me almost colliding, Mary-Ellen's shouting at Angela to get her act together before she gets moved back to level four, and the countless amounts of girls puking. I begged her to let me be on this team. My family has paid so much, taken time off work for the weekend competitions. Besides,

I'll be so happy in April when I'm vying to be number one in the world, I remind myself.

The taillights of the cars blur red in my vision on the highway. When we get home, my muscles have stopped twitching but my feet have swollen, stretched full against my sneakers.

"Some of the other mothers mentioned the team going to Houston for a week. Apparently, Mary-Ellen brought it up. She wants to take you guys to do Worlds choreography camp with BDM Allstars."

"Really?" No one mentioned it to me, and I figured the girls would have considering BDM—Basic Diamond Material—are the current world champions. Their choreography is always top-notch, and since our team hasn't done so well in competition this year, it'll do us good to have a new routine. Then again, seven days with just Mary-Ellen and Heath and nonstop cheer is overwhelming. I decide not to even consider it until I'm sure it's happening.

I bathe in cold water with Epsom salts, the rest of the night spent packing my things to go back to RR. It'll be strange to be locked in there when I was just filming this episode. I'm already used to being home, but it took me weeks to get used to RR. I just want to be in one place again. Consistency.

It's well past one a.m. when I hear Mom and Dad fighting. Arguments are an anomaly in this house, an activity they do so rarely it sparks my interest and gets me to crawl out of bed when I'm supposed to be asleep.

I sit by the second-floor railing, watching their lit-up reflections in the kitchen from the dark front windows.

"Adam, she's fine," my mother snaps. "She doesn't need to go back there and be left alone again! She's home. She's at cheer. We can watch her. She's missed enough school."

"You don't think I want her here? We trusted this program, Eloise. We need to let them make sure she's okay. Neither of us is in a position to judge her health. We didn't even notice she was sick in the first place!"

Dad never uses Mom's first name. I haven't heard it in ages and I'm not sure what it means.

"You're sick! Those IronMen you do. Nuts! And we don't send you away to some . . . some ward where children die."

"We're not keeping her here. She will finish their program and then come home. The girl who died, that's what they're trying to prevent. They will make that call, El. Not us."

Mom's reflection crumbles. She starts crying, sobbing, gripping Dad's arms for support. "I don't want her to leave again," she says, softer. "We just got her home. She should be with our family."

"We asked for Thanksgiving and they gave it to us when they shouldn't have. Now quiet down before you wake the kids."

Asked for Thanksgiving?

A creak sounds behind me and I whip around, afraid I've transported to the middle of a James Wan film, some ghost creature poised to attack me. But it's just K.J., wearing boxers and a video game T-shirt. *To Game or Not To Game*, it says, with the second option crossed off. He's so lame, yet he has so many friends. I don't understand it. I only have Rowan.

"She's been crazier since you left," K.J. says, squatting

down beside me. "She sits in your room and sleeps in there sometimes too."

Silence blankets us for a few moments.

"Are you happier when I'm away?" I ask.

He peers at the reflection, Mom and Dad holding each other. "Thought maybe I would be, but Mom acts like you died and Dad just watches more triathlete programs. It's worse, if you can imagine that." He turns to me. "Can you do me a favor? Like a blood favor?"

"A *blood* favor?"

"Yeah. We have the same blood, so it grants me one favor, as your big brother." His eyes meet mine, both of ours the same shade of brown. "Don't fuck any of my friends."

I twitch at the word *fuck*. Rowan has said it a thousand times and I've thought it myself on occasion, but there's something about it coming from my brother's mouth that creeps me out.

"I won't," I say. "Favor granted."

His eyes bore into mine. "I'm serious."

"I know. I don't want them, K.J." *Sometimes, I wish I did,* I think. *But I don't. Fucking them is the farthest thing from my mind.* "I swear on our blood."

He nods and I half expect us to hug or have a grand gesture of best friends from here on out, but he straightens, gives a wave, and disappears behind the door to his room. Mom is still sobbing and the sounds are painful. Mama bear being torn away from baby bear. I climb back into my bed and lie awake, appreciating that it's my bed alone and no one else's.

The Blue bed in RR always felt eerily split between myself and Alyssa's corporeal form.

Mom chooses the back seat on the return trip to RR. Dad drives and I take the front seat because I can barely move. I hobble to get around the car, every muscle pulsing with pain.

"Only a half hour left," Dad announces. "Last chance to use your phone."

I pull up Twitter, hurrying before I get too nauseated. *One week. Then I'll be more active. Sorry for the disappearing act, but good news coming soon. #CheerChampions #Texas?*

I check out the fastest replies.

U are so amazing!!! I love u sm. Plz notice me!

I just fell off the treadmill. NBD. :D

OMG OMG OMG NO WAY!!!!! #blessup U R MY FAVORITE ON THE SHOW.

Like this tweet with your nose if you see it. (:

I laugh at the last one and tap the heart with the tip of my nose. Dad passes me a weird look and I go to nudge his arm, but my muscles cry out in pain. I pull open the console, hoping for Advil or an extra travel muscle roller, but instead I see RR's stamp, the back-to-back *R*'s, and recognize the paperwork. At a glance it looks like a packet of instructions for this weekend. I pull it out and click the console shut.

I start reading. Then rereading.

"Did you guys go through this?" I space. "It's a whole list of things I was supposed do over the weekend. It says . . . *No exercise for more than a light half hour.*"

My father pulls over to the side of the road. He looks at

it, surprised. My mother has no response. I suspect it was her who stashed it in the console.

I begin to hyperventilate. "They're not going to let me out in a week! This was a test and we failed it! I already gave my interview and got my spot on the team back . . ."

Dad and I turn our heads to look at Mom in the back. "I assumed it was just a recommendation," she says. She won't look at me, only Dad.

"Mom! I'm freaking out here!"

"It's fine, honey. We'll sign it. They won't know."

My father and I scowl together, the resemblance undeniable in the side mirror.

"What if they see my interview on tape?"

"How would they see that, Shoshana? Calm down. We can pull you from the program. *We* are paying *them*, remember?"

I'm going to have to lie. This weekend home was meant to have a regimen, including monitoring my social media. It doesn't say anything about not posting, thank God, but we basically broke every rule in the book. I'm going to have to cheat the rest of my recovery at RR.

My father's ears go red, but he holds it in as we drive. Mom doesn't even think she did anything wrong, and that's the worst part. RR is strict. They'll pry it out of me.

You can tell them the truth, my conscience offers. Of course it nags me to do the right thing now. *You could stay with Rowan and forget the show.* It's not an option. I just started filming and Rowan and I are on iffy terms. Maybe if I could talk to her about it . . .

I glance at the form again, the signatures they're going to forge. I broke the rules. Now I'll have to channel Rowan to cover my tracks.

18

Rowan

What Nurse Schultz says: "There's a visitor here to see you."

What she means: not a visitor at all, but a familiar freckled face with dark brown eyes and relentless curls. The magnet in your chest is pulled to mine and we meet halfway down the front hall. Desperate, relieved. You're back and I'm sorry. We fall to the ground in a tangle of tripping legs and impatient arms.

"I love you," I say, and you parrot it back. *I love you.*

How many times do we say it? *I love you. I love you. I love you.*

So many people say those words but, most of the time, they're empty. We mean it. We reinvent it, give the words new life. Honey drips from our lips—"DSL" lips, I was told in fifth grade by a male classmate—and now my lips are new too. They bear no resemblance to how they were in fifth grade. They're fully yours.

We stand and hug again.

"What are those?" I ask, feeling the papers in your hand brush against my arm. You give them to Nurse Hart.

"A list of what I had to eat over the weekend. Instructions and stuff. It wasn't as liberating as you'd think," you say, a tad fidgety.

I take you up on your old offer of hanging out while being babysat by the nurses. It gives us a chance to catch up, for you to finally tell me everything about the show, why you're here, how home was.

We sit on the stiff leather common-area couch, the both of us positioned pretzel-style, facing each other. Robinson oversees us. I'm quick to fill you in on the App game, about how Sophie, Donna, and I already guessed your life. Now, you'll just be adding the popcorn details.

After you've gotten through the majority of it, I say, "Mary-Ellen sounds as F'd as King Joffrey."

You play footsie with me, keeping your voice low.

"I'm sure plenty of people have considered poisoning her like Joffrey too. That person being myself on occasion."

"So why not join a different gym? If she's the one who caused your breakdown, then you shouldn't be anywhere near her, right?"

I sound like one of the nurses, I know, but that's who I am when it comes to you. I don't want to see you have a breakdown, on TV or in real life. I need you to be rainbows-and-unicorns Shoshana, so I can be hanging-on-by-a-thread Rowan. If you're the one hanging on by a thread, that means my thread is somewhere blowing in the wind.

"It's not that easy," you say. "There are only so many teams that are good enough to make top ten in the world. Even if I found another team who wanted me, I'd have to move. I'm pretty sure my mom would do it, because she's crazy, but my dad and my brother wouldn't want to. After eighteen, I age out anyway. I'm already on the show. People would call me a traitor if I left."

"All of this is worth a chance at the world title? I might get it if you were guaranteed to win, but you're not."

"That's the thrill of it," you say, eyes lit up like coffee being doused with cream. "Anything can happen. CheerWork from North Carolina won Worlds three years in a row. A three-peat. But last year, they dropped one stunt and Teal Allstars became the reigning champions. One mistake and it's all over."

"Harsh," I say, attempting to braid sections of my too-short hair. "Why did they make your team—"

"GE."

"GE—a show? You've never even won Worlds. You came in sixth. And don't get me wrong, sixth in the world is—well, shit, it's sixth in the world. I can't even do a cartwheel. But why would someone film you guys instead of a team that actually wins?"

"You said yourself it's like *Dance Moms*. Why did they choose Abby Lee Dance Company?" you ask. "Because she makes good television. So does Mary-Ellen."

I feel like the lesser one for once, a new balance blooming between us. I let go of my hair and pick up yours. "She went to jail. Abby Lee. For fraud."

"Mary-Ellen does criminal stuff, too, puts all her money in different bank accounts so when they freeze one, she can pull money from the others. But plenty of people have tried to sue her. It's like trying to sue God."

You know I don't believe in God, so you add, "Or take down the prime minister."

"That's been done before," I say.

"Yeah, but the likelihood?"

I nod in agreement. *Cloudy with a chance of not likely at all.*

"Besides, that same question can be asked for our fan base. Why don't girls like Elly stalk teams who actually win Worlds? I mean, they do. But the show makes them feel like they know us, like we're friends. They see all the hard work we put in and it's like you always say—we're in the age of 'pics or it didn't happen.' It doesn't matter if CheerWork does twice as much conditioning as us. If audiences don't see it, it doesn't count."

We push on, catching up on lost time. We talk about all the random stuff we've thought of in the last week and haven't discussed. The Big Bang theory. The necessity of separation of church and state. What we'll name our kids. Yours: Aviva for a girl. Jewish, and for your favorite season, springtime. Me: Sam or Taylor or Blake, something that can suit either gender. All the things we want to try before we're has-beens: Skydiving. Cliff diving. Diving anything. Learning to ride ATVs. Taking a trip to Bali and camping out on the beach. Learning to surf. Going to Hell in Grand Cayman, just to say we've been to Hell and back.

I mention the millennial fame complex, doing something to live out my inner celebrity, but you don't know what that is. Strange considering . . .

"Considering what?" you ask.

"Considering you're already famous. Well, mini-famous."

You frown and I use my hands to smooth out the W-shaped wrinkle between your eyebrows.

"What is it? The millennial fame complex?"

"It's like, all those famous people we see in magazines, in movies, on our phones. How many girls with hot bodies do you follow on Instagram? How many times do you check Instagram a day? An hour? It's conditioning your brain. When you see all those people with insane bodies and sports cars and they make life look like a Kool-Aid commercial, you start thinking it's real, that somehow fifty percent of people live that way. That's why so many people are depressed and desperate to be famous. They think more followers equals being better, more relevant, happier. Hence—the millennial fame complex."

"Sounds like the reverse of my personal project," you say, more to yourself than to me. "But we're not even millennials. We're Gen Z. Why? Do you think I have it?"

"No," I rush. "If you cared about your status, you would've told me you were famous the second we met, Shosh. You don't have it now, but it's an epidemic. You can still catch it. I think all of us have it. I do, a little."

You start carpet angels on the floor and I face the window. It's an ironic reversal, the snow beginning to dust out there. Not like "Winter's coming." Death. Ninth-grade symbolism. Yada yada. The girls around here feel that way about summer. *Summer's coming.* Less clothes. Stomachs exposed. The crackly winter air our version of safety.

"So, what else do we need to discuss before you vacate the premises?" I ask.

"I feel like we've covered every topic known to man."

"What about bananas?" I say. "Did you know bananas are scientifically proven to make people happier? I read that somewhere. But it doesn't mean you can eat ten bananas and expect to feel better. So, what's the point in telling us that? Plus, eating them in public is like licking a lollipop. Perverts think you're doing it as some sort of *come and get it.*"

"*When you're ready, come and get it, na-na-na-na,*" you sing, sleepy.

"What comes after all this?" I ask. "After the show? Say you go back home and win Worlds. What then?"

It's time we be real with one another, get to the big stuff.

"I don't even know what you want," I say truthfully. "Out of life, I mean."

"Neither do I." You sigh and sit up, move to rest your cheek on my shoulder. I stroke the baby hairs by the base of your neck, those cute relentless curls. "What do you want, Ro?"

You, I think. *I want us to be together, in whatever capacity that fits for us.* I pull your head up to look at you, face-to-face, not caring about Robinson or any of the passing girls who might see. You lick your lips, like your body has processed what I want before your head can. There's a rush of *this is it* and I feel like I need you in this innate biological way, like an anemic needs iron, and I close my eyes and the space between us so easily, it's near habitual.

My lips press with light pressure against yours.

You taste sweet, like mango ChapStick, and you feel warm, like a radiator. It only lasts a few seconds, but it's enough time for me to confirm I'm definitely not straight. My toes curl and my chest swells and I get this spontaneous heat low in my belly. I want to keep going, but Robinson clears her throat and I pull away, staring at your full, lax lips.

Your cheeks and neck are patchy red and I have no idea what you're thinking.

I want to say, "I've kissed girls before," meaning *it wasn't one bit like this*. But Robinson calls, "Rowan, go get in line for lunch," and I do, though not before I glance over my shoulder to see the surprise resting on your face. Probably you're shocked because I don't whine or backtalk to the nurses as of late.

"Have fun with the Reverse Heathers," I say, loving to watch you process your feelings. "Almost all of them are Blue now."

You bite your lip. I assume it's because you're coming to terms with all the *What If*s that have been running through my head this entire time.

What if RR isn't the end for us?

What if we are *us*, just somewhere else?

What if us means something you never even thought possible?

19
Shoshana

She kissed me. She kissed me in the TV room with no warning. She kissed me in the TV room with no warning and I felt nothing, same as all the rest.

I still don't know why she did it. Was it a game? A test of my loyalty? A sudden burst of inspiration? Was she missing touches from one of her old boyfriends on the outside? What was it for? What does it mean?

The rest of our reunion was great, enough to keep me buzzing all the way into Personal Projects, even among the confusion.

My photo collage is still there, and when I tape Rowan's photo on, the one she let me take this afternoon, it already looks important. "What do you hate most about yourself?" I asked, and she told me to take a picture of the zipper on her jeans, her camel toe. Didn't say why, but muttered something about vulnerability. We haven't talked about the kiss. An hour went by, I snapped the photo, and we parted ways with an elbow squeeze. Rowan was slightly happier than usual, but besides that, everything appeared to be in order.

I hot glue flower petals and sprinkle glitter along the sides of the photos. The stickers overlap a bit, but I like it better this way. Messy.

"What is that?" Crystal sneers, arms folded. The picture of her scars is surrounded by hearts and next to one of another RR girl's stretch marks.

"It's psychological training for self-confidence," I say, holding it up. "It romanticizes the features people are usually told to dislike about themselves. We've been trained to think glitter and butterflies are beautiful. I think we can train ourselves to do the same with what we've been taught is ugly."

"Nurse's pet, much?" she snorts.

Brandy comes to my other side. "How long do you need to look at it before it works?"

"I doubt it really clicks that way," I say. "It's just supposed to be a nonconformist thing." I was trying to take after Rowan.

"Where are you?" Crystal asks, scanning the photos.

"Oh, I'm not on it."

"So you love everything about yourself?"

"No!" I sound as defensive as I feel. I hate a lot of things about my appearance, like the freckles on my lip, my brown eyes I always wanted to be lighter, my ratty frizzy hair, my thick bumpy nose.

"I guess I never really thought about including myself," I confess.

I hand Brandy the camera and position myself before I tell her to click. I upload the photo to the computer and print it out on a black-and-white page.

They stare at my side profile. The left side.

"Your connected earlobes?" Crystal asks. "Your hooked nose? Your bony forehead?"

"It's the left side of my brain," I say, cutting her off before she can make me insecure about one more thing, then silently add *connected earlobes* to the list of weird, could-be-better parts of my body. "It's where my thoughts are formed. Where the conscience is."

"That's your Achilles' heel?" Crystal laughs. She goes back to the Reverse Heathers, her new team of Blue girls. Brandy makes a face. *Ignore her.* I make an equally annoyed face. *I plan to.*

Nurse Robinson and Hope hang my poster on the art room wall with the other personal projects and art creations. I'm not proud enough to boast about it. I'm no van Gogh and Rowan is ten times better, but it cheers me up. Without my phone, I'm bored again and missing it more than I did the last time. I feel like I'm walking around without glasses on, lacking something vital. Everyone's back on Instagram and Twitter and Tumblr and buzzing about me. They think I'm home and I'm not.

If I could spend all day with Rowan, using our imaginations to burn calories, things wouldn't be so bad in here. Nothing is when you have a best friend. When I first joined GE, I thought I'd make some. Friends, that is. At tryouts, Mary-Ellen singled me out as the best and she said it in front of everyone, told them I was going to be on her top team, that she had her eye on me. I expected to meet nice, agreeable girls, because if Mary-Ellen liked me, the rest had to.

But on a team where everyone's told they're replaceable, it made me into a bull's-eye for target practice. Like New Girl but worse. Nobody spoke to me. Nobody clapped when I got new skills. When Angela had her sweet sixteen, she didn't invite me, and when all the girls came to practice the next day wearing matching pink sweatshirts like the Pink Ladies, Angela's name on their backs, I had to fight every instinct not to cry. It reminded me of my bat mitzvah. Mom said I couldn't give away anything to my friends, like sweatshirts or socks. Too many feelings would be hurt. At the time, I'd thought she was exaggerating. Lesson learned: she wasn't.

I didn't have any real friends until Rowan, though I'm sure I thought I did. Girls to partner up with on the occasional school project, to see a movie with in Watchung or get fro-yo with from Yogurtland. But it was never easy with them. And with Rowan, it's so easy. She's smart. Steve Jobs smart. Okay, maybe not that crazy, but the way she thinks is fascinating. And she doesn't care about all the trivial crap most teenagers do. We can hug and cuddle and we know what's important and what's just for shits and giggles. She's my first real friend and I can feel how rare that is. Anorexia can be so lonely. I never thought I'd find anyone who understood me the way she does, and if I do find someone after her, it won't be for another seventeen years.

"TWINS!" She jumps me in the hallway after Personal Projects is up. "We're having twins!"

I'm like a spooked horse the second I hear her voice, afraid she'll launch into talking about the kiss and I'll have to squirm, fudge, evade questions not to hurt her. Until she brings it up, I do my best to play along casually.

I rub her belly. "Now you're *really* going to get fat."

I must say it because I'm nervous. My mouth just moves and Rowan's immediately sours.

Just kill yourself, my conscience fires. I attempt to recover. "Sorry. You were saying?"

"Twins. Two new girls. Tomorrow."

"You won the lottery."

"No." She shakes her head, regaining her smile. "I'm not gonna mess them up. I'm going to be good. Take them in like I did with Sophie."

Like you did with me? I think. *Am I one of your projects?*

"Even if their answers are wrong?" I ask.

"I'm not even asking questions," she says.

"Turning over a new leaf?"

"Like Robert Downey Jr., baby."

"You seem good," I tell her honestly.

I'm not sure what happened during my weekend home, but Rowan's a lot nicer to the nurses now and vice versa. They're in synch or something. Making jokes that I'm out of the loop on. Some part of me wants to ask her about it, but we're good, and I don't want to screw that up. I just tell her the truth: she seems better.

She doesn't respond. Just lifts her fingers to her lips and pretends to smoke, blowing out invisible clouds. She's always looking at things I can't see. Special eyes, only for her.

"Do you ever get fan mail?" she asks, kicking off her socks in the living room. She says in the summertime she wears rings on her toes, gets henna tattoos as prep for real ones she'll have when she turns eighteen. No sleeves or tramp stamps, just tiny geometric shapes behind her ears, one at the back of her neck, or the moon phases running down her spine—all to help her play the role of mystery girl. I can't imagine her inked up, but I believe her when she tells me she will be.

"Sometimes," I say. "Not a ton. But people send fan art and stuff. It's cool when it's good and creepy when it's bad. One girl sent me Ring Pops because the camera guy caught me eating one backstage. I guess someone said it was a luck thing, that I *had* to have a Ring Pop for every competition, and it kind of blew up. Really I just felt lightheaded and the staff handed it to me for the sugar."

"What about real letters? Like the horse-and-buggy ancient-practice kind?"

"A couple. The shorter ones are good. Once in a while, they're too long. I once got this girl's English essay on how I was her role model. It was eight pages all about me. She kept quoting me and I sounded awful."

"Are you popular at school?" She starts tackling all the questions she has. Previously, we pretended like outside school didn't exist. The word was banned from our vocabulary. My backstory was I came from Narnia where I lived with Mr. and Mrs. Beaver. Rowan was raised by wolves, obviously.

"Most of them know who I am, but that's because of my brother, K.J."

"People know me too," she says, "at school. Probably as a wendigo, but still."

"It counts," I agree, and the two of us keep talking until our voices grow hoarse and the nurses tell us it's time for dinner, then shower, then bed. Neither of us mentions the kiss.

Monday morning I have group therapy, which Brandy convinces me to go to early so we get the good seats with our backs against the couch. Until the other Blue girls join us, she tells me about her bipolar disorder, hereditary from her uncle. Bipolar two, which she sarcastically calls "diet bipolar," whatever that means. It's the reason she's been here so long. Just when she begins to get healthy, a wave of depression hits and she won't be able to get out of bed for days; she won't eat, won't speak unless spoken to. I haven't seen her that way, and she says I probably won't if I'm gone in a week.

I'm the first person she's met who's famous. I tell her she's the first person I've met who actually enjoys RR.

"They care about you," she says, talking about the nurses, "believe it or not."

Not, Rowan would say, though maybe not anymore. She still doesn't like the nurses, but she doesn't hate them either.

The Blue girls wander in, clumps of a whole waiting to be assembled. Crystal and the Reverse Heathers enter last after Walsh and Hart, who complete our disproportioned circle. One of the main reasons Gray girls don't have group therapy is because it has the possibility to turn into a screaming match, an uprising against the nurses. Donna and Rowan and now Sophie could stand in a line and interlock their arms. *Red rover, red rover, we call Nurse Hart over*, and take her out by themselves.

But most Blue girls see the light at the end of the tunnel. They have hope, so they take this seriously.

Sabrina Hoffman is the first one to stick a hand in the air and ask to speak. She goes on and on about her fear of restaurants. Going out to eat like *oh no, everyone must be watching me,* and I silently shake my head knowing there are millions of people who actually watch my every move. *Try having cameras around you all day long,* my conscience challenges, grumpy from too little sleep.

"Shoshana?"

"Huh?" I say automatically, looking around the circle.

"Do you have anything you want to say to Sabrina?" Mrs. Walsh asks.

This is the part where I say something profound, a statement that will drop jaws and leave everybody frozen. But I think about the show waiting for me and just tell her, "No," and she lets Sabrina continue. I don't speak until we go around and talk about the days since last group therapy, which for me was before my weekend home.

"It was good. Fine. I went to see my coaches and my teammates. Ate Thanksgiving dinner with my family. My brother is kind of annoying, but yeah, it was nice."

That's all I contribute and we move on. The rest of the girls talk about their addictions to diet pills, scamming celebrity secrets on websites, MiraLAX. The girls with bulimia grumble about their love of food and their equally strong love of puking it back up. To my surprise, so do some of the ana girls. The disorders here seem to cross like embroidery. I didn't know it was so nuanced. As I imagined it, anorexia and bulimia are two sides of the same coin. Turns out, it's more of an eight-sided die, where you can toss it multiple times and wind up landing on different illnesses at different points in your life. That scares me—the idea that this could spiral, get worse in new, unimagined ways. The proof is in the pudding, as some girls open up about their medical issues. Osteoporosis. Heart irregularities. One girl with diabulimia, a word I've never heard before—diabetes type one and she deliberately underuses insulin to try to control her weight. Two girls have eroded esophagi, the skinnier one saying she has acid reflux so bad she feels like her body is burning from the inside out.

I feel grateful. I haven't had anything like that. No extreme medical consequences from my eating disorder. Nothing more than fainting and losing some hair.

"I've been to nine different treatment centers in the past five years," says one girl. I feel bad for not remembering her name. Even in secluded RR, I've been living in my own world. Plus, she has one of those faces, totally androgynous, no defining features. She must not talk often though, because I would have remembered her thick Southern accent.

"My pops used to have an eating disorder." She gazes around at us, hazel eyes blinking tears away. "They say sixty or seventy percent of eating disorders are genetic. I bet a lot of y'alls' family members probably have one, and y'all don't even know about it."

"What's her name?" I whisper to Brandy.

"August? April? Some month."

The girl looks over at us. Shoot. She keeps going on anyway.

"So, I guess I'm worried if I have a baby one day, they'll have it, too, and end up here, doing this."

"That's too far ahead," Crystal interrupts, craning her neck to the ceiling like she's *sooooo* over this. "A person dies every sixty-two minutes from an eating disorder. Get to, like, twenty-five first. If you live that long, then worry about it."

While the nurses reel Crystal in, I whisper to Brandy again. "How is Crystal Blue?" She's not lying about the sixty-two-minute thing, I've heard that before, from Kelly; it's one of her special dietician facts. But I have no clue how Crystal has made it this far in RR.

"Just because she's getting better doesn't mean she's getting nicer," says Brandy.

We listen to another girl who goes to private school with secret underground sororities. The girls in her Alpha Gamma Psi group made her sit on washing machines naked and circled all the places that jiggled with a Sharpie. They spawned her E.D. by controlling what she ate and how much she exercised. It stuck.

I know it's called group *therapy*, but some of these girls here open up like they're talking to Mrs. Walsh privately. I would never mention my breakdown to them. I couldn't.

When the hour's up, Nurse Hart pulls me aside to check in and go over my weekend home. It's an informal conversation, but I can feel the pressure of it, how it will determine my future. I explain what I did, leaving out the part about cheering so hard I still feel sore everywhere. When she asks what I ate for lunch on Saturday, I tell her mac and cheese with a half a peanut butter sandwich and apple slices and chocolate milk. I studied the sheet of meals I was supposed to have in the car before we got here. Mom and Dad don't get it. The nurses are like the LAPD, checking fingerprints and conducting random searches. I needed to be prepared for this exact moment. So I memorized the meals like I used to do with my school exams, with mnemonic devices.

"How did you feel at home? Anxious at all?" Nurse Hart asks.

"A little. Just when I first got home. After a couple hours or so it wore off."

That lie is more believable than saying a flat-out no. What patient wouldn't be anxious about going home for the first time in months? She needs to believe this and buy the lie. Rowan taught me how to do it best, lying. It's all in the details, like any good story. So I go over the food, the Thanksgiving celebration, even my interview for *Cheer Champions*. Keep as much true as I can. When she sends me on my merry way, I know she bought it. And my *knowing better* gut isn't sure how to feel about it.

Over the next few days, I eat when I'm supposed to, talk to Mrs. Walsh openly about Mary-Ellen, and make a plan with Rowan about how we'll keep in contact after RR. She'll be able to receive letters from me, and once she's Blue, she'll be able to write back. She demands at least one letter per week, but I swear I'll send one every day.

I follow the rules and the nurses set my release date for Tuesday the eighth, two days after Hanukkah starts, six days from now. It *should* go by fast, but it moves slower than I expect. I wish I could sleep in my Gray bedroom, because being Blue doesn't feel like the real RR. I want to remember Rowan, what it's like to lie together under her words, to whisper goodnight when we're dozing off.

I walk around the red rubber track with Brandy, cold to the bone even with layers of sweatpants on. It starts snowing again and the nurses allow all the girls, even the Gray girls, to come outside and stick their tongues out for the first snowflakes of winter. Several of them don't, afraid even the snowflakes will have calories. Watching from the window is "August or April," who's probably missing her southern weather.

Rowan stands on the track beside me, smirking with a black beanie over her purple hair. "You're beautiful in snow," she says, pushing me into a pile of white.

I get up, brush off my wet hands. "How come whenever I call you beautiful, you tell me to shut up? But when you call me beautiful, I'm just supposed to accept it?"

She blinks snow from her lashes, water droplets swimming down her cheeks. "Because when I say you're beautiful, I don't mean the traditional *Sports Illustrated* kind or the Jennifer Aniston 'let's get the Rachel haircut' way. I mean beautiful like . . . I feel different when I'm with you. Less shitty. And unless you mean it that way, you're just like my mom. When she says I'm beautiful, it makes me feel like this"—she pinches

233

her cheek in reference to her skin, her exterior—"is the most important thing about me. And it's not."

"When I call you beautiful, I just mean—"

"You see my button nose and blue eyes and blonde roots and think it's beautiful because that's what you associate with it," she fills in.

"Would you let me finish?" I laugh. "I mean you're beautiful as in, despite being obviously pretty and wanted, you cut off your hair. You tell people not to look at you. You always try to be the opposite of what people expect, which must be tiring, but it is beautiful."

She stops blinking, snow coming down faster around her, like she's making it happen. A storm.

I think she's about to say I can call her beautiful if that's really what I mean, but she pulls me close for warmth and says, "Walsh thinks I cut my hair off so no would want me. So I can be ugly and let live, because people let ugly things be without touching them."

"She said that to you?"

"No. But I can tell she thinks it. She thinks we starve ourselves to hide our bodies. She's right about that when it comes to me."

I've never known Rowan to be this honest. Totally upfront.

"That wasn't my first kiss," I blurt, sensing I owe her the same. "Well, it was my first kiss with a girl."

Already off to a great start, Shosh, my conscience chimes. I need to get this off my chest, but I haven't worked through what to say or how to say it.

She shifts her weight from one hip to the other. "And?"

"And I don't know," I say, until I realize I'm lying again, an instinct to keep her happy. "I mean, I didn't love it. But not because of you. I've been kissed several times and I haven't liked any of them. Yours was probably the best, but it was still a little . . . repulsive? That's the wrong word. I guess slimy is more accurate. No, that doesn't sound good either. I like cuddling, you know that. I love being next to you and with you. It's just anything more than that with anyone makes me feel off, like I'm acting, pretending to feel things I don't."

Her lips part, forming a little *O*. "So you're ace?" she says, her eyes sparking like blue flames.

"I thought we agreed no more *Gilmore Girls* references?"

"No." She bites back a smile. "It's not a pet name. I mean *ace*. Like, *asexual*. How didn't I see this before, Shosh? You're totally ace."

I get the same kind of panicked, unsure feeling I used to get when Mom looked at K.J. and me when we were little, wondering where all the singles went from her wallet, and although I knew K.J. periodically stole money from her to save up for video games from GameStop, I would never tattletale on him. He said if I did, a monster would come eat me in the night. I feel like a monster is here and I want to hide. Deny.

"It's not a bad thing." She rubs my arms like I'm cold, although really, I'm sweating through my winter jacket. "You can still have relationships with people. With . . ."

The word doesn't pass her lips. But because it's her, I can

hear it. *Me*. However much she wants to finish that sentence with it, she's not letting herself step into the equation yet.

"How are you so sure?" I ask. "About me being ace?"

"I'm not saying for sure that's what you are. Only you can decide that. But think about it. You don't like talking about sex. You don't seem interested in it. You find kisses, even ones from my hot, awesome mouth, repulsive."

Throwing all the information right there in front of me—it makes me truly consider what she's saying. How I've never had any real crushes in school, though I chalked that up to slim pickings. I thought I wasn't into dating because I was too focused on cheerleading. That one day, I would be . . . and I'm still waiting for it.

"*Asexual*," I say, just to hear the word spoken on my own tongue.

"Sexuality is fluid, Shosh," she says, stroking my upper arms. "That's why I've decided to start calling myself queer. So I don't have to explain to anyone if I change my mind. And who knows, maybe you'll like sex later on in life or feel differently in different situations, or maybe you won't—who gives a fuck? It's all right, any of it. You don't have to justify yourself."

She gives me a quirky smile as if the speech sounds nice to her own ears.

"Feel free to chime in here, but I know you love what we have," she says, "the intimacy of it. That's why I wouldn't say aromantic. It's common for people to mistake themselves as ace if they're traumatized, like if they've been assaulted, but that's not asexuality. So unless you were . . ."

Her sentence trails off, less abrupt and more as if a new thought has crested, forcing her to consider the lightbulb of a fresh idea as she watches snow melt at her feet. She stops touching my arms and I hear "*No, no, no*" slip from her lips and then, "Is that why we're connected?"

But I don't understand why she's suddenly so upset, upset enough to rush away like lightning strikes where I stand. After a few steps away, she pivots and races back. More seriously than I've ever seen her, she takes my hands. Her eyes glassy, her pupils wide.

"Did someone do something to you?" she demands. "Huh? Speak up, Shoshana. For once in your goddamn life, spill."

"Do what?"

"Look, there are . . . a lot of–of sickos out there," she says, panicked. "If someone did something, you can tell me. Even if you can't remember it, I'll believe you. People like us were meant to find each other and if you were raped, too, then we can figure—"

"What? No!" I raise my voice and then lower it, realizing how the girls around us have encroached our space. They stand a few feet away, eyes lingering, pretending they're not listening. "Rowan, I haven't"—I make my voice a whisper—"I haven't had sex. You know that. And I haven't been assaulted."

Her pupils dilate. The tension drains from her soft features but builds in my hawklike ones, like the pain is transferring.

Is that why we're connected?

People like us were meant to find each other.

Raped, too.

The *too* seals it. Her words are an admission. She's been raped. She hasn't told me. I suspected something but never asked. The reveal of this information must dawn on her, because as quickly as the relief flooded in, the terror is back and blacker, lighting up her eyes and making her shoulders tremble. She realizes what she's confessed and she thinks she needs to be the strong one, as always.

She starts to let me go again so no one will see her step falter, not even me, but I crush her against my chest. I hold her, tighter and tighter so she can't breathe or tell me to stop. I don't say I'm sorry. I don't say anything. I just hug her with every fiber of my being and, for the first time, I'm glad there's more fat on me to hold her with. When my muscles ache, I remember what she did for me—when she saw my bare scalp and kept right on talking, reassuring me she didn't care about anything other than us—and I will do the same for her now.

I take her hand and her cast and start spinning us, round and round until it's all white except for our focused faces. Rowan's pink cheeks. Her black, snow-dusted beanie. A single tear pushing past her pale-blue iris.

We spin and spin like teacups, brimming with hurt. The nurses shout for us to stop before one of us gets injured, but we don't listen. We keep going until we're unable to see anything else. White snow. White noise. It all blurs and burns away, the rest of the world going with it until the only thing left is us.

20
Rowan

Walsh comes in for an emergency session with me Sunday morning because I'm finally ready to talk about it. *The Red Roof Inn.*

It was after I had completed treatment at two different centers, neither of which worked. After Mom started having sleepovers at her *friends'* houses and leaving me alone at ours.

It wasn't a surprise when I got a DM on Instagram, a *Hey beautiful* from a stranger named Sean. Guys DM'd me all the time. But his pictures weren't the typical douche-y jock photos. They were mostly of nature. No shirtless selfies or bio packed with words like *swole* or *gains*. I liked that, and so I answered *Thanks* and, upon rechecking the one photo he had of himself, all lanky arms and boyish charm on a park swing, added *You're not so bad yourself.*

He told me he went to St. Peter's, the all-boys school two towns over, which was when I said whoever forced him to attend there needed to spread Jesus's love like a hole in the head, that I was terribly sorry for whatever crimes he'd committed in a past life to lead him to this torture. But Sean actually believed in the Jesus stuff, and whether it was because he was hot or just because he was someone to talk to, I didn't fault him for it.

You probably could have guessed this by now, but I hate

girls who have best-friend boyfriends. The girls who never talk to other girls. Antifeminist. But with Sean, I figured I might be one of them. You only need one partner in life. A companion to pick you up when your head is down. He convinced me we were that for each other.

So, I fell in love with the person on the phone—*warning, danger, danger*—and sadly predictable, I know. If I'd been watching myself as some naive girl in a Lifetime drama, I would have walked out of the room or shut off the TV. I would never have bought it. Because *no one* is that stupid, especially not me.

But understand this: I was lonely. Not bored. That's not the same thing. *That* I could have dealt with. But being lonely, especially when you're a teenager where everyone seems social 24/7, it's like a bad omen for the rest of your life. Cats. Sagging skin. Knitting. I didn't want it.

Sean texted me nonstop, in class, when I got home, before I went to bed. We made phone calls in the morning, agreed I could be his bad, emo, non-Catholic influence, and in return, he would be my saint. Watch over me. Protect me. I even told him about my parents and that my father was cheating on my mother, and he swore it was not my fault, that life was hard for everyone and I couldn't claim responsibility for their mistakes, that he would never do the same to me.

I believed him because I wanted to believe him. Simple as that. People will believe anything if they're desperate. I talked myself into the possibility that this something was real. That I could have something good and pure and the universe could only fuck a person over so many times. I bought into the idea that my limit was up.

We made a plan to meet up at a diner closer to him than it was to me, but only after he went to church on Sunday. And here we are, Shosh, finally getting to why Sunday is my dark day, why it's strange that out of all seven days, I met you on the good Lord's day too.

I got to the diner first. Sat in a corner booth at the back, wanting to watch him walk in so I could size him up before he could do the same to me. Someone came in, but it was a man, older than what Sean should have been by ten or fifteen years, with brown hair, not blond, and a mustache Sean couldn't grow.

He saw me and waved, then walked over and sat at my booth. I couldn't catch a fucking breath, Shosh. I'd seen *Catfish* once or twice, sure, but those people were dumbasses. They didn't even look the other person up on social media or talk to them on the phone. I had done both. I had researched.

"Hello, Rowan," he said, and the fact that he knew my name was startling. I had my hands wrapped around my water, beads of the chill dripping between my fingers. I wanted to scoot out of the booth, but I couldn't. Couldn't get up. Couldn't look him in the eye. I wanted to go home and I wanted to scream and I wanted to die right there on that red leather cushion. Sean wasn't in high school. Sean wasn't even named Sean. Yet he knew everything about me, which was evident when the waitress came by and he ordered me plain lettuce for dinner, aware of how much I hated eating in public.

On the phone, Sean talked like a teenager. Sure, he was a

bit mature, joking about other teenage boys being clowns and too young to understand real faith, but I never thought it was because he was a fucking adult.

He asked how my Spanish quiz had gone the day before, asked if Carly was still neck-deep in her frog biology extravaganza. I said I didn't know. He said, *"Figures she is—it's very 'Carly.'"* I didn't feel good about any of it, so it doesn't explain why, when he paid for the uneaten vegetables and walked me to the door, asking if I wanted to "ride around for a bit," I nodded and got into his piss-colored Toyota Corolla, let him take me to the Red Roof Inn where he was camping out.

I didn't protest when I saw the lingerie hanging from the bathroom door, the framed picture of whitewashed Jesus propped up on the nightstand. Didn't scream when he pressed our thighs together on the bed or when he ran his hand along the waistband of my jean shorts and said we should pray together first. I didn't say no when he told me to lie still and unclench my muscles, that it'd only take a few minutes for him to be *free of his sin*. As he saw it, I was doing the Lord's work. I was making him clean again.

After that, I can only grasp details. Little things, like the brush of his caterpillar mustache on my shoulder, the crushed can of Mountain Dew on the nightstand and the nutrition facts on the back: 170 calories and 46 grams of sugar. His golden cross dangling from his chest as he hovered over me, trailing my skin like an extra finger. Lying there, I questioned if he was right in a way, that there was another presence with us. Nothing godly, nothing good, but something demonic. Dangerous.

He took me home after and I never saw him again. Alone in bed, I lay with one comforting thought: *At least I burned some calories kissing and fucking and sweating.*

It wasn't rough. Not some big, strong man who got impatient with waiting and started to ram himself into me. Sean took his time. He acted as if he really did love me and in the Lifetime version of this, he would have become obsessed with me, stalked me, and ultimately gone to jail. But Sean was smarter than a Lifetime antagonist; he didn't reach out to me again and his Instagram was deactivated. It was like he'd never existed at all.

Weeks passed. When I turned sixteen, I'd seen every part of my city from various rooftops, never having the resolve to jump. But when I was up there, I'd think about Sean and I'd want to do it. My body still remembers his hands. They've never really gone away. I used to like sex, Shosh. Not for the first ten or twelve times I did it—I don't believe any woman does when she's bleeding and it feels like a razor blade making tick marks on your insides. But once you're a bit settled, it gets good. Since Sean, my body has betrayed me. Since Sean, I've tried, because even douche-y school boys can get it up for the witchy goth girl. Since Sean, I've falsely believed I could get used to it again.

But also since Sean, I have found the power to leave boys with blue balls, because it's not my job to be that moist hole and it's my choice who gets to touch me. That's the only positive thing I've taken away. That now I know I don't have to wait till he's finished or be satisfied with whatever he wants. My opinion, my pleasure, matters just as much as his. More so, because it's oppressed and because it's mine.

The reason I like you—*like you,* like you—was a mystery to me initially, Shoshana. I thought maybe it was because I was bored, because I was tired of men, afraid of men, really. But no. I like you because I like you. Because I'm attracted to you. Because you're interesting to me. That doesn't just go away because you're asexual or somewhere on that spectrum. I still want you. But now, I get you, understand a bit more about why you are the way you are, why cheerleading is the center of your existence. Remember how I mentioned that world, the world where we could choose our feelings? Yeah, well, that's not the one we're living in.

I tell Walsh all of it. About Sean. About you. About how I want to get better, but I don't know if it's possible. Walsh doesn't bring out the dolls this time. She just listens.

At the end, she says, "I just want to tell you how well I think you're doing." Her eyes float to my cast. "And that I think you're pretty great."

I cross my cast over my chest. All the nurses have been sucking up lately, just to pat me on the back for doing what every other girl in the program does: listen.

"And you'll do okay without her," Walsh adds.

When you leave, will I be okay? I don't know. Maybe I'll revert to the me before you turned up, destructive and so angry I wanted everyone and everything, including myself, to disappear. Or has a new layer of Rowan set the groundwork, a foundation that will withhold through this next period in the A.S.E., After Shoshana Era?

"Here's hoping," I say, but I let myself linger on the thought of you, here with me until then.

I know you aren't certain what you want, Shosh, and while I know that means we can still be together, be partners in crime, be lovers in whatever sense you'd consent to, I don't think you're ready for this. Which is perfectly understandable given you're seven-fucking-teen and haven't tried anything with anyone. You need time to figure it out. I'll wait for when you do, for when *our* time comes, because I believe it will.

Nurse Robinson and Nurse Hart are off duty for the night. My mind itches to make a new escape plan. But if I did, you would say no. Or you would say yes, even though you want to say no. And without you, there is no plan.

Sophie and Donna are already in their beds when I open the door. They wait for me to decide what to play, what to say, what to do. I face Donna, thinking it took her two, maybe three days to get over Jazzy. It will be near impossible to forget you, but as with all things, I can see it happening. You'll get busy with the show, with your family, friends, a future partner, little Aviva down the line.

I, Rowan, will be a reminder of that short period in your life when you were sick. Or maybe you'll recollect that you weren't sick after all. That this was only a mistake on your parents' part. I believe you'll try, at first. But life has a funny way of throwing things off course. And like I said, we're going in two different directions.

"She'll write," Donna promises, like she can tell where my mind is tonight.

"Like Jazzy wrote to you?" I sigh, sitting on the ladder.

"Jazzy isn't Shoshana. We didn't agree to do the whole pen-pal thing. Have a little faith."

Have a little faith. I almost laugh. Can I have faith in things? Can I even hear that word without gagging? As a little girl, I must have had some form of it because I sang "Rise and Shine" and "Give God the Glory, Glory" with the other Sunday school kids. I believed because I was told that those things exist. Like God and Santa Claus and the Tooth Fairy. I'll never understand why parents make those things up, pretend there's magic when there isn't. Kids don't know anything. If you didn't tell them about Santa Claus, there would be no Santa Claus to miss. If I hadn't met you, Shoshana, there would be no Shoshana to miss.

Sophie sits up in her bed, *your* bed, and puts a hand on the ladder by my leg, her red hair brushing the wood. "Is she the person you love most in the world?" she asks me.

"There's not much competition," I admit.

"I miss my mom so much."

"Me too," Donna agrees. "What's your mom like, Sophie?"

"Shy," Sophie says. "She doesn't talk to any of the other moms at my school. But she cooks and cleans and takes care of us."

"Is she the one who gave you your carrot-top?" I ask.

"No. That's my dad."

"My mom is strict," says Donna. "Insane really. But after being here, I almost miss her curfews."

I say, "My mother tries too hard or not at all, depending on the day."

I lie down in my casket and Sophie climbs up to snuggle me, not worried about getting in trouble. I've taught her well.

"You have us," she whispers. "I know I'm not Shoshana, but you remind me of Farrah, so it works both ways."

"Farrah?"

"My big sister. I bug her half the time too. And she doesn't come to family dinner anymore because she's always hanging out with her boyfriend. But you remind me a lot of her."

"Because I have priority issues?"

"Because you don't care about things."

"Everyone cares about things," I say.

The three of us keep talking, loud enough to be heard by the nurses at the end of the hall. But I'm more curious if you can hear us downstairs, Shosh. It's your last night here after all. What are you thinking about? Are you talking to your bunkmates? Are you already asleep? My guess is the third. You could win a hibernation contest, easy peasy.

I try to count the days we've been together on my fingers but every number I come up with feels wrong. Not enough. We've been together for such little time and already we have to say goodbye. In the last week, we've talked about all the things we want to do, but will we actually do them? Will we ever lie on the beach and throw french fries at seagulls? Or go into the city to the Stardust Diner? Will tomorrow be the last time you stand in front of me, a concrete being?

Sophie sings "Sweet Pea" and I hear the ache for her

ukulele. She says she played every day when she was home, but that she doesn't want to anymore. When she's fast asleep in my bed, I trade places and claim yours. It no longer smells like you. Just another RR casket, a plain mattress belonging to hundreds of girls over time. Now it has my handwriting scrawled above it for anyone to read, though it's only meant for you.

Your parents will be here in under an hour. Sayonara, Shosh. You'll return to real life as usual. The thought makes my stomach ache so badly I have trouble eating breakfast. Even more than usual.

We didn't bake a cake this time, but the nurses brought in Dunkin' donuts for breakfast and some of the girls like Donna are over the moon. I take small bites of my jelly donut. My body is all twitchy like it was after the Red Roof Inn, like I'm already grieving.

The nurses, for all their sucking up, don't let me leave until I've finished my meal. And I still have to wait for you to finish yours, which in the end, leaves us with ten minutes before you go. It's still early, so you have bags under your eyes and mint breath from brushing your teeth like an Olympic scrubber both before and after your meal. We sit on the bottom steps, facing the door, debating what to say to each other. In the window, the snow has stopped. Now, it lays in clumps on the ground mixed with dirt and car exhaust.

"You won't forget about me out there?" I ask.

You rub at your eyes, still tired. "Not a chance. I friended you on Instagram and Facebook. The second you get out of here—"

"I'll accept," I agree. "And you'll write me letters until then? Give me something to survive on?"

"Every day," you swear, and I do my best to believe you. You reach into your back pocket and pull out a small scrap of folded paper. You hand it to me. *One secret.* You saved it. You're trying to cash it in. I don't know what secret to tell you.

"I'm scared," I say, taking the scrap. "Of being here without you. Of being here and never feeling better." My face feels hot. My eyes burn. "It's not a huge secret, I know, but I haven't really told you how I feel. I guess because I'm supposed to be—"

"The tough one? You don't have to be," you say and wrap your long arms around me. I take a few deep breaths, trying to remember everything about us in this moment, somehow knowing it will never be this way again or, at least, not for a very long time.

"You're the strongest person I know, Rowan," you say.

I roll my eyes. "Here come the pom-poms."

"No pom-poms. Just what I've thought since the moment we met."

"They're here," Hart interrupts.

I grab your hand and squeeze. "Click your heels three times and say, 'There's no place like home,' and when you open them, you'll be back to your normal life and this will all have been a dream."

You smile at my reference, take my hand like you're going

to bring me with you, and close your eyes. You click your black Adidas once and I trace your profile with my eyes. My heart is so full, like a mother watching her child's first steps. Even though I'm terrified to be alone and go back to the way things were, you do seem happy. You deserve to be happy.

You click your shoes again and I hear your parents coming up the steps. They're not allowed inside the center, not while the other girls are here or it would make everyone cry for their families. Everyone except me.

Your ears prick up. You feel close, *are* close, only seconds away from seeing them and being out again, and I want to keep you and say they can't have you, that you are mine, that you have never belonged to anyone else. But through the window is your mother's profile and you look so much alike, so plainly related, that I know you are not mine. You never have been.

I crumple the *one secret* paper in my fist and let go of your hand, full knowing you can't take me with you. We're standing side by side when your heels make their final audible *click,* and then *poof,* you're gone.

21
Shoshana

Just like that, I'm home. I have my iPhone, computer, all the technology at my disposal. I can eat however much or little I want. I will pick up school in three weeks, after holiday break. Everything is in motion again. Normal.

Except for Rowan.

She's not here and I wish she were, even if it would be weird seeing her outside of RR. I'm skin hungry for her, a term that usually doesn't relate to me, but Rowan explained it and it fits here. I'm longing for her body, her warmth, her arms around mine. Her reassurance, mostly. Around her, I'm *in*, I'm *one-of*, able to escape my aloneness. Without her, my mind can send me spiraling inward, a reflective mirror that Walsh claims "warps" when I look at it.

Mom lights the candles at dinner and we all recite the prayer. "*Barukh atah Adonai, Eloheinu, melekh ha'olam, asher kidishanu b'mitz'votav v'tzivanu l'had'lik neir shel Hanukkah.*"

"Amen," we say and get our gifts. K.J. gets a new video game and I get new cheer shoes, a new laptop case, and a new uniform that fits. The price difference doesn't pass K.J., who leaves his new game on the counter and goes downstairs to play the old ones, pissed. Mom must have paid a fortune to have my new, larger uniform shipped fast, because they usually take a few weeks, even months to come in. My eyes linger on the basement door, thinking of how I could go sit with K.J., make a joke about switching gifts, ask to play the new game with him. I always longed for us to be friends, but neither of us can seem to bridge that gap.

"Try it on!" Mom squeals, rubbing my arms. I'm shoved into the bathroom to change. The uniform is still tight, just like all competitive cheer uniforms, but now I can move my arms without feeling like I'm going to rip the mesh. I lift up my elbows and swing them around, get a sense of the flexibility and range of motion the spandex gives.

"Open up," she calls eagerly. I unlock the door and let her look at me, wrapping my arms around my stomach.

"Oh, stop that," she chides, moving my hands to my sides. "You look *beautiful*."

"I barely have ab lines," I complain. My stomach is pudgy, no muscle to it. Same with the backs of my arms. The urge to drop right here and give my mom twenty is tempting me. Dad comes up behind her and stares. He's been watching me like a hawk since he picked me up from RR. He's like Nurse Hart, eyeing me at dinner like I'm going to push peas into my ears to avoid eating them.

Nurse Robinson sends me check-in emails, asking me how I'm doing. I reply generically and, on occasion, provide extra details for reassurance. I write about it to Rowan. All of it. I write and write, but with each passing day, I have less and less to say. I try to keep it up, but it's so much more difficult than talking to her. There's no *her* to bounce from. It's just me and my brain and a scrap of paper—an odd and uneventful combination.

I start a letter today to tell her the big news.

It happened in bed two nights ago, when I was lying down with my head on the pillow, eyes glued to Tumblr. My fingers moved automatically, pressing keys, punching the enter block, and I almost didn't expect to find anything when the page loaded.

Asexual. One word, but there were thousands of posts for it. Most of them were questions from accounts in the community, strangers asking strangers for advice on how to deal with the events of their lives. One post read: *If your parents aren't accepting of your identity, I'm your new mom. Drink water. Take your meds. Make sure you eat. I love you.*

That one was my favorite. I guess my own parents would be accepting, but I'm not a thousand percent sure. They're cozy with our Republican neighbors. They want me to have kids and a family like they do. I bet they'd even like me to be more Jewish; Dad would anyway. Me being ace might not be bad news, but it wouldn't be good. It'll throw a wrench in their plans for me and my life. That wrench scares me enough to stop me from telling them.

Under an anonymous account, I asked HellYeahAsexual, who by their posts seemed kind and open, about how they knew they were ace. They responded with: *Only you know what your body likes and what it doesn't. But for me, I knew bcuz I always liked snuggles and wanted that to be the big event of the evening. Sex never interested me.*

That's me, I wrote back. *That's me to a T.*

I write to Rowan to tell her this, heading toward my revelation but preparing to start out slow.

Dear Rowan,
Rowan,
Hi. It's me again.

Hey Ro,

Have you ever gotten letters from anyone besides me? I have from some of my grandparents on birthdays, but never from friends. This is still so strange. Feels like we're in the 50s. 60s? Idk.

When we go to Houston, I won't be able to write to you for a whole week. There won't be a mailbox or the time. But I'll be thinking of you every day while I'm with the team. I promise. If anything, they make me miss you more. You'd have so much fun meeting my teammates/castmates. A lot of them are worse than the RR girls. Hard to believe, I know, but seriously, they spend hours poofing their hair and pinching their lips to make them look plumper. It's the reason cheerleading isn't taken seriously. Then again, I do the same for competitions. All of us do. Teams with full uniforms (stomachs covered) never score as well as the ones who show skin. Judges like it. Most cheerleaders do too. But then you see the ten-year-olds trying to be sexy and it's bizarre. Imagine Sophie in a miniskirt with red lipstick, and choreographers telling her to lean over and arch her back and sex up the moves. Like Nicki Minaj with braces. Crazy.

This one girl on my team—everyone calls her Ginger—is twelve, and last night, my first real practice back, she got yelled at for dancing too provocatively. You should see the move she's been given. It's like—how can you do that move without looking like a stripper? Did I mention she's twelve? She's also really good. Better than me. But I guess that's not the point.

Anyway, I'm beating around the bush!

Here's the big news . . . the big "coming out" thing.

I feel like it's both a cheat to put it in a letter and also the perfect place to voice my thoughts so I can state them adequately.

Since I've come home, I've reentered the Tumblr trenches and done a bunch of research on labels. You might not even know all the terms I've seen—there's an overwhelming number of them and I bet you think that's good. You'd probably say there should be seven billion definitions, huh? One for each of us on the planet because all our sexualities are different? I'm not disagreeing with that, but a small part of me likes being in a box with others. It's kind of like a little box family, I guess.

What you were talking about in the snow—when you said there may come a point where I have sexual desires, that maybe I'm not asexual—that appears to fall closest to "graysexual" or "gray-A." I thought you'd want to know that word, if you don't already.

That's not what I identify as, though—at least for now. At the moment, maybe for always, I'm ace.

All of this is still hard for me to accept. Not sure if or when I'll feel okay telling people, especially my parents. They won't have a clue about these terms. But I'm glad you know now.

That's all for this edition of "What's Shoshana Up To?" Lol. It feels like I'm writing into the abyss, but I know you're out there, somewhere over the rainbow. It'll be easier when you're Blue and you're allowed to write me too.

"In case I don't see you—'good afternoon, good evening, and goodnight.'"
Recognize that one? If not, figure it out. It's a good one. You'd like it.

Love,
Shoshana

With each passing day, the letters get worse, until it's reached almost two weeks and I'm scraping the bottom of the barrel. I should have spaced it out. Instead, my first two letters were four pages long. Now I get three lines in and want to call it quits. Rowan is going to be bored out of her mind. All I do is talk about myself, my day, how I'm feeling, what I'm doing. Sometimes I ask how things are going there, rhetorical questions she can't answer, and then it's back to me again. I'd never be able to have my own reality show. It'd be like watching paint dry.

On my way to the car for practice I spy Breezy on his front porch sitting with Corey. They look over at the same time and I give a small, polite smile, embarrassed.

"I really should get my license," I say as I slide in next to Mom. I'm a late bloomer. The other juniors have all been hitting the road for weeks. K.J. has a license. He's a senior like Rowan—if Rowan doesn't get held back after all of this.

"When you're ready honey, but don't rush it," Mom says. It's the wrong answer. She's supposed to tell me yes, that it's been too long already and I need to be an adult. She's supposed to help me parallel park with trash cans. Not encourage putting this off.

"Have you given any more thought to where you want to apply for school? College tours will be hard enough with the competition schedule, but we can schedule private ones or look at the schools near the competition locations."

"I haven't thought about it," I cut. With everything that's been going on, I haven't considered the colleges I might want to attend. Should I stay in New Jersey and go to Rutgers like K.J. apparently decided last week? Should I get as far away as possible? What am I even going to major in?

"Well, your SAT reading comprehension was surprisingly average. We should try to get that up."

"Yeah, okay."

Tonight I'll write to Rowan about all the bad and shitty things about being home, like SATs and college prep. How am I supposed to win a world title while simultaneously giving interviews to deans on my biggest role model? There's too much pressure.

I open the car window even though it's freezing and my practice uniform is basically a bathing suit. Mom tells me to shut it, but I ask her to wait a minute. Just until my body stops threatening to be sick. Luckily it settles by the time I get to the gym.

"Listen up!" Mary-Ellen yells. Our team circles around her

and she motions for us to sit on the floor, preschooler-style. I think she likes towering over us. I've got four inches on her standing.

"I know you're all excited for Houston next week. The crew will be coming with us. We're flying. They're driving."

Some of the girls laugh.

"Two of you will be in charge of a handheld camera. You'll be documenting everything from JFK Airport to the transfer in Philadelphia. Then the cameras will switch to two other girls until we arrive at our hotel. Now, I did not pick these girls. If you're upset"—she mimes zipping her lips—"keep your whiny traps shut."

Next to me, Bri and Meredith bounce on the mat anxiously. My bet is Bri is out, but Meredith will score one simply because the girl can dramatize a No. 2 pencil.

"Meredith," Mary-Ellen announces, reading off her phone. Bingo. "Ginger. Angela. Shoshana."

The girls behind me mumble "fuck this" and "every time" but Mary-Ellen looks around, shouting, "What did I just say?" and everyone shuts up real quick.

"Meredith and Ginger, you get the cameras first. You're responsible for them the moment you get them until the second you pass them over. Unless you want your parents paying thousands of dollars for your ungrateful asses, learn how to take care of something."

Heath walks over, bare feet thudding on the mat. "All right, I think that's enough talk. Let's get to work."

What little patience Heath and Mary-Ellen had for my

recovery has dissipated. I'm expected to keep up with the team now. Not just keep up, but be as good as I was before. Better, actually, because *before* was when I had my breakdown and was starting to suck.

As I tumble, I shut my mind off and rely on technique to get me through. Squeeze everything in my hollow body layouts. Legs together in the back handspring. Set with my chest up for jumps to tucks. Heath has me work on standing fulls again. In the routine, I'm still toward the front, though not in the center as I was before. Ginger has taken that spotlight.

The cameras aren't in the gym today. They only come about half the time, with no warning of which days it will be. I can tell when I walk in the gym, though, based on Mary-Ellen's hair, that she knows. If it's blown out to give her thicker-looking volume, that's a day we'll be taping.

The schedule mostly depends on Lorri and the equipment, but they usually never miss a big competition. The season is set up with Worlds as the finale. Twenty-two episodes. They started filming in August and plan to go all the way to April.

Heath works out the tumbling counts so Ginger and I don't clash if we go on the right numbers. Apparently Bri says it still looks "sick" and puts our tumbling at the max start value if I do my double at the end of the pass. BDM Allstars will help with making our stunts more unique. We'll be ready for Worlds if we concentrate.

On our three-minute water break, the girls huddle in clusters. I stand alone, pretending to check my phone like I have a ton of text messages coming in. I have none.

I picture Rowan in a cheer uniform, a sparkly bow on her purple head. Never in a million years . . . but I bet she'd do a wicked impersonation of all of us, especially during the interviews that always make us look slightly dumber on cable.

"So, where were you?" a voice asks. Angela. She has her arms crossed, annoyed.

"What?"

"For the last two and a half months? Where were you?"

I pull on my ponytail, smooth the flyaways behind my ear. "Just away."

"How far away are we talking? In state? Out of state?"

"You never talk to me," I say. She doesn't. Not unless it's about stunts and what I'm doing wrong. "Can we go back to that?"

"Can you tell us all why you left? We're a team you know. You screwed all of us over." Bri steps behind Angela to back her up.

"I'm sorry," I say. I really am. This is a team sport and I let them down.

"Just don't do it again. The closer to Worlds you fuck us, the worse it is for all of us. Imagine the reverse. If you wanted to win and we left you in the cold. Any chance of making top three, gone."

"I get it," I say. My conscience absorbs their words like a sponge. Blackmail for later. *Failure. Fraud. Letdown.*

Bri moves out of my way, but Angela hesitates. They both stick up their noses as I pass. I feel like I can't breathe, but I press my thumbnail into my side, creating moon-shaped indents that bring me back. I use this method too much. I remember Walsh, all those sessions I opened up. I should be better. But I cheated the system on my weekend home. I lied. Which means what? I'm no different than I was before?

Dad stays up late with me after practice, flipping through triathlon magazines, the two of us stretching and icing. He's in impeccable shape, better than I used to be and certainly better than I am now. But two weeks before his IronMan in January, he'll stop everything. No hard exercising until the big day. Cheerleading isn't like that. Worlds is a three-day competition. You have to be able to hit the routine three days in a row, only a total of seven minutes and thirty seconds across seventy-two hours. Dad goes for seventeen hours. But he doesn't have any teammates to rely on. Whether he performs well or not, he does it alone.

"Are you sure you're feeling okay?" he asks for the thousandth time.

Mom brings over a bin to ice my feet again.

"She said she's fine, Adam. How many times are you going to ask her?"

Everything about this moment feels like old times. Dad turning on an IronMan documentary. Mom licking my practice wounds. K.J. nowhere to be found. Except Mom and Dad have quiet tension for the first time in history and I'm not motivated to ice and stretch and prep for practice tomorrow.

I'm not blind to the fact that my family is rooted around me. Mom made it so and Dad and K.J. just went along with it.

Without cheer, we'd have to figure out a whole new dynamic. What would we talk about at the dinner table?

These are the thoughts that come to me, Rowan. It's strange how you can feel so sure of who you are one minute, and the next, you have no idea. Sometimes when I hear myself talk, I'm thinking, who is this person? I feel like I don't know her.

You are the most self-assured person I know. I remember what you said about the people living inside you—not in the spirit way, but how you're always transitioning into someone new. Maybe I'm just in a transitional period. I keep asking myself, who am I without cheerleading? I don't know the answer, but when I'm 40 I will and I'll let you know.

I love you. I wish you were here. I know I keep saying that, but it's true. Even though you would be so bored you'd pull your hair out.

"All wisdom ends in paradox."
Know it? Figure it out.

Love you, love you.
Shoshana

22
Rowan

The twins are here. Identical Olsens, except not actually pretty or blonde or all that skinny. They're wavy-haired beings, jutting out their hips as they walk, with real love handles to grab onto and thick farmer's arms. The craziest thing is that, from what I can tell, there isn't a single way to differentiate them. Imagine all the fun I could have, making them pull pranks on the nurses. Who's getting healthy and who's not. Old Rowan would have lived for it. But I told you the truth, Shoshana. I'm not going that route. Not this time.

Donna, Sophie, and I form a cult. No one comes in. No one goes out. I know I told you I'd take the twins under my wing, but that would be a gateway drug. I'm supposed to be focusing on myself and I can't do that if I'm concentrating on all these shiny new objects. Sophie, with her own sneaking strategies, finds out their names. Miriam and Mable, like an old grandmother and a maple syrup brand.

"I don't care how stupid their names are," I tell her. "We're not messing with them or befriending them. It's just the three of us now."

"Yeah," Donna says, scolding Sophie. "We're supposed to be Rowan's 'ana sponsors.' You can't be tempting her with enemy information."

"The twins are our enemies?" Sophie asks, putting an arm around me. She's been craving reassurance lately, worried about her place in our triangle and if it'll be revoked.

"Space," I insist, shaking her off. Through the window, I watch Robinson approach the edge of the parking lot, the black pull-out mailbox at the start of the street.

"Yeah. Space," says Donna. "Rowan's waiting for the next letter from Shoshana and can't deal with your neediness right now."

Donna and Sophie are never allowed to read your letters. I don't let them. But that doesn't stop them from waiting with me like puppy dogs as Robinson gets the mail. Either they're so bored they're living vicariously through me or they're placing bets behind my back about how many envelopes I'll get before they stop coming.

Sophie tries to hug me again, harder, and for a little girl with no nails, she scratches my arm damn hard.

"Hey!" I spit, stepping out of the way. To my and Donna's surprise, Sophie falls through the two of us, flat on her face with a hard thud.

Donna and I stare. Our minds calculate the reason why Sophie didn't catch herself as she starts mumbling baby talk, contorting her body into new, painful positions. Donna reaches a hand out as a reflex, trying to stop Sophie from hitting herself as she pounds her clenched fist against her forehead. Then Sophie punches Donna on the arm so hard Donna screams.

I yell for the nurses and Donna begins bawling, irises

leaking a pitcher of tears as she says, "I'm sorry. I'm sorry. I didn't mean to touch her."

Every brain wave inside me is in command mode.

Grab Sophie, they say.

Grab her.

Hug her.

Hold her until it stops.

Being there for someone physically is just about the only way I know how. But Sophie is spasming and so it's Donna I grab onto, gripping her from behind and squeezing tighter and tighter until she's miming Sophie's calls of helpless pain.

The nurses must come at some point—probably only a few seconds after it starts—but it feels like an eternity that we stand there, hovering overhead, watching her. Donna and I are frozen like we're witnessing a car wreck, our interest matched only by our horror, and Robinson has to set down the mail so she can forcibly pull us apart. My arms lock with refusal.

"Please let go, Rowan," Robinson says.

She only left us unsupervised for a minute, I think. *A minute.*

I release my hold on Donna and every part of me exhales, collapsing in on itself. Nurse Hart moves to Sophie with a medical kit and I can see blood dribbling like baby drool from Sophie's mouth. The rest of the staff observe the scene like it's normal, like it's not the most fucked-up thing they've ever seen. I guess it's not, which is a sickening thought I have to table for now. Hope is the only nurse on my level, with her left hand covering her mouth, looking ghostly ill. Kelly puts a hand on Hope's back to brace her.

When Sophie stills, the nurses turn her onto her side. She doesn't even look like Sophie. She just looks like a body. When the body blinks hard and breathes normal again, the nurses start asking it questions in soft voices.

"What's your name?"

Sophie.

"How old are you?"

Twelve.

"Where are you?"

No response.

"Sophie, where are you?"

I don't know.

Donna is sobbing in our room when I get up there and I don't blame her. What just happened didn't feel real. Sophie— completely possessed, a body with no being. I climb under Donna's covers and hold her again, lightly this time. I put two and two together about the blood from Sophie's mouth. It came from splitting her lip on her braces when she body-slammed the carpet. Maybe, *just maybe*, I could have prevented that if I'd caught her. That small detail leaves me nauseated and teary eyed.

Don't die, I think. *Don't die. Don't die. Don't fucking die.*

The thought goes nowhere. Not to God's ears or Sophie's. Yet it's pure instinct to will it.

My heart weighs heavier in my chest now, like it's wet. We're all F'd up. Coming in here and leaving the same. But Sophie wasn't totally F'd. Not yet. After the first seizure, they said medication would solve it, so she believed them. She trusted them. Now she'll know better. She'll be worried that what happened to her today could happen to her at any time. She'll be embarrassed that Donna and I saw her that way. I know by putting myself in her size-five shoes.

Nurse Hart comes into our room. She says Sophie is okay, they're taking her to a hospital, they'll get her the help she needs.

Donna asks when we can see her again, to let her know we're sorry, and Hart says they'll pass along the message. Sophie's parents are coming soon and they'll decide if they want to take her home and out of RR's program. Hopefully, though, she'll be staying with us.

Hart hands Donna an ice pack for her arm.

"If it happens again, what are we supposed to do?" Donna asks.

"In here, you shout for us, just as you did. We don't want any of you getting hurt and that's our number one priority. But if you're somewhere outside one day, at a restaurant or in a classroom, you want to remove any sharp objects so the person can't hurt themselves or anyone else, and you dial 911."

"What good is modern medicine if it can't help her?" I speak with the sharpness of a blade on my tongue.

"It can help her. It's just not perfect. If you want to find a more permanent cure, there's plenty of room for more scientists in this world." She squeezes my shoulder and gives Donna a wink, leaving us alone.

"And then there were two," I say. Donna doesn't laugh. She's digging herself into a hole of sadness. I'm freaked out, too, but mostly I'm thankful Sophie isn't going to die today. She's going to be okay. Donna doesn't seem to think so. She holds her bruise like it's a token Sophie gave her as a symbol of their profound friendship.

Relief is what I feel when Mrs. Walsh comes and has an emergency session with Donna, talking sense into her so she exits the therapy room looking a hundred times better.

I go in and Mrs. Walsh is sipping tea. Mint, by the light-green color.

"Did Donna make it all about her? The *could've, should've, would've* thing, because that's really not my taste or my angle on it. I mean, it's not about either of us. It's about Sophie's brain not working as it should."

I fall over the side of the orange loveseat, lying back like a real psychiatric patient, hands behind my head.

"It is not either of your fault," she agrees.

"You know this is exactly the kind of thing that always happens around me. I'm a magnet for it. The apple doesn't fall far from the anorexic, psychopathic, trouble-magnet mother."

"How long has it been since you've spoken to her?"

"Last time she called was five days ago and by the time the nurses forced me on the phone, she had to go. Last time we talked-talked was two weeks ago. Ten minutes total—three minutes of a heartfelt conversation, followed by seven minutes of fighting."

"Does that upset you?"

"We're on the basic level of human decency," I say, "so it's whatever. She gives me my space and I give her the house when she wants to bring her friends over. We're even."

I leave a long pause after I speak, so Walsh will ask me questions or add a note to the conversation. I refuse to be the patient who doesn't shut up for the entire hour.

"Is that how you typically think of your relationship with your mother? Even?"

"She plays nice. I play nice. She yells. I yell back. Yeah. It's symbiotic."

"Would you say that's been healthy for you?"

I choke out a laugh. "That's a pretty pointed question."

"It's just a question, Rowan."

"No," I snap. "But she's my mother . . . she pays for food and she doesn't beat me. That's kind of a decent setup compared to other people's lives."

"What about emotional support?"

"Emotional support? For what?"

"Being a teenage girl. The things you've been through."

"She asks me about school sometimes, if that's what you're talking about."

"Does she know about Sean?"

I sit up in the seat. "No. And she never will."

Walsh doesn't know my mother. If she found out, it would only be a sign of my failings, her daughter dragging herself into trouble. That, or she'd go crazy. Flip out and try to find him, put him on death row. She's unpredictable in the best and worst ways. It's what my father used to love about her. It's also what made him cheat and leave.

My mother and I haven't spoken seriously in a while. She might actually be wondering about me in here, the way I occasionally, by accident or on purpose, wonder about her out there. We have a phone call later today and I'll admit, I've thought about secretly dialing your number, Shoshana. You had me memorize your cell anyway and I doubt the nurses have memorized my mother's number. She doesn't call enough. Maybe that's too expected, though. Maybe they'd notice or maybe you wouldn't want to hear from me. Perhaps Sophie's collapse is some sort of omen, a premonition to stay away from you, before something else happens, something much worse.

Shoshana

t takes two flights to get to Texas, where we'll train with BDM Allstars. On the first flight, I manage to snag the extra seat with strangers, separated from the team so I can listen to music and books and fall asleep with my mouth open without worrying about being secretly filmed by the other girls. But in the Philadelphia airport, Meredith passes me the handheld camera and the object makes me overwhelmingly popular on flight two. I'm forced to squish between Bri and Nicole, two girls desperate for more airtime. I haven't even buckled up when they start yelling at me to turn on the camera.

"Hey," I say, holding the device against the small TV screen in front of me. "We're on the second flight now."

Bri and Nicole lean into the shot and wave at the lens.

"Hey, peeps," Bri says, in full makeup and designer sweatpants for the plane ride. I'm in regular sweatpants and Nicole's in a casual off-the-shoulder top with a carefully selected neon green bra strap showing.

"We should do that whole 'I'm on a Boat' song by T-Pain, but instead, sing 'I'm on a plane,'" Nicole suggests.

I roll my eyes before I remember I'm on camera.

"The camera crew is stuck driving," Bri says, also ignoring Nicole and addressing the audience. "Sucks to suck. It's like, a twenty-four-hour drive too. God, with all that equipment, from the microphones to the lights and the green screens. They're probably piled on top of each other like sardines."

She knows the crew is going to watch this, doesn't she? They'll be deciding what to edit for air.

"They're going to interview some BDM people too," Bri adds, flipping her braids. "This is kind of fun, controlling the camera."

She grabs it by the lens, ripping it away from me.

"Stop!" I wrestle to get it back, afraid she's going to damage it and Mary-Ellen will be pissed. Both our hands are on the camera, the red light still blinking.

"Don't be such an attention whore," Bri insists.

"I just don't want us to break it," I warn.

She tugs harder. "Then let go and *we* won't."

I obey, worried she'll fling the thing into a passenger a few rows behind us if I don't give up. She holds the tech out in front of her face, whitened teeth glistening.

"Now that the real host is here, welcome to Brianna, Nicole, and Shoshana's crib."

I don't miss the way she says our names out of order from our row to tack mine on last. It's little things like this that get under my skin. Pinpricks. It shouldn't matter. I'm the bigger person. But no reminder about starving children in third world countries with "real problems" makes the pinpricks sting any less.

A part of me wishes I was more like Bri or Nicole, because they don't see things the way I do. That must be why Rowan wanted me this way. Smart. Experienced. In constant pain. *Misery loves company.*

"As you can see, this is our row." Brianna amps up her Valley girl impression. I wonder if she realizes she's just role-playing a more extreme version of herself. "We know it looks small, but there's actually a trampoline, a hot tub, and two tennis courts underneath here." She taps the seat where the life jackets are.

"We're supposed to be answering the questions they gave us," I say, anxious to get the safe-in-one-piece camera back.

Nicole scowls. "We didn't get any questions."

I pull up the list Lorri forwarded to my phone, already saved, and read the questions aloud.

"How are we feeling about going to Houston? Is there any competition between Garwood Elite and BDM? Are we excited or nervous to be working with a coed team? Will the boys be a distraction to us? Are we aware spots will be shifted when they redo the routine? Do you think there will be a new center flyer?"

Nicole starts swearing. "Fuck yes. I'll be center."

"Calm your tits, they're not changing you," Bri says. "What was the first question again?"

I grab the camera and hold the shot evenly between the three of us. Bri releases control and lets me moderate the panel. "How are you feeling about going to work with BDM Allstars?"

The girls run their mouths until the flight is halfway over, never letting me get a breath in or make it around to any of the other questions. We touch down and I hand the camera over to Heath. He asks if I got good stuff and I shrug. We'll see what footage Lorri can salvage.

Mary-Ellen rents a van and we pile in, bags lying under our feet, forcing our knees up to our chins. I feel for the crew. We're only in the van a half hour and I'm nauseated. Twenty-four hours must be a devil's playground.

Our team slowly turns to ice cubes as Mary-Ellen amps up the air conditioning. No one wants to ask her to turn it down, and if we ask Heath on the passenger's side, she'll know we're just too afraid to ask her. Either way, it's a lose-lose situation.

Our team splits hotel rooms, Mary-Ellen naming the group leaders and giving them room keys. I'm not a group leader. I'm bunked in with Angela as my queen, meaning I'll have to ask for her permission every time I want to leave the room to call Mom and Dad with privacy.

Garwood Elite is its own kind of RR.

At night, my cell phone collected by Mary-Ellen and Heath, a tactic used to hone our focus on tomorrow's choreography camp, there's nothing to distract from how lonely I feel. How cold it is to sleep without Rowan in my vicinity.

In the mornings before choreography camp, I do my own hair and makeup. The other girls all help each other, a semi-circle of hair lines and extra hands for perfecting eyeliner. No one volunteers to help me. I even out my eyebrows on my own, hairspray my poof until it's rock solid, pump coats of mascara on as I dream of Rowan's lectures. It's for the best, I tell myself. If someone on the team did help me, they might see my bald spot. It'd be hard to come back from that.

BDM are as good as their competition history and consistency shows. Their stunts are insane. They're a coed team, the boys tossing the girls in the air like graduation caps, watching as they spin on the way down and catching them a few feet above the floor. Angela and Meredith ogle as the guys tumble and we watch their new routine. It's out of the park, bat-shit crazy. As long as they don't have any major hiccups, they'll win the large coed division for sure.

The tumble track I sit on sinks beside me, indicating someone has sat down or that I've just gained pounds upon pounds on the spot. I see the red-and-black uniform, the yellow lettering that says *BDM*, the logo, and the men's pants.

"Hey," the cheerleader says. The one word bears his full Southern accent. Like April or August's from RR. "I'm Travis. You're Shoshana."

It's not a question so I just nod.

I watch the BDM stunts go up, their flyers linking arms, lifting their legs in sync and turning their heads with a snap. It has a strong effect with the music. I bet here they're trained like Navy SEALs. The girl crying in the corner with a mental block would indicate yes. It's just as hard to make it here as it is at GE.

"Don't talk much in real life, do ya?" the boy asks. He's supposed to be tumbling during this section, but since the stunts are being fixed, he's allowed to hang out on the sidelines and watch.

"I speak," I admit, finally looking at him. I'm shy again and it's ridiculous. I don't want to be silent anymore.

"Y'all in a fight or somethun'?" He nods to the rest of my team, stretching together on the floor. He's in great shape, like all the boys here but stockier. He vaguely resembles the B version of the gymnast Jake Dalton.

"No fighting. I'd just rather focus on cheer than how you and the rest of the boys look in tight pants."

Rowan would be proud.

"Believe me, we don't wear these pants normally. We wear shorts an' no shirts, all skins. But the coaches said we gotta be in full uniform for the cameras. I'm sweating bullets here."

He is. Sweat drips down his forehead, into his dark, thick eyebrows. He looks at my Garwood Elite sports bra and then across the floor.

In the corner of my vision, I see Lorri pointing at me, motioning for the cameras to get a shot of me and . . . what did he say his name was?

Now I get it. It clicks inside my brain. What's-his-face came over here for his five minutes of fame. He'll be able to tell all his future dates he was on a TV show, play them the clip of this moment, and they'll think he has girls like me lined up around the block. Rowan prepared me for this. The millennial fame complex.

I keep a sour look on my face so they know I'm not into it. They rarely use video of me when I'm without the halo of angel-Shoshana, something I noticed watching the last few episodes before my breakdown. They really did me a favor by only using shots where I acted decent.

"You as good as they say?" he asks. "'Cause I heard you've been benched a while."

"I'm fine," I say, scooting off the tumble track. "And I wasn't benched."

Mary-Ellen calls us to the floor. She says we're doing a run-through and letting BDM Allstars pick us apart. The boy on the tumble track watches me sidelong while I get into position. I'm not ready to go full-out yet, but I'll have to do at least the stunts. I can mark the tumbling and pray as few people notice as possible. The boy will notice, though. He'll watch me the whole time so the cameras will watch him.

"Don't be nervous," Heath whispers as he passes me. "Let your body run on autopilot."

I roll my ankles out, stretch my wrists, crack my neck and back, and shake out my hands. *No nerves. Autopilot. Right.*

Someone yells, "Come on, ladies!" and I smile, hoping it looks like I'm having fun. Heath and Mary-Ellen are up front. I get on one knee in my starting position. *Hands on hips. Breathe. It'll all be over in two minutes and thirty seconds.*

There's a pause just before the music starts. When it thrums to life, we're sent into motion at once. Lifting, flipping, cartwheeling into new positions. I throw a warm-up pass for running tumbling, but complete the Arabian so they can see the visual effect of my flip over Ginger's.

The pyramid hits and my bases and I toss Nicole's kick double basket as high as we can. As soon as the dance music blasts, the tightness of my body gives out and my motions get sloppy. I hold the end pose with unsteady breath.

The feedback from BDM is immediate and no-bullshit, exactly what we need. Everyone, especially the coaches, agrees we should keep the tumbling section with Ginger and me, but our opening stunts need work and so does the dance where we all looked exhausted. Tumble track boy is still staring at me, observing my chest rise and fall, my cheeks rouge with blood.

"Look alive, superstar," Lorri tells me. I must seem like I'm in pain, which I am, but cheering is the part I like. It's the rest—the downtime at hotels, the meals where I sit alone or at the end of our group table, the constant awareness of my wrong gestures and voice—that I'm not so crazy about.

Before RR, I could grin and bear it, but after Rowan and how close we are, I feel more on my own than ever. It's like when the boy from *Room* goes outside and everything is different, and even though he misses being in Room, he could never go back because now he knows there's so much more to the world. I can't go back to pretending these girls are my friends, not when I know what real friendship feels like.

The physical labor of cheer helps me not think so much, mainly because it's hard to think of anything besides *don't throw up*. When the choreographer comes in midday, he works us until we're five feet under. Not six, because then we wouldn't be able to carry on. Just five, enough to leave us dizzy and dehydrated, but not enough to kill us.

Everyone in cheerleading knows this choreographer: Hooper Ernst. He's got a cheeky dipped smile and a big jolly gut, but he doesn't play around and he doesn't give a shit about danger. He wants the wildest routine imaginable. The same "wow" factor Heath and Mary-Ellen crave, that the judges applaud.

Hooper positions us where he pleases and we stay silent. Stand still. He places me in the very back, just another consequence of being tall, large. Ginger keeps my old spot in the center and I watch her learn special choreography while I copy my counter partner on the right side.

The girls lean closer into Lorri's shot of Hooper and Ginger working together. It's hard to believe some of them were on the show before me. I remember I used to think Angela was the coolest person ever, the pristine perfect cheerleader. When did that stop? I barely remember it, or register her presence as she passes me each day in the gym. Is it a good thing I no longer praise her and my teammates, or is it another part of me that's lost?

Five more days of choreography camp puts me on robot mode. Breakfast. Cheer. Lunch. Cheer. Dinner. Conditioning. Sleep. Repeat. My body is exhausted from the practice beforehand and each day I slip a little more behind. Mary-Ellen watches from the side, conversing with Heath. When we get back to the GE gym, they'll rearrange what they want, maybe switch spots. It's likely I'll stay in the back. *Where I belong*, Mary-Ellen must think.

I spend more time with BDM Allstars in Houston than I do

with GE. Their Southern hospitality forces them to socialize with me. That includes Travis, tumble track boy, and his sister Carmela, who's also on the team.

"So, what's it like to win?" I ask her on our water break. She's a two-time World Champion with a natural blonde bob and black eyeshadow. She's incredibly tiny, one of those graduation caps they toss to the sky.

"Everything they say it is. Sweet. Unforgettable." She points to the Worlds' glass globe and a banner hung above it in the gym, the picture of BDM with gold medals around their necks and rings on the fingers. In the photo, Carmela is crying tears of joy.

"It was also a big F-U to CheerWork. They're hungry for us. I like rubbing it in."

Rowan is like that, too, I think, smiling. I try to imagine myself falling on the mat, breaking down, not because I suck, but because we've won Worlds. The image is too far off to be clear, but even the distorted glimpse ignites a fire in my belly.

"And you like being on BDM?" I ask.

"Yeah." She looks at me, pointedly. "Thinkin' about makin' a switch? 'Cause the coaches here would take you in a heartbeat. I don't know why they moved you to the back. I saw your pass at Worlds last year. It was nuts."

"It's a little late for switching gyms," I say. By the time I got down here and moved, I'd almost be aged out. I'd also feel like a traitor, and K.J. would kill me for moving our family away from Rutgers.

"You know that feeling when you're behind the curtain,

ready to go up the stairs, and your stomach gets all tight with butterflies, but then you get out there and perform and in a matter of minutes it's all over?"

"Sure," I say, but usually it's less butterflies and more dread—not wanting to fuck up.

"Well, your life doesn't change afterward, does it? Same with Worlds. I bet you thought being on the show would make your life better. That you'd be happier or other bullshit. But are you?" She cracks her neck, speaking so much like Rowan I almost feel like she's here, possessing Carmela. "Same with winning Worlds. It's a great thing nobody can take away from you, but it doesn't make the bad days go away, or make it any easier to win the next year. Really, the best it's for is braggin' rights. *World champion.*"

"It does have a ring to it."

She laughs, but it's not Rowan's "ha" kind. "My rings are sittin' at home in a box collecting dust."

"I'd never take it off," I say, staring at my bare fingers. The coaches call us back to the mat and Carmela waits for me to finish my water. Either it's her Southern hospitality or the bloom of a friendship doomed to end through long distance.

Back at the hotel, I take an extra-long shower, muscles pumping to repair all the tears I built in them today. I change into pajamas, brush my teeth, and get in bed. The rest of the team stays up gossiping about BDM boys and watching *John Tucker Must Die* on the hotel flat-screen.

I snake down to the floor, still wrapped in my blanket. I used to be a big fish in a small pond at Jersey Heat, the first cheerleading team I joined with fifty cheerleaders in the program total. Now I'm a small fish in a big pond at GE, with fifteen hundred cheerleaders divided into almost seventy teams.

Angela and Bri are on the bed, giggling. *Any chance of making top three: gone.* They want those rings just as much as I do. For all I criticize, they're right about me not flaking out on them again. Teammates need to rely on each other, even if they don't get along.

There's more to the world than cheerleading. I know that. I understand how all of human existence is going to live for a while and then we're going to die like Rowan said, and a Worlds' ring or a TV show won't change any of that. I understand it won't make my bad days go away and that people cling to these things to distract themselves from universal truths. But this matters to me. Regardless of what happens in the end, I can't do what Rowan wants. I can't stop caring about what other people think or say "fuck you" to strangers' opinions. Was Rowan ever able to do that? Has anybody actually been able to? Doubtful. If they were, what did it take them to get to that point?

I bet it takes a massacre.

24
Rowan

Houston, Texas: land of chicken-fried steak, humidity, the nation's only funeral museum—and for the last week, you. That's why the letters have stopped. Or that's what I tell Donna and a newly re-medicated Sophie to get them off my back. We watch over Sophie like worrywarts, not just Donna and I, but the whole RR clan. Sophie says she doesn't remember anything of what happened, but the stitches in her mouth, the bruising on her lips, are proof enough. And if they weren't, Donna's grotesque yellow bicep that she keeps poking to watch change color does the trick.

Sophie has apologized for it a gazillion times. I tell her all apologies are overkill or useless after two times, but she still says "I didn't mean it" and "I'm sorry if it happens again."

We're all worried it's going to happen again. Sophie, rightly, is freaked out most of all. Donna and I crawl into her bed, squish her in a Smurf sandwich, and lie in silence so the nurses will spare us the lectures. But I suspect they'll be more lenient with us post-seizure, give us a bit of time to recover, reconnect.

Days pass without word from you. It snows again and you're not here to make it special. Donna, Sophie, and I build the world's most pathetic snowman, but it's mostly Donna and I while Sophie sits and presses ice to her plump mouth.

I can't escape myself in here anymore. Games no longer take me away. Nothing does. Instead, I confront this place head-on and go through the motions of eating and bathing and shitting and repeating. At weigh-ins, my scale reads a number that skeeves me out, but when the bathroom mirror shows me a body distinct from the one that arrived here months ago, I feel oddly okay. It's a new body, a new Rowan. A Rowan who might not die from this, who might not want to.

Nurse Hart says my mother is on the phone, so I grab the corded RR machine and press it to my ear. She's already talking, in the middle of a sentence about needing to return something to Forever 21 and the death of my goldfish Larry.

"I'd been feeding him," she says, "but turns out you can feed the suckers too much. The little shit ate himself to death."

The irony of that sentence isn't lost on me.

"I gave him a proper burial," she says. "Said a prayer in the Lord Christ's name."

"Well," I bite my lip to keep from mouthing off, "then I'm sure he's in fishy heaven."

There's silence and I wait for her to scold my tone, for this to turn into an argument and then one of us to make an excuse to get off the line. Instead she pauses, her voice thickening as she asks, "You want me to pull you out?"

Blood pulses under my cast. I let out a laugh. "Did one of your boyfriends break up with you?"

She'd never offer to pull me from a program unless

something severe was going on and she needed me to come home and distract her.

She spits out a curse. "How dare you. Do you know how much you cost me in medical bills? All because you refuse to eat a couple bites of dinner."

Guess who I learned that from, I think. I say something just as true, but slightly less harsh. "Dad's the one footing the bill."

The words piss her off anyway. Any mention of my father usually does, but particularly when it's in reference to his new family or the money he makes as a lead contractor, enough to pay my treatment center costs and fulfill his part of child support. He only does it to keep good faith with his new family, but it's something.

I can tell she's about to pull the *I'm your mother and what I say goes* card, but before she can, I hang up. I want to vomit at how much I'm thinking like Walsh, but the truth is, I can't go home for a week only to spiral out again. It'll land me right back here or in an identical treatment center, and this can't be my life forever. If it is, it's no use. I need to break this pattern, wheel, whatever the fuck. I need a new Rowan to take over. One that's strong enough not to let me go back on this.

Nurse Hart drives me to the Medemerge up the road, where I'll be upgraded to a removable splint instead of a cast. She lets me play music on the radio, smiling when I skip the top hits for an 80s station. I roll down the window, float my cast along the air to "Everybody Wants to Rule the World." Nurse

Hart keeps her hands on the wheel, steady as granite. She could turn her hands off the ten and two position, make us crash, make it all end. She doesn't, though. She's stable.

After a half hour in the waiting room with sick children and check-up teens, the Medemerge nurse comes out. I sit on crinkly white paper and let her saw off the fiberglass. My arm feels strange, like it's being born again. New baby-pink skin. Pinker than the rest of me. It smells rotten.

"Would you like to keep the cast?" the nurse asks. She cut directly down the middle of *Shoshana loves you,* a clear sign from the universe if I read into it.

I tell her no and she tosses it in the garbage before sliding a Velcro splint up my wrist.

"Two visible hands," Hart commends.

"All the better to eat with," I snort.

Once we're back outside, Hart clears her throat in a way that makes me sure she wants a cigarette. She resists and the two of us walk toward the car.

"When we get back to the center," she says, "you're going to pack your things."

I meet her gaze, confused for only an instant before I get it. My mother. She's never been known for her selflessness. Probably called back the moment I hung up and demanded my release. I'll leave tonight. Go home, stop eating, be sent away again. This emerging layer of Rowan will be discarded and I'll fall back into the old ways, old habits, just like that.

"Is she coming tonight or tomorrow?" I ask, feeling out-of-body mad. Sophie's and Donna's faces appear in front of my eyelids. Mostly Sophie's baby brace-face. I didn't know I cared enough to worry about goodbyes.

"No one is coming, Rowan. You're moving downstairs. You're going to be on the Blue schedule."

I freeze. I've only imagined this moment a thousand times and it's already over. I wasn't prepared. I want to ask her to re-create it and tell me again.

"Seriously?"

"You'll eat in the Blue kitchen, unsupervised. But I'm warning you now, we will be able to tell if you're not eating what you should. If we catch any tricks, anything with the other girls, you'll be Gray again. Got that?"

I nod. This wasn't what my cynical mind expected at all. Why now? Do they really believe I have the power to change? Do they really see me out there, in the world?

Hart and I walk the rest of the way to the car. She warms up the engine and motions for my seatbelt.

"What happens now is completely up to you," she says, eyes on mine. I soak in the power. The choice. Turn the wheel or get better. My call.

"Are Donna and Sophie Blue?"

She shakes her head. No elaboration necessary. I'm Blue. They're not.

Hart pauses in the driver's seat to use a lens cleaner on her glasses, then we're in drive and creeping closer to RR. I enjoy this, the in-between, not Gray anymore, not Blue yet. For a moment, all of the Rowans are here again, beneath me, lifting up this new Rowan I'm becoming.

25
Shoshana

Each night, curled in the safety of my own home, my un-bunked bed, the tears come. Squeezed out of me, like oil from a rag. In Texas, I dug my nails into my thigh so many times that a flock of V-shaped birds has bloomed beneath my spandex.

Mary-Ellen is the only one who really sees me, I think, pulling the covers tighter around my too-soft body. *I'm not cut from strong enough cloth. I am jeans that rip, a zipper that won't pull over its seam. I am a safety pin, temporary, something she no longer needs.*

In the morning I'm in better spirits. I believe I can hold the thread of worry in my mouth a little longer, the string tightening around my teeth, sewing itself through my cheeks until my jaw is aching and wired shut. Mom can tell something is off though. She asks, "Are you feeling all right?" and presses her palm to my forehead, like the problem might be physical. I imagine confiding in her, letting the thread tumble its way off the spool. *I want to quit. I hate it at GE. None of the girls like me. Please, I want to be a big fish again.* But I am wound too tightly to let go.

Mom drops me off at the gym for yet another practice and I watch Ginger and Angela giggle, reaching for the front door with their heads buried in their phones. Have these girls spent a full week away from technology? Have they lain beside a friend with no screens in their way? Created their own games to pass time?

Was I like them before RR?

"What's wrong?" Mom asks.

This time, I have to give her something. "Mary-Ellen," I say. "She's just really tough, and a little scary sometimes."

Mom sighs, grateful, relieved. If this is all it is, she thinks she can contain it. "Mary-Ellen is just a person, Shoshana. Like me and you. The only power she has is the power you give her."

I nod, but when I head inside and spot Mary-Ellen across the mat, beady eyes looking right through me like I might be a speck of lint under her shoe or a bad tax return, I hand her the strength of an atomic bomb.

My phone vibrates. *@CheerCarmela has followed you on Twitter.*

Since practice hasn't started yet, I duck into the cubby room and check out the verified page. I recognize her teary-eyed World Champion profile picture. Ten thousand followers. I feel flattered that she liked me enough to track me down on social media, so I direct message her.

@CheerCarmela Hey! Thanks for helping out the team. Like I said, I'd ditch GE for you guys if I could, but first I'd have 2 slit Mary-Ellen's throat.

I consider writing *stab* instead of *slit*, but I think Rowan's wrong on that one. *Slit* sounds better. Carmela will get the sarcasm anyway, so it really doesn't matter.

"Level-five bitches! On the mat!" Mary-Ellen shouts.

I slide my phone into my bag, grateful that we all have

to go without technology during practice. Even Mary-Ellen abstains from checking hers. GE has its own rules, and no screens is one I can back up.

The twenty of us warm up, holding splits and handstands, throwing backflips and baskets, jumping with our toes perfectly pointed. Our gazes linger by each other's hips, our thighs, our pierced and unpierced belly buttons. For a second I look at Mary-Ellen, her coarse hair like a ruffled cape around her shoulders, her neck hung low like a turkey snood, and label her the plastic surgery *before* photo—what she wouldn't give to be young like us.

Then I catch her eyes and drop them like they're something too hot to hold.

Heath pinches my cheek. "Pay attention, Bagels and Lox."

In between our jumps to tucks, Nicole tells me, "Add a full twist to yours."

"You first," I say.

"You have it though, your problem is just mental. I physically can't do it."

She makes it sound like a mental block is easier to work through than a physical one. Like I can just choose to get over it, to throw the full twist after my straddle jump. I don't know how to explain that a mental block is worse than a physical problem. There's no material solution, no technique to correct to set your mind straight.

Ginger does a toe to full. Nicole and I watch her prepubescent body fold like a binder, her ribs shining like high-priced needles. She's tiny, gorgeous, everything we've dreamed of being, maybe were once, long before now. Ginger does our best skills without even trying and it solidifies her place as center flyer and center jumper. I peek at Nicole's body, also slimmer than mine, and try to suck in my gut. Maybe if I were thinner Mary-Ellen would treat me like she does the other girls: not well, but not as severe.

Maybe I'll just skip a few bites of food at home while nobody's looking, I think.

"Bagels and Lox, standing tuck fulls, let's go," Heath tells me. He comes to my left side to spot me. Compared to six months ago, his arms have to do way more work. I'm one of the largest girls on the team now, maybe *the* largest.

A hefty exhale escapes his lips each time I set my arms up and he has to get his hands under my back, around my waist, and push me up, giving me the height to land on my feet. I do, but I still can't commit to it without him standing there. My mind begins to unpack the trick like it's a bag, spilling the contents across my brain to mess up my thoughts. I break it down: swing, set, pull, twist. But then I'm standing there too long, not going, trying to work up the nerve to chuck it. Heath and Nicole and Ginger shout, "Go! Do it! You have it! Come on, already!" And Mary-Ellen just stands on the other side of the mat wiping the grime from under her nails with the edge of a nail file. Not even worth her time.

Eventually, Heath and my teammates catch on that they're not helping and leave me to stand there alone, afraid. I'm a long ways off from competing a standing full: one more skill I won't have in time for Worlds.

"You just have to get this in better shape," says Heath, coming back like a boomerang to knock his knuckles on my head.

In better shape. Does he mean my mind? I solidify that I need to eat less, only a half a sandwich tonight, not a full one.

We run the routine a couple times and I throw my skills and land them, but not well. Once upon a time I stood out on the mat. Like Ginger. Now I'm just trying to not draw attention to myself, my body moving to the rhythm of the bodies around me like water. I'm as still as possible—no ripples, no waves.

Mary-Ellen starts watching me again. I can feel her red-laser eyes pierce my skin.

Afterward, she says: "Not even close. Go again!"

Afterward, she says: "What did I tell you girls? An ugly hit ain't winning us shit!!"

Afterward, she says: "Pick it up! What are you bitches on, level two? Shoshana, let's go!"

We all give more until we're sore and panting. Heath calls for a water break. I wonder, if it were up to Mary-Ellen, if we would eat or drink at all. Maybe they'll invent artificial cheerleaders one day and she'll coach those robots to a world title.

I'm chewing my cheek until the pain draws me back into our practice space. An hour and a half left. I think I can make it.

On our water break in the cubby room, Ginger taps on her phone. A flood of messages appears, which slightly depresses me since she's twelve and I'm seventeen and I don't have anyone texting me. Except, that isn't exactly true. When I unlock my passcode, my phone opens to dozens of notifications. No, not dozens. Hundreds. Over six thousand . . .? Nearly all from Twitter?

Lorri has texted me ten times. I glance at her last one: *Call me immediately!*

I pull up my Twitter account, where most of the traffic seems to be coming from.

"You wrote this?" Meredith asks before I can read it.

She holds up what looks like a tweet sent from my account. A wheezing pain begins building in my chest like a widening cloud. I'm going to puke and not the way bulimics do, not the *I'll feel better afterward* kind. I'm going to be sick. Really sick.

Because I didn't direct message Carmela. I tweeted at her. Publicly.

Slit Mary-Ellen's throat. That's what I said and they think it's a real threat. They think I'm a psychopath, far from the good girl they thought I was, now a creep, a traitor, a loser, a freak. Parents are sharpening their pitchforks online and they want me off the team, off the show, ASAP.

I delete the tweet from my account, but it's too late. It's been up for people to screen grab and retweet. *@ACETravis* retweeted my original tweet and wrote: *It's true. She hates Mary-Ellen. Told me herself that she hates her whole team. Probs only there 4 TV publicity.* And his tweet has been retweeted over a hundred times. More and more people are tagging me in posts every second. It's suddenly hard to swallow, like there's no saliva on my tongue.

All I want for Christmas is to see @ShoshanaWinnick get kicked off Garwood Elite for being a disloyal bitch. #ShoshanaSlitsHerself

Everyone @ the CheerWork gym wants to go home but we're too into #ShoshanaSlitsHerself! What a brat! That's NO team spirit.

They're still in practice apparently!! Have fun, traitor. There's a crowd of ppl waiting to CHEER you out the door!

The hashtag *#ShoshanaSlitsHerself* is trending . . . nationally? Can that be right? Even non-cheerleaders seem to be clued in to what's happening. I'm the entertainment. My head pounds and blood laps against my ears so loudly I can't hear what Nicole beside me is saying. The words I read on the screen are not real. How can they be, when they're all in an app?

I shrink down to my knees, into a ball on the cubby room floor. There are no cameras here, but there might as well be. The overwhelming sense that I am being watched has not left me since RR. No, since before that. When I first stepped into GE's gym.

Someone says, "Give her space," and people move away. But I feel more like an animal at the zoo, something slimy that nobody cares to touch. The waterworks start up, hot and fast, and pinching my thigh doesn't block them out. Everything I've kept at bay bubbles up and I can't remember the last time I screamed, like really screamed, except in fourth grade on Halloween when K.J. jumped out from behind the basement door in a Joker mask and I lost it. Why am I thinking about that right now? What is happening to my brain?

"May the Lord have mercy on your soul," Angela hisses.

"She should've prayed to Jesus with us at all those practices," swears Ginger.

"We all wanted her gone anyway," says Bri. "Now we'll get our wish."

I don't see it coming—the way I lunge at them, grabbing somebody's hair and not caring whose it is. Black dots float in front of my eyes and suddenly I am being plucked into the air like a doll, which is fitting because I feel as un-lifelike as one. Restrained by multiple pairs of hands, I do the only thing I can think of. I chant her name in my head. Or maybe I say it aloud. I can't tell what's real and what's not anymore. *Rowan. Rowan. Rowan.*

I curl up, wanting to die, wanting nothing at all except to not be here anymore. *She must hear me,* I think. *She'll hear me and make this all go away.*

Just before I black out, I see Mary-Ellen standing a few feet away, her arms crossed, her chin raised, her nose pointed up in the air like she can smell my fear, like she's just waiting to taste it.

26
Rowan

Having August as a roommate is a different experience than having Sophie or Donna or Jazzy or you. She's quiet, most interesting when she opens her mouth and an unexpected, thick Southern accent pops out. I like that she's from Tennessee, that she fills out the stereotype. Hunting, fishing, dirt bikes. She doesn't talk much. Actually, she doesn't talk at all unless someone asks her to. I do quite a few times, always sticking to safe subjects—what our hometowns are like, what we do in our free time, what we used to love when we were little, what we used to hate when we were little, what we love now, what we hate now.

August flosses her teeth beside me in the Blue bathroom and I run cold water over my fingers, using them to slick back my half-purple, half-blonde hair. It's a strange sight to see so much of it growing back in.

We walk into the living room for our phone calls and August grabs her cell phone first, calling her "old man" or "pops" who shouts so loud into the receiver that I can hear him from half a room away.

"Cheaney came looking for you. I told him to knock off," my mother says first thing on our call. She picked up, which is a start, but I can tell she's mad I didn't come home. My release could be on the horizon now. It's already been two weeks and I've been obeying all the commandments. Certainly the nurses are considering it.

"Good. He's not my boyfriend. Tell him I said so if he comes again."

"Count on it," she says. "Still no word from that friend of yours. Shakira?"

"*Shoshana*," I correct. There have been no letters, not so much as a whisper from you for the past two weeks. "And no, nothing."

I'm Blue, so I could write to you, Shosh, but what would I say? If you realized you're better off without me, I'm not going to convince you otherwise. You probably want a clean break, or maybe you extended your stay in Houston and need to focus on cheer right now. It's hard to know anything from in here when I'm trying to get better. Avoiding social media like a red-tinted spider. And if you're trying to stay better like I think you are, I can't fault you for breaking that promise.

"What did you do?" my mother asks. She figures I drove you away or killed you. Fifty-fifty.

"Why do you always assume it's my fault?"

"Blood of my blood," she says.

"Well, you're wrong." My finger creeps closer to the "end call" button. She thinks every word that passes her lips is one hundred percent fact. Meanwhile, she's never even met you, Shosh. The idea that she could be wrong—it's like the thought has never even occurred to her.

"Just because she hasn't reached out lately doesn't mean

she won't," I snap. Maybe I do fault you for breaking that promise though, Shoshana, just a little.

My mother snickers in that hissing, spitting way, the one that assures she's in a cruel mood. "Right, like how I used to believe your father was working late contracting jobs and not fucking around with itty-bittys your age."

"Shoshana's not fucking anybody," I say.

And she says, "Everybody's fucking everybody."

We simultaneously make excuses to get off the phone and Hart gives my shoulder a quick squeeze before I go find August again.

August and I walk side by side into Personal Projects. The nurses said I have to learn how to be productive again, be a student, be consistent with a structure, which I've loathed in the past. Get used to it, they said, and I am.

For the past two weeks, I've scavenged every corner of my brain for a personal project. I've started ones, my favorite being a research project on the pubic-grooming habits of women who *do* watch porn versus the ones who *don't.* Still, to the nurses' relief, I abandoned it within the hour. As we walk, August throws me the bone of "Use your family. That's what I'm doing."

But what is there to say about my family? I know you ten times better than I know my mother or father, Shosh, and you know me ten times better than they do. So, maybe, when August says family, that's who she really means. You.

August pivots in front of the art room, meeting me toe to toe, blocking the way with her body. She's one of the only girls in RR who might have a shittier life than the one I've led. This is her tenth treatment center and she was only six and a half the first time she was hospitalized. We don't talk about this one-on-one, but during group therapy, she opens like a book.

"Maybe you ought to sympathize with your Ma more. Interview her for your personal project," August says, knowing a few basics when it comes to me.

August is, for all intents and purposes, me 2.0. We both want to do better despite everything that's come before. We also think we understand shit we have no fucking clue about. Recently I've seen that, how I'm still seventeen, how I assume I know it all. What on God's earth do I fucking know about existence? Nada. No more than anyone else, at least. And even if I swear I do one day, the next day will bring some change that will cancel it all out. In the end, I'll know nothing. You'll know nothing. We'll all know nothing. Bet on that.

August spins on her heel and I follow her in, considering what interviewing my mother might look like. It would probably be like one of those "ask a relative about where you're from" assignments we had in middle school. I'd just make up happy endings, write stories I wished would come true, and never really ask.

Behind the art room, inside the computer lab, August and I take our seats and get to work. Her suggestion has given me a new idea, about the stories I used to write, about the ones I might write now.

"Can you girls help us, please?" Robinson asks. She's pulling personal projects off the walls to replace them with new ones. August and I, along with the rest of the Blue girls, start peeling the construction paper off the paint. We tape new projects in the now open spots. The new ones seem brighter, more neon, making the room look like confetti cake, sprinkles of colors between the beige walls. I tape up a red poster with Brandy's name on top. *Commercial Sells Best* is titled above the research, a bunch of book jackets and their corresponding sales. The results are pretty bad for literary writers: the stark shallowness of America today.

August wanders around, sniffing at reports and drawings. I trail my trimmed nails over the sheetrock, mapping the maze of projects. Then my finger stops. It rests next to your name. The bottom of the *S* snakes under *hoshana* and my eyes dance across the whole project until I find you, a picture of your side profile.

I haven't seen you in what feels like years. This is the closest I've come to contact. My first thought is that I miss the bump on your nose, miss your cheeks, miss your touch. Then, I'm missing everything.

"Is that hers?" August asks, pronouncing it *hurs*.

I point to your name, tempted to say "No shit, Sherlock" or "I didn't know you were blind," but I keep asking myself, "What would Shoshana say?" before I open my mouth. I realize you'd say nothing. Certainly, not anything cruel. So I let you guide me through this, trending upward. That's the bittersweet part of our separation—I can still see you and hear you and feel you, even when you're not here.

I find my photo on your board, my crotch hot-glued

between a pic of love handles and a double chin. On the edges of my photo are stickers of caterpillars and suns, glittering grass and watering cans, things any five-year-old would die to decorate with. My zipped-up jeans are creased and faded from washes, but they look sea blue because you've colored them in. And even though you're not here to explain, I understand exactly what the purpose is, what your art is trying to say. My body isn't something to fear; it's something to love. For the first time, I see myself through your eyes: *beautiful,* the way you said it covered in snow.

I've already chosen to get better. I'm Blue. I'm on the up-and-out. But today, I choose it again. Staring at your art, I choose it, Shoshana. And I'll probably have to choose it a bunch more times, maybe every day, every hour, every goddamn second. No overnight success—isn't that what they say? There's no instruction manual for this get-better shtick. If there were, I would've fixed myself the first time. I wouldn't need RR. I wouldn't need you. Now I rely on those things, day in and day out. Rely on your voice to be there in my head, to lead the way. I may walk this path alone, but I can only see the road, Shoshana, because you've given me the light.

Shoshana

Mom and Dad are in the dark. The sneaking, the hiding, the avoiding, the way I held peanut butter against the sides of my teeth for over an hour last night before I was excused from the dinner table, then scraped it back out with a toothbrush so hard I chipped one of my back molars. They have no freaking clue.

Nobody knows what's happening with me. I'm in shock, I guess, or *they* guess, meaning Mom and Dr. Colwell, our pediatrician. Mom will abide by anything he says, so when he's the one to claim "it's just shock, it'll pass," she believes it.

I don't. I know better. I've learned from Rowan and her windmill brain, always turning, always instructing me that, when you want something bad enough, you'll find a way to make it happen. Right now, the only thing I want—the only plausible thing that doesn't involve a time machine—is to disappear, to get rid of this hideous body that I somehow tricked myself into believing wasn't horrible, wasn't ugly, was worth anyone's time.

Foolish. I've called myself that word two dozen times today, and yet, it feels too kind. *Foolish* has an undertone of playful school children, easy-to-correct mistakes. I don't deserve that luxury. There's nothing easy to correct here.

Most of the day I spend lying in bed on my right side, though sometimes I get bed sores and switch to my left. I can't find motivation to go outside or even downstairs, and since my mouth is now a one-way traffic lane for calories, I'm even stricter with what I swallow.

Mom and Dad aren't clever enough to catch my schemes. Even with Dad watching my every move, he doesn't know where I hide the food. The best spots are in obvious places, like the liquor cabinet they never use. Sweatpants with Ziploc bags taped inside the pockets. A dark cup they think I'm drinking out of when really I'm just spitting food back into it.

Look at me now, I think. *Rowan would be so proud to see the accomplished liar I've become. Look how good I've gotten at playing this game.*

Last night, I dreamed I was back at the GE gym, only Rowan was there with me and I wasn't surrounded by a swarm of pointing cheerleaders. The place was empty and Rowan was holding a knife. She asked if I wanted to hold it and I said yes. Our hands brushed when I took the hilt. Then I looked at her and then the knife and I turned it so the knife pointed at me.

I waited and waited for the impulse to do it, but just as I was almost there, about to *stab*, not *slit*, Rowan swiped it back and said, "Gotcha!" and patted me on the back for playing along so well, for my progress since RR. I felt myself sink with disappointment and woke up with the same feeling.

There's a light knock at my door—two knocks, one word. "Shoshana?"

Mom doesn't wait. She comes in and sits down on the bed,

tears in her eyes that have lingered there ever since she picked me up from the gym a week ago. Being aware of her pity only amplifies everything I feel for myself: embarrassment, anger, regret, shame, disgust.

"Please come downstairs. We'll put on some junky TV and have popcorn. We'll just relax and cuddle up together."

Relax? I want to laugh, but that would only result in more tears. Doesn't she see how much work she is asking me to do? First, I would have to get up from bed. And even if I could sit up, she's asking me to walk downstairs and sit where there are people—possibly K.J.'s friends if they come up from the basement. I can hear their rowdy howls, their roughhousing, from two floors up. Don't get me started on the popcorn.

I make a moaning noise. It's meant to say, *I heard you. Thanks but no thanks.*

"Shoshana," she says, firmer this time. I guess she didn't get the message. "Get up. Right now. Quit acting like your life is over. I know you don't have perspective on this yet; you're young, but one day you will, and you'll be sorry you wasted so much of your life in bed."

Attempt two—the hard approach, I think. *She's finally realized her soothing methods aren't working.* This won't work either, but it at least gives me the itch to speak.

"The internet is forever, Mom. That's the point. You didn't have technology growing up. You don't understand."

At middle school assemblies, they used to warn us about how the World Wide Web is forever. They said our posts might one day be used to deny us jobs or admission to schools. The information, even if you delete it, is still out there, and so we needed to keep it all clean.

Mom didn't grow up with a reputation to protect online. She doesn't understand what this means, the severity of what's happened to me. The online persona is just as important as the in-person one. Maybe more so, because it's the version everyone sees. And when everyone sees it, everyone believes it. And when everyone believes it, they can usually will it into existence.

I am example A. Strangers think my life is over and they're right. It is.

Mom folds her arms over her chest. She still wants to fight. "Things weren't so easy in my heyday either, lady."

I mumble, "Not this way," and she tucks a loose strand of hair behind her ear.

"I don't understand how you have the energy to argue with me, yet you can't pick your head up from that pillow."

I close my eyes.

"Shoshana."

I open my eyes. "I want to change my name."

"Your name?"

"Anytime anyone googles me now, all they're going to see are articles about what happened. I need a new name. A new identity."

"What is this—a bit? You're not changing your name, Shoshana. It's a beautiful name and it's you."

I cover my ears and curl my legs under the covers. "Can you just bring me a bagel?"

Another trick that kills two birds with one stone: asking her to bring me food. This way, she thinks I'm hungry, that I want to eat, that I'm still healthy, but it also gets her to go away.

Before RR, I cut down on food because I wanted to be a better cheerleader; now, I do it because it's comforting. Ever since *#ShoshanaSlitsHerself*, I've forgotten what it feels like to be warm, to bathe in sunlight, to have my cheeks glow red with blood. My brain has made a box for what happened and filed it away in a tight corner of my brain marked "Do Not Open." I keep it closed by making rules to avoid it all, and the first rule is no eating more than two hundred calories per day.

I've done that for a little over a week now. No one can tell as long as I keep myself nested in covers.

Mom returns with a peanut butter bagel and, after small talk that spirals to nowhere, leaves again. I manage to crawl out of bed this time, but only to the bathroom to ball up the bagel dough, let it plop, sink, and sit for a minute in the toilet before flushing. I make sure to leave smears of peanut butter on the plate so it looks like I made a common man's mess.

In the mirror, I pull at the skin that clings to my face, hollow eyes and flat cheeks. The box marked "Do Not Open" springs up, jack-in-the box style, revealing the Twitter fiasco. *Like I said, I'd ditch GE for you guys if I could, but first I'd have 2 slit Mary-Ellen's throat.*

Why would you ever write that? my conscience pests. *Why? Why? Why? What's wrong with you? Do you ever* think *before you* act*? What happened to "if you don't have anything nice to say, don't* say it?" *What the hell, Shoshana? Is this what you wanted? Is this what you did because you know it's what you deserve?*

Make this go away. I beg a genie who never comes.

What if I had never sent that tweet? I will live with that *What If* in my mind for the rest of my life.

In the reflection, I watch myself touch my neck, my arms, my hips, my thighs. I part my hair to find the bald spot on the crown of my scalp, the ugliest part of me. I stare at it and bore my eyes into it, refusing to blink.

A seventeen-year-old girl with a bald spot. How disgusting. How grotesquely unnatural.

If that were the only thing wrong with my appearance—a bald spot—I could fix it. Get extensions or a wig. But that's just the tip of the iceberg when it comes to my obvious flaws.

Look at yourself, can you even stand it? My conscience slithers between my ears. *Who would want to be friends with you? Rowan doesn't. She never liked you. She only tolerated you because you worshipped her, you lazy ogre, you asexual freak.*

That last one takes the kicker and I physically shrivel, sinking down onto the cool tile floor. With sluggish movements, I drag myself into the molding shower and reach up to spin the knob, water spurting from hypothermic cold to skin-searing hot.

"You can drown from drinking too much water," Rowan told me once. I open my mouth to the drops above me, let them slap my tongue and slide down the back of my snotty throat. *How much do I have to gulp down to get the job done?*

But internal drowning isn't my cause for getting wet. It's

my hair. The bald spots are more visible when I'm drenched, and I want to see the damage. I want to see just how much of my scalp is on display.

Two hundred extra strands shed before I get out, and when I see how little there is left in the mirror, I snatch the pair of yellow scissors from the left-hand drawer, sick of being Shoshana, sick of clipping it every which way to hide the truth.

With a steady hand, I lift the longest piece straight above my head, sliding the scissors all the way down until they're a half inch above my scalp. The stands are stuck helplessly in between the blades, no choice in the matter.

In my head, I count down from five. I don't make it to three before I ball my hand into a fist and hear the first whizzing snip.

Rowan

When I finally get a letter, it's not from you.

No, this letter is from my mother and it's a total of twenty-two words. *Thought you would want to see these. Come home already, little boat. I'm bored without you and desperate for advice on Wyatt.*

I'm shocked she spent time writing it, addressing it, locating a stamp. That's a lot to ask of her these days. Plus, she stuck two photographs in the envelope. It almost makes me forgive her for bringing up Wyatt, her ex-boyfriend scumbag who literally makes me gag upon mention.

August bends over to see the first photo in the envelope. *October 1999* is scribbled on the back with the word *Halloween*. I'm only two years old, in a stained pumpkin suit that hides everything except my tiny legs and chubby arms. In one hand I hold a baby trick-or-treat basket, and in the other, a fistful of my father's blond locks. I sit on his shoulders and my mother is tucked small and safe under his arm. We look cohesive, perfect, the American dream. Just like your family, Shoshana, but even then, we were a raggedy bunch. My father dressed up as a construction worker and my mother went as a waitress. Even for a day, they couldn't pretend their lives were any other way.

August snatches up the photo, squinting at my father. "Your dad looks like an off-brand Heath Ledger."

"If I had a dollar for every time my mother wished he had a heart attack too——"

August covers my mouth with her hand. Her fingers smell like lemon. "Don't speak ill of the dead."

I peel her hand away. "I'm not. I'm speaking ill of my parents, the living."

August gives a stern *you know what I mean* look and I ignore her. As it turns out, she's not really Rowan 2.0. Together, we check out the other picture. Ironically, it's of my mother and father's wedding day. They're standing in front of a small church that desperately needs a power wash and my mother is blissfully grinning at the camera in her white satin dress.

There was a woman who came to RR once, to teach us poetry as a special elective. She brought the poem called "I Go Back to May 1937," by Sharon Olds, as the example. This photograph feels so close to the one mentioned in that poem. And I see what Olds was saying, how sometimes, our parents' lives before us feel like ghost stories. This photo of them, so in love, so clueless, is like seeing ghosts. I have that same urge as Olds, a desperate craving to tell their old selves, *Call it off. You're too young. You're too malleable. You'll get divorced. You'll bring a kid into this world who, most nights, will long for nothing more than to fling herself out of it.*

I wrote a poem about suicide during that poetry class. No one understood it. The translation for *colgate* in Spanish means "go hang yourself," but without the context, I got questions like "What did you mean in sixth grade, your best friend told you to Colgate?" or Alyssa's more philosophical "Why does it end like that? With 'Colgate. Number 1 brand recommended by dentists?'"

That woman never came back to RR. I think she's some unpublished poet from outside the area who got scared off by Alyssa's work, a sonnet about a woman who morphs into a toddler. That, or RR didn't pay up. You might think this place has our best interests at heart, Shosh, but first and foremost, eating disorders are a business. The more girls they send away, certified better, the more their statistics improve. The more their statistics improve, the more girls come in, and the more money they make. I'm not saying it's all bad. I'm only saying, it's not all good.

I stare at the photo of my mother, who is, I admit, undeniably beautiful.

Forget what I said, I think to her and my father, the ghosts, because I am like Olds. Bad lives make for better stories. I'll walk away from this better than I was. I'll turn whatever my life has been into something bigger, better, brighter.

Like that, RR becomes my own solo self-care writer's workshop. That woman who taught us poetry neglected prose, and I swear, when I start writing it, I don't put the pen down for days. The nurses and August say they've never seen me this quiet, that it's startling them. You haven't seen me like this either, Shosh, because it's completely new for me. All my energy poured into something. The stories go on as far as I can gas them and I sleep with my notebook tucked under my pillow.

My personal project is a fiction story. "The best fiction is far more true than any journalism." That's what Faulkner said—according to Hart, who quoted this to me—and that's how I feel, writing the characters who speak to me with voices so loud I can't ignore them. I let my imagination run wild and start a story that's main plot revolves around a talking pumpkin—inspired, I suppose, by that Halloween picture of little me.

But the story is not about the pumpkin, or the fact that it can talk. It's about the mother and daughter who find it abandoned in a lonesome patch, who sneak it out together and use the pumpkin to repair their relationship. It's what August wanted me to do with my mother in my personal project: make peace. Somehow, I'm able to do a part of the healing on my own.

"I'm surprised they're letting you do that," says August, scrunching her waves and whipping them into a microfiber towel.

"Letting me do what?"

"Write a story as your project. There's no research in that."

August blows out a large exhale. Being in the same space as me all day is rubbing her the wrong way. You'd be fine with it, Shoshana, because you used to conform to whatever we were doing, whatever I wanted to do, and you'd make the best out of the situation. I think about that a lot. About *you* a lot. I didn't always treat you the best. More than that, I used you, in the way you always feared. Friends use each other, yes, but I did more than that. I molded you like clay, remaking you into a vision of goodness, anything to avoid my dark place.

I owe you all sorts of apologies, which I plan to give, if I ever get the chance.

"There's no research in it," I tell August, "but there's art. Besides, I think we both know I shouldn't be on the computers right now. They may block some sites, but that's a slippery slope for me."

"So, what happens when they let you out? Are you going to live like a hermit?"

I wind my hair around my ear, checking to see how long it is. "If it keeps me from coming back here, yes."

Hart had us do a mindfulness session yesterday where she talked about body neutrality, how babies and toddlers eat instinctually because food is just food and not a moral issue to them. There we sat, watching our bellies rise and fall, imagining our bellies as the bellies of babies. *What do you need? What do you want? How can I best give it to you?* Since I've been looking at my body like it's separate from my brain, like it's a baby I'm trying to keep alive and happy and coo-coo-cooing, I've been eating with less grief. A ridiculous technique? Definitely. Working? For now.

At dinner in the Blue kitchen, I eat until I'm full and nearly miss the calorie goal. The chocolate chip cookie puts me just over the edge, and I think they'll want me to eat some of the popcorn with our "twenty-five days of Christmas" movie tonight, *The Polar Express.*

Donna and Sophie sit on the floor in front of August and

me, resting their heads on the couch cushions between our knees. It's nice when we get to be all together like this. I stroke Sophie's red hair and she climbs onto the couch to sit between my legs, back leaned against my chest. She's warm and I'm warm and I feel like this is exactly where I'm meant to be.

During the commercial break, Donna throws popcorn at my mouth for me to catch, missing half the time because her aim sucks and I'm a moving target. Sophie wants to join in, but I advise her not to for fear of her splitting her mostly healed stitches on a kernel.

We're in motion, yelling, laughing, hanging monkey-style off the couch, which is why we don't immediately notice the front door open, the three figures filing in. Two are parents, and parents are never allowed directly in the center.

My whole world stops when I see the phantom in the front hallway, faintly recognizable, closer to the first day I met you than the day we said goodbye. But even that feels too generous a statement. Dark circles curve under your eyes like mirrored eye shadow and your lips are cracked and peeling and blue, frozen from winter air. Most notably, your hair has been cut short, shorter than mine, chopped unevenly. My eyes linger there.

You don't see me at first. There are too many of us crammed into one small space and, by the crazed *holy fuck everyone's here* look on your face, you expected us to be in bed already, tucked in, lights out. I read your mind, your plan to sneak in unseen after hours, not judged.

Your mother's and father's faces have a swollen pallor to

them that scares me. Your mother is crying and your father is fighting the same fate. You frighten them both.

A nurse clicks off the TV and ushers everyone back to their rooms quickly, the girls simultaneously groaning about missing the other half of *The Polar Express*. As we start to creep to and around the stairs, you spot me and catch me by the arm, forcing me to look at you. I feel your fingers tighten around my wrist brace, how thin your own bundles of flesh have become since I last saw you. Your attempt to hide the obvious weight loss under sweatpants doesn't work. Your neck is far too narrow.

"Hey," you say.

I'm too wigged out by the haircut—by all of it—to formulate a response. This is not the Shoshana I know. Maybe that's the point, the angle you were going for.

"I missed you," you say, then slam your fist against your forehead like it's a punishment. "I missed *us*."

I know I should be formulating a plan to help you. That's what best friends do. I imagine going Gray again, being reincarnated, déjà vu, back to start. But I can't bring myself to backtrack. My first instinct is to pull away from you because too many Rowans have suffered too much. Too many Rowans have been ruined and this layer cannot be another one undone.

"What happened?" I ask, and your knees give in, sinking into me. I hug you back and you're laughing and laughing until you're sobbing and sobbing and coating my skin cells with your slippery clear tears. Your tall body hunches over my shorter one but now you feel so fragile.

"I don't know what to do," you choke, tears bursting out

of you. I remember I thought you never cried. This must be everything you've ever dammed, gushing out in a Niagara Falls event. "I want it to end, like you said. I want to be gone."

"It's okay," I swear. It's a false statement that pops out, a childlike reflex. I rub your back as your nails dig into my shoulders.

Nurse Hart studies me carefully and I nod at her that I'm okay. She takes your parents outside to talk, leaving me here with you and Robinson, who watches from the sidelines, holding her emotions back as she sees you, the good patient, and all her hard work unravel.

They didn't fix you. They have to start again. This job is never-ending for them, and for the first time, I have to admire the nurses here. Robinson and Hart and Schultz and Kelly and Walsh and Hope. They could make a hundred girls better today and they'd still have a new batch of a hundred more tomorrow.

"Promise you won't leave me," you say, grown fingernails raking red lines down my arms.

I brush away your tears, but what is there to say? We both know the one thing you want is the one thing I can't give you. I can't stay or be your strength. Not when a part of me is starting to believe I did this to you.

Whale sounds of agony pour from your throat. "Promise!" you demand.

I remember your eyes being innocent. Now, they're anything but.

I don't promise, not to you, but silently, to myself, I make a promise that I will get out of here and get better. I will be more than this—for the both of us.

29
Shoshana

Two showers. Three breakdowns. Four times the effort to get out of bed. Five meals choking down Ensure before I relent and consume foods that aren't liquid.

Rowan comes to visit sometimes. Always when I'm at my worst—a tip she receives from the nurses, her half-friends now. She'll knock on the door and won't ask me what happened, even though I can tell she wants to. She's been Blue for a month, twelve of those days being ones I've been back for. She gets to go home tomorrow morning, so I've come up with one final plan to make it all okay.

I was too weak to run away with her before. But now I'm not. I'm ready.

I play dead, a plan of my own creation to get the nurses to bring her to my room of solitude. They're hoping she'll pull me out of this depression. Or maybe Rowan is the one who thinks she can pull me out of it, and the nurses are cautiously letting her see me, thinking she can handle it. Either way, they all want me Gray again. But to be Gray, I'd have to be something. At the moment, I am not even good enough for that.

Tomorrow, on the outside with Rowan, we will be nothing together. Combine two nothings. You get something: enough.

"You finally learned silent treatment," Rowan commends,

kicking her feet up on the edge of my bed. She's still Rowan. Little feet and skinny limbs, but her Kool-Aid hair has faded, making her almost shiny blonde. I'm bonier than her now. *An accomplishment*, I think. Or maybe that's her role—The Extremist. Maybe I'm supposed to be the chunky friend who sits and watches from the sidelines, the good angel on her shoulder.

"Are you going to grow it out?" I ask, reaching to flick her nearly chin-length hair.

She pulls down two of the front pieces, measuring their uneven length. "For a little. Maybe I'll go as short as you, Hathaway." She reaches over, ruffling my spikes, expecting me to laugh, to tease, to play the game. But how can I? My entire life has been ruined and she doesn't even know it. Soon, she will. If she agrees to run with me, I'll tell her everything. For real. She'll understand why I am this way, why anyone would be if they were me.

"Let's go," I say, and she doesn't need to ask, *Go where?* She can still read my mind. She knows I'm not talking about downstairs or to watch Ms. Matusick's dance class or anywhere within a hundred miles of this place. I mean out of here. Out of this center. This state. This country. She sees right through me and that, if nothing else, has remained the same between us.

Nurse Hart is at the door, but I don't care if she hears. Let her lock the doors, handcuff us to the bunk beds. If Rowan agrees, we'll find a way out. The two of us, together, will always find a way.

"Please," I add, and my voice cracks, desperate. She's the

one person I have left in the world. Everyone else is stained with what happened, with the show, with pitchforks. My mother with cheerleading. My father with his competitive drive, embedded in me. My school, my town, my life. I need a new one. We can be greeters, like she said. Live off hipsters in LA. Live a simple life on some farm where we do nothing but garden and trace sketches of Frida in the dirt. *We are always one decision away from a completely different life.* Someone said that. I can't remember who. But her decision will change my life forever. It has to.

"I need you to say yes," I warn. "Say yes and I'll do whatever you want for the rest of—"

"Eternity?" she catches, biting back her smile. She's not getting it. She's not taking me seriously. Or worse, she's playing it off. The way I once tried to do with her planned escape. Instead I snitched. How badly I wish I hadn't. How badly I want to skip back to that section of our story and make up the rest.

"Yes," I say. "Eternity. My life. It's yours. Take it."

"You sound like Donna." She chuckles.

"I'm. Not. Donna."

"No, you're not," she agrees, getting more serious.

"Please,"—I take her hand like a lifeline—"I'll do anything. I'll make sure you stay healthy, if that's what you want. Or I won't let you eat. I'll kiss you and like it. I'll be who you want me to be. Just please say yes."

"No."

She says it plainly, not particularly soft or stern. It's just a word. No. Simple. Final. Two letters from the English alphabet that, when put together, represent the gesture of a shaken head, and still, my brain can't make sense of it. She can't say no. This is not "two roads diverged." This is one road. One us. This is what she wanted.

"Yes," I snap, gritting my teeth. I look at my *tsk-tsk*. It's gone. So is my faith. The only God I know now is one I question too much to believe in. "After everything I've done for you — jumped out a window, followed you like worship, reassured you. You owe me this," I say.

I mean every word.

Rowan stands, nonthreatening, just ready to leave. "This is my fault," she says. "I manipulated you, Shosh. I was using you to make myself feel better about all the things that hurt. I was pointing out your issues to avoid facing my own. There is no us. We're two people and I shouldn't have tried to make us one. I'm sorry. God, there aren't enough ways to make it up to you, but I am really, truly sorry."

"And what are your issues?" I spit. "Being raped?"

She flinches the tiniest bit and I know I'm being cruel, but I feel nothing. My mouth is the weapon. *Fire*, I demand. "That no one wants you now? That no one will ever love you because you're a cold, heartless bitch?"

"That's enough," Hart says from the doorframe, ready to pull Rowan from this pointless rescue mission. Rowan stays, holding a hand up to Hart. A signal.

"I heard about what happened to you out there," she says. "Blue girls have computers, you know. The trending stuff, the show and the team firing you. I didn't even look at their screens, but the girls told me about it. They made you want to die, didn't they?"

Her voice is honey smooth. Gentle. Water meant to douse my fire, but it leaves me steaming instead. She's saying this in front of Nurse Hart, confessing that the Blue girls broke computer rules and assuming they won't get in trouble. That's how close they are now. Like we were. The betrayal is all too much.

"Get out," I hiss.

She stands still.

"Get out!" I scream, and Nurse Hart pulls Rowan toward the door.

From out in the hall, she says, "I leave tomorrow morning. Don't let that be the last thing you say to me."

"Oh, what? You think I owe you some famous last words?" My mouth tastes bitter, ugly as the rest of me. "How's this? Go fuck yourself!"

She shakes her head, thinking those magic thoughts I can't hear. "That anger you feel . . . I've had it before and it almost tore me apart. But I'm here now. I'm okay, just like you will be one day."

Something—whatever of me is left intact—seeps through the anger and melts at this. Could she be right? Am I not completely doomed without her?

The fact that she's the one delivering that message makes me, just a little bit, believe it.

She must see the switch in my eyes, the one from bleak nothingness to a speckle, a grain, a pinch of hope. In return, she offers the tilt of her lips.

"Promise?" I ask, still in an angry tone I can't yet lose.

She didn't promise to stay here with me when I first got back, even when she could have and revoked it later. I know she won't lie. She will only promise what she believes to be true, in her heart.

She nods, uncrossed fingers in view. "Promise."

Mom used to say a good night's sleep could cure anything. But every day I wake up from now on will be painful, at least a little bit. Even with the small hope Rowan has given me, I don't see any pain-free life for me, even a month, a year, a decade down the road. All that said, there's something okay about it. I don't know what's right for me anymore. The gut instinct, the knowing better, it's gone. Possibly for good. There's something unsettling, but also nice there. It's entertaining, imagining where my life might go when I don't have to be perfect.

I run downstairs to catch Rowan before she leaves and she's there, waiting for me next to the door. A woman who could be her twin, just a little taller with laugh lines and a skirt that's up her thighs, stands on the front porch. Everything about her screams of Rowan. Long hair in an oddly girlish ponytail. Bangle bracelets that chime like the ones I wore in elementary school. It has to be her mom. She has a small cross tattoo on her left collarbone, just as Rowan once mentioned.

With her duffel bag over her back, Rowan moves in for the hug first. I can't speak or communicate how much I already miss her and who we were in here before all of this happened. I really wish I hadn't told her to fuck off.

"You'll find me in the future," she says. It's not a question.

"I'm not sure I have much of one." I try to say it as a joke, but there are tears shining in my eyes again.

She lifts my chin, like I'm better than I think I am, like I'm worthy of more than this and will be more, not a doubt in her mind.

"Yes. I'll find you," I say, not sure when that will be.

"Not if I find you first." She winks and the *Stand By Me* reference nearly shatters me again. We do our handshake, the one where we spit saliva into our palms and slide our hands to grip the other's elbow. Then we intertwine our arms, her wrist fully healed and my entire body in the process of sewing my internal wounds. I squeeze her hand like she squeezed mine that night on the ledge of the bathroom window, holding on for dear life.

There's no way to make her stay, so the best I can do is send her off like it's my choice. Pretend to know where this is all leading. Pretend to be in on it, just as she taught me.

Rowan's mother glances at me through the entryway. She's filled out the final paperwork, her signature a scrawl Rowan could forge in an instant, I'm sure.

"Try not to look at it," Rowan advises me under her breath, side-eyeing her mother.

We both manage a sly grin. For a sad second, it feels like the old us.

"You know"—she nudges her shoulder into mine—"in

the multiverse, there's a version of us who never met, and a world where you win Worlds and I take church seriously."

"A world where we ran away together."

"Yes." She smiles, but it's without teeth. "One for that too. But from here on out, it's all choice. We're not fated anymore, Shosh. We never were, really. We created that. So we'll create this too." Rowan gulps down her seriousness and her face turns playful, almost sad. "Who knows, maybe I'll be back here with you in a week."

My voice is stern, forceful in a way I didn't know I could be yet, when I say, "You won't." And most of me now wants her to go. To be decently happy and healthy and prove to me that it's possible for me, for any of us, to do the same.

Rowan drops my hand, hugs the nurses, hugs me again, and heads out the door. Her mom leans against their small red Toyota, which is pulled up to the front of the parking lot, engine left running. They get in by stepping through the open windows, either because the doors don't work or because it's tradition. *Maybe it's a way they measure their size,* I think. *At what point are they too big to climb through the spaces?*

I take the RR stairs two at a time, back to the Gray girls' bathroom, the previously unlockable window where we stood that night, ready to blow this popsicle stand and run for the LA hills. From here, I can see Rowan bobbing her head to music inside the car. She's laughing—the last glimpse I'll catch of her for likely weeks, months, maybe years. Her expression is one I label as not happy, but satisfied.

I try to hold on to it.

Nurse Hart is already calling me down for weigh-ins with the Gray girls.

Somewhere out there, in the multiverse, I imagine a world where Rowan and I both die from this. And that could still be this one, this world. But there's also a multiverse where we both live. One where we all do. Donna. Jazzy. Brandy. Crystal. Sophie. August. It's too late for Alyssa, but the rest of us can still make it. *Just do it*, Nike-style. Just eat, just breathe, just be okay. From inside RR, a real part of me believes we've all got a bit of a better shot.

Before breakfast, I move my stuff to my old bunk bed, resting on the lower mattress and staring up at Rowan's handwriting. Tucked under the memory foam is that black Sharpie. I etch out the *Mad* and replace it with *Still*.

So now it reads: *We're All Still Here.*

30
Rowan

One Year Later

Don't take me for a fool. Even now, I'm well aware that my college acceptance was crazy, Shosh. All luck, really. I mean, my grades were shit from time off and my brain was mushy from starvation, but luck be a lady, 'cause UMD, for whatever reason, still accepted me. Sent a personal letter and everything. And a presidential scholarship.

I would never have gotten in before RR. But after I left, I wrote an essay, the kind of essay a person can only write after they've come through the other side of something shitty and stroked the new, plush green grass. I could have turned in my personal project, but these common apps don't want talking pumpkins. They want the truth, so I gave it to them.

I wrote about the girls in RR. I wrote about you. I wrote about the pain I felt. I wrote *out* the pain I felt, and then the anger, and then the empathy I felt for *your* pain and *your* anger. I sat with it a while. I still sit with it sometimes, but now it's out of my body, on the page, a totally different life-form. I wrote about how much I liked running away from my issues and why I really wanted to go to college, because at least then I'd be running toward something good. Admittedly, college isn't the coolest place for a destination, but hey, there are worse places to be. We both know that.

What I'm sure of: we both remember everything in there, the way it happened, the way no one else can replicate it. I used to believe our existence was pointless, futile. Though it may be still, it's whatever we wish it to be, whatever story we write. How did I never see that?

These new people at UMD are strangers turned friends. Not like you, who I met because we share the same disease—no offense, Shosh. The longer you're sick, the harder it is to separate the label from who you are. But it's not who I am, and I make new friends now for other reasons. Education. Art. Music. Maybe there will come a time when I'll be back at RR. Hopefully not as a patient, but maybe I'll be the one teaching sonnets to the Gray girls, hearing their *colgate* versions and doing the translation: *Please make it stop hurting.*

Don't for a minute think I've forgotten what that's like, the hurting. 'Cause I haven't. And I still feel it, like a live coil around my chest that shocks me the minute I forget it's there. A year isn't enough time to distance myself from pain that strong. But you see, Shoshana, there is this thing called credit. Look it up. We all deserve more of it for surviving day after day on this insane planet, day after day in RR.

You deserve so much of it, Shoshana. You really do.

My mother says I loved you like she loved my dad—instantly, sexually, too much. That's why we weren't meant to be. That's why we couldn't make it work and why you won't ever call. But to hell with that! She doesn't speak for me or for you. In fact, I told her she was wrong the first time she said it, right after she picked me up from RR. And I've told her every time since then, because I finally have faith in something: us.

It's a Sunday, what I now allow to be my day of rest, when you prove her wrong. When the caller ID says *Unknown* and I just know, like you always said I did, that it's you. I'm well aware that the moment I press that green button, there will be a new us. Two New Girls who find common ground in born-again lists, the things we want to do and the places we want to go, now that we're on the outside. You reach out for me today, like I always knew you would. The only task I'm given is to pick up.

And I do.

RESOURCES

National Eating Disorders Association (NEDA)
Helpline: 1-800-931-2237
For crisis situations, text "NEDA" to 741741
www.nationaleatingdisorders.org

National Alliance on Mental Illness (NAMI)
Helpline: 1-800-950-NAMI (6264)
nami.org

National Sexual Assault Hotline
1-800-656-HOPE (4673)
rainn.org

National Suicide Prevention Lifeline
1-800-273-8255
suicidepreventionlifeline.org

ACKNOWLEDGMENTS

My first and largest thank-you is to the person reading this. Thank you for finishing this book. I know it's not easy to finish things these days and I'm so glad you saw Shoshana and Rowan through to their final pages.

There's no adequate way to express my gratitude to all those who have helped shape this book, but first and foremost thank you to my agent, Kaitlyn Johnson, who plucked me from the slush pile and cheered me all the way to the finish line. Thank you to my all-star editor, Mari Kesselring, who made this book a *gazillion* times better than I thought possible, and to the whole team at Flux, for bringing it into the world.

Countless hugs and squeezes to the writing teachers and professors who changed my life, including but not limited to: Cathy Hoffman, Liz Coleman, Lorraine Savoy, Alisa Zonis, Laura Friedland, Mary Bannon, Tom Bailey, Gary Fincke, Catherine Dent, Silas Zobal, Melody Moezzi, and Nina de Gramont. My warmest thanks to the entire Susquehanna University creative writing faculty and my cohort at the University of North Carolina Wilmington.

Bottomless thanks to my sensitivity consultants, Nicole Gapp, Marnie Fisher, and Maggie Moore. To my therapists, Becca and Nancy, my goodness, what I don't owe you both. Thanks, also, to the friends who have touched this book in some way, big or small: Ailene McNamara, Patrick Durney, Susan Browne, Lia Correa, Andy Keys, Rebecca Hannigan, Christopher Sturdy, Nathan Conroy, Alexis Olson, Elly Cowell, and Paul Dickerson.

Lastly, thank you to my parents and grandparents—Joanne, Todd, Mort, Elise, Rhoda, and Lester—for encouraging my writing from the start. I love you all, and I thank you infinitely.

ABOUT THE AUTHOR

E.J. Schwartz is a recent graduate from the MFA program at the University of North Carolina Wilmington. Her writing has appeared in the *New York Times*, *Barrelhouse*, and *Necessary Fiction*, among others. She was born and raised in Scotch Plains, New Jersey. *Before We Were Blue* is her first novel.